BLUE
MOUNTAIN

CHECK R PRESS

Meet the Best Bad Mama-Ever

BLUE
MOUNTAIN

LISA MICHELLE

Lisa Michelle

Blue Mountain editing by Murphy Rae, Chelle Northcutt, and Lillian Schneider, www.murphyrae.com
Formatting by Elaine York, Allusion Publishing
www.allusionpublishing.com

FOR NANA,
WHO TAUGHT ME WHAT LOVE IS.

Deep into that darkness peering,
long I stood there,
wondering, fearing, doubting,
dreaming dreams no mortal ever dared to dream before.
Edgar Allan Poe

PART I

CHAPTER
ONE

Nana's real name was Effie. Effie Hobbs. At least that's what I thought for thirty-seven years. The truth arrived a few days before she faced final judgment, though I'm certain it wasn't forgiveness or atonement she sought. I suspected she craved recognition after being locked up in the Calaveras County Detention Facility. Either way, I couldn't let the truth be buried with her. So when her attorney, Ed Manetti phoned to tell me that Nana had been moved to Mark Twain Hospital in San Andreas and allowed death-bed visitation, I jumped in the truck, suppressing visions of my sweet Nana chained to a bed.

Mark Twain Hospital isn't much of a hospital, and San Andreas isn't much of a town, despite the fact it's officially the county seat, but they're the best we can do in Calaveras County.

Driving way too fast when I hit the downhill curve reminded me that I needed to replace my squealing brakes. I rolled through the stop sign at the bottom of the hill as a dark rain hit fast and heavy. The world became smudged and blurry.

The storm felt personal, as if it had saved its fury just for me. Such a perfect cliché to follow this morning's front page news.

CARNAGE IN CALAVERAS COUNTY

Property owned by Effie Hobbs of Wilseyville is currently being searched in an effort to locate missing veterinarian Mark Williams, according to the Calaveras County Sheriff's Department. Early investigations, assisted by cadaver dogs, have discovered what allegedly appears to be multiple human bone fragments from dozens of sources possibly making this the worst mass murder in Calaveras County history.

That didn't prove a damn thing. The discovery was nothing more than a variety of bone fragments. Horses and cattle died on the ranch and Nana fed them to the hogs. Hell, she'd even toss them a fresh roadkill deer once in a while. Pigs will devour pretty much anything placed in front of them. Nana would say, *"A hungry hog will go through a bone like butter."* It was possible that the remains weren't human.

Am I kidding myself?

A lightheadedness took over. I rolled down the window and let the vicious rain slap some sense into me. Wind accompanied the hum of mud tires on wet pavement, as soothing as a cryptic lullaby. Experts wouldn't go as far as to arrest Nana and tear her place apart if they didn't have decent proof, right? They'd be opening themselves up for a huge lawsuit.

Mass murder, the paper had reported. That meant more than a few victims. Christ. Was Nana a serial killer? The possibility made me nauseous, and I leaned my face toward the open window. Took a deep breath of cold rain. How many people do you have to kill to be classified as a serial killer?

My heart ached. I sucked in three healing breaths, like my therapist, Maureen Yamaguchi, had prescribed.

Rumor was, Maureen had left a successful private practice in San Francisco and come to Calaveras after one of her patients committed suicide. I wanted drugs, but Maureen insisted on meditation and bullshit focused breathing. When Maureen swore daily affirmations would bring positive energy into my life, I couldn't help but roll my eyes. I counted three full breaths, slowly in and slowly out.

"Nana is not a serial killer. Nana is not a serial killer."

Guess I felt a little less like driving off a cliff.

The geriatric ward was on the third floor and I was too impatient to wait for the clunky elevator. I took the stairs and had worked up a light sweat by the time I reached the third floor but still couldn't shake off the cold. My heart raced—not only from the exertion, but mostly from holding my breath to avoid the foul odor not unlike fermenting earth that smothered me the moment I exited the stairwell.

At the end of the hall, a hefty guard sat outside of what I guessed was Nana's door. He stood as I approached. Spread his feet shoulder-width apart. His chubby hands pulled on his gun belt like a potbellied Barney Fife.

"Hi, I'm Jessica Williams. Attorney Ed Manetti said he notified you guys I was coming to see Effie Hobbs," I said too loud and too fast.

"You're the murderer's granddaughter?"

I bit my cheek and chewed on his offensiveness. Getting used to Nana's preconceived guilt rubbing off on me was tough. I'd been condemned by friends and acquaintances and now this ill-mannered asshat. I'd had enough.

"She's been convicted?" I rubbed my brow. "I missed the entire trial?"

Sarcasm—the weapon of the weak, I know, but burying my fist in that dough-belly of his wasn't an option.

"I doubt she'll live long enough to be brought to trial. Photo ID?" He tucked his chin and glared at me as if I'd murdered children. I never carry a purse or my wallet, but Ed Manetti had suggested I bring my license.

I forced a smile, pulled it from my coat pocket, and handed it over. He inspected it with two hands.

"Jessica *Juniper* Williams?" He raised a brow and seemed to be suppressing a smirk.

"Yes." I dropped my head, looked at the warped industrial tiles, then thought better of it.

Nana believed that looking away from an opponent was the same as kneeling. Stand your ground with your chin up, chest full, and eyes locked like you're ready to take on the world. Easier said than done. *"A rabid dog never looks away. If people think you're dangerous, they become cautious real fast."* One of many Nana-isms.

He handed back my ID and didn't say or do anything except look at me for what seemed like a long uncomfortable while. His disgust was tangible. I raised my chin and locked onto his beady brown eyes for only a second then weakened and looked away. He opened the door and said, "Go ahead."

I pinched the crucifix hanging from my neck and walked in.

The room smelled like someone had tried to sterilize stagnating shit. A sickening feeling made my stomach churn as Nana shivered under a white blanket. Seeing how fragile and pale she'd become snatched my breath away. Fragile was something she'd never been, and it was hard to tell where the blanket ended and she began. I dragged my hands down my face—held tight to my tears—then touched her white hair, pressed and parted from sleep. She looked up at me. A smile cracked her face, something usually reserved for special occasions. Her scarred upper lip pulled tight and noticeable.

A faded blue hospital gown hung low and crooked above Nana's chest. "How you feeling?" I bent and hugged her tight. Maybe a bit too tight. Her bones seemed to give a little, and I caught myself wanting to squeeze harder. I loved this woman more than anyone or anything in my life, but I let her go. "You're cold."

"Cold is good." She took a ragged breath. "Helps me remember. They say I got the cancer."

I slipped off my wet coat. Hung it on the back of a chair while trying to come up with an encouraging response. "I talked to the doctor, and he says—"

"I'm gonna die. Doctor knows it and so do I. It's time anyhow."

"Don't say that." God and Nana were all I had left. Months before Nana had been accused of murder my life had turned to absolute shit. All because I'd chosen the wrong man to love. Soon as I thought things couldn't get any worse, they did. Immersed in chaos and sucked down the sewer pipe, I was drowning in an endless sea of churning human waste.

"What's going on, Nana? Is it true? What they're accusing you of?" Her face became brittle as her eyes narrowed in on me and she tilted her head downward like a lion stalking prey. For once, I held her intimidating gaze—refusing to weaken and look away. Just like she'd taught me. "Come on, Nana. Time to fess up."

With her middle finger, she wiped dried saliva from the corners of her mouth. Squirmed while clearing her throat and looked about as guilty as an innocent woman could look. "You won't like it."

"I love you. No matter what."

"Love..." She grinned and grunted, then went quiet as if contemplating the meaning of life. "I read your book you know."

"I know. You told me it was s-h-i-t."

"The story *was* shit. Boring as hell. But you write well enough." Her gnarled fingers shook as she reached for me. The cold from her hand ran through mine as I cradled it. Admired the scars and age spots accrued through a lifetime. Hands that constantly smelled of garlic. Hands that gently brushed tangles from my long hair without pulling or whacking me with the brush if I didn't hold still. Dry and calloused hands that were soft when wiping away my tears. Arthritic knuckles that like her refused to bend.

"Know what makes a good story great?" Nana asked.

"Marketing," I sneered.

"A personal connection to the truth. It allows the author to understand and share the gritty details." She squeezed my hand with surprising strength. Her dark blue eyes, now a milky gray, looked past me to somewhere far away. "Jessica?" Wide-eyed panic struck Nana and caught me off guard.

"I'm right here, Nana. Right here." I kissed the top of her hand.

"I have something for you."

"Okay." I'm ashamed to admit that my mind immediately went to something monetary. But I'd helped with her banking the last few years and knew there wasn't much left other than the ranch. Blue Mountain was just over two hundred acres of high country situated in a northeast section of Calaveras County. Most folks think of Mark Twain and jumping frogs when they hear about Calaveras County, but seldom do they know the truth. The truth lies in the name. *Calaveras*—Spanish for skull.

When the county legalized marijuana growing, Nana was offered fifty thousand dollars to lease her ranch to a grower named Ping Vang. She told him to his face to "shove his dope money up his ass." She'd never let them destroy Blue Mountain.

With Nana's signature, I'd used Blue Mountain as collateral to hire Ed Manetti.

"Ever since you were a little girl, you wrote stories. Stories about trees and horses. Remember the one you wrote about the fly?" Nana asked.

"No," I said, believing Nana was confused.

"The fly that got caught in the spiderweb. Remember? The fly fought and fought until it almost destroyed the web and the spider had to turn it loose."

"Oh, yeah." Wonderful, Nana's memory was better than mine. "That story was a so bad."

"Yeah. But you were brave and kept writing. So now I have a gift for you. The story that will make you a writer. But you have to be brave. Braver than you've ever been in your whole life."

"Okay."

"Record what I tell you and keep your mouth shut about it until I'm gone. Then you write the story. It's a goddamn good one." Her chin dropped to her chest. She squeezed her brow and closed her eyes tight.

"You in pain?" She didn't answer. I watched her jaw muscles lock. "I'm getting the doctor."

She shook her head. Slow at first, then defiantly. Her eyes still closed.

"Few things are as attractive or as profitable as tragedy," Nana said, her mouth twisting like the words left a bitter taste. "They'd never admit it, but people like me fascinate run-a-the-mill folk. I shock them. Make them question their safety. Sometimes even their sanity." She opened her eyes and found me. "I'm like a car wreck—they *can't not look,* and when they can't see, they create gore all on their own." She grinned. "Death is the ultimate truth of life. Can't remember where I read that, but it's damn sure right. My story, Jess—is the most valuable thing I can leave you."

Her honesty exposed me. She was right about society's fascination with death. It had always captivated me. Looking at Nana dying in that bed, I thought I'd come here mostly because I loved her and also to decipher if she was capable of killing, but something told me she could unravel my own truth. She always had. I reached inside my coat pocket and dug out my cell phone.

"Promise me, Jessica, you won't share what I tell you with anyone, especially the law, until I'm gone."

"Fine. I swear I won't. I have a recording app on my phone." She had no idea what an app was—I just needed to talk. To focus on anything but the facts that would overwhelm me in an instant if I let them. "Good thing I charged the battery on the way over." I opened the camera, went to Nana, and leaned in close. "Smile. I'm gonna take our picture." Nana squinted up at the phone.

"Swear to me." Nana said and refused to grin as I snapped the camera a few times.

"What?" I asked.

"Swear to God you'll keep my story secret until I'm dead." She sounded serious.

"You don't even believe in God."

"*Yes, I do!*" She slapped her hand on the bed. "Just don't buy into the wrathful God created by sermon or scripture."

"Okay. I swear to God. Whatever you want—I won't tell anyone." The words hung in the air a long moment. It was hard to swallow the fact that Nana believed in any sort of higher power. "I'll bring my Bible next time."

"Please don't."

"Why not?"

"Unlike you, I don't have time to cherry-pick my way through scripture." She was right like always and kissed my cheek.

I opened the voice recorder on my phone and pressed record. Goosebumps pricked my arms. It was like I was willingly stepping into a bear trap as she began to put the gruesome and jagged pieces of truth into place.

CHAPTER
TWO

Winnie

N ana was not born Effie Hobbs. Winifred Mudgett was her name and her date of birth unclear—somewhere around 1935—New Jersey. The family survived thanks to Franklin D. Roosevelt and the Public Works Administration for creating public housing. In Atlantic City, poverty didn't promise unhappiness, but it most likely contributed to Winnie's troubles. Along with a father who refused the few jobs he qualified for. He swore he could not survive spending day after day doing mundane labor meant for monkeys. Public Works offered a weekly paycheck, but according to Mr. Mudgett, working for anyone other than yourself was for suckers. With ambitions of opening his own cinema, Winnie's dad squandered what little money they had in the stock market.

Mrs. Mudgett worked long hours and sometimes covered the night shift as a laundry lady at the Thomas England Military Hospital. The few hours a day not spent working, cooking, cleaning, or clashing with Mr. Mudgett about money, Mom slept. She never ever smiled, smoked a lot, and was always too worn out to notice Winnie.

Fury seemed as much a part of Winnie as a second skin, and her younger sister Nell was an easy target. The one-year age difference between them caused a competitiveness that more often than not was ruthless. Winnie's attacks started with what she called "pranks." Cutting off one of Nell's braids while she slept, then making it up to her with a compassionate cup of hot cocoa that masked an entire tin of chocolate flavored Ex-Lax.

While Nell soaked her sore butt in a warm bath, Winnie came in.

"Get out!" Nell threw the soap but missed.

"I'm sorry." Winnie dropped her head and wept with her hands in her coat pockets. "I thought it'd be funny."

"There's nothing funny about it, Winifred. You're an awful girl. Hateful."

"I know. But I love you. I do, and I'm so very sorry. Truly. Can you ever forgive me?" Winnie sobbed.

"Yes. But you have to swear to stop tormenting me."

"I swear it." Winnie pulled her hand from her coat pocket and wrapped her pinky around Nell's as she pulled a toad from the other pocket and tossed it into the tub. The sharp screams drowned Winnie's laughter.

Punishments went from stinging wooden-spoon spankings to bruised beatings with the belt. Not even standing out in the cold for hours or depriving the growing girl of food for two days taught Winnie a lesson.

The final straw came before Christmas. Winnie was nine and knitting a scarf while Bing Crosby sang "White Christmas" on the record player Dad had just bought with Mom's S&H Green Stamps. Mom was furious and threw a hot iron at him for using her stamps without permission. She'd been saving for over a year to buy a radio and threatened to move to California over the deal. At the top of his lungs, Dad reminded Mom that he'd relinquished his mother's fortune and his inheritance when he married her. Mom had been quiet for days after that.

"Who's the scarf for?" Nell asked, inspecting Winnie's work.

"Me," Winnie answered.

"You should increase the tension. Tighten your stitch." Nell turned to go, but before she took one step Winnie plunged the knitting needle deep into the back of her thigh, then swore it was an accident. Swore she stood and stumbled and never meant to stab her own sister.

Later that night, Winnie snuck from her room and sat with her ear against her parents' door.

"There's something very wrong with her. No one likes her. She's never even had a friend—not one," Mom said. Winnie wanted to bust down the door. Explain that she didn't have friends because she didn't want them. Plain and simple. She preferred her own company over that of idiots.

Her father refused to defend her. "Making friends with Winnie would be like trying to befriend a snake. I hate to say it but she reminds me of my mother. Is narcissism inherited?"

"Oh God, don't say that," Mom said.

"We're both in denial because she's so smart. Her grades are fantastic, but she couldn't care less about anyone. Other than herself. What about when she lost at Monopoly?"

"She's competitive. What's wrong with that?" At least Mom took her side.

"Throwing the board and all the pieces across the room then choking Nell is not normal behavior. And not fair to Nell. Winnie's worse than the plague," Dad said.

Before hurt could infect Winnie, she got mad. Bolted down the steps and snatched the kerosene lantern and matchsticks off the kitchen table. She spent most of the frigid night on the roof. A shovel rested against a stove pipe and Winnie used it to pry up rotted wood shingles. After shoveling the shingles into a nice pile, the kerosene from the lantern fueled the spark from the match. It was an intense work of art when it went. Lit the dark like a magnificent sunrise. Winnie never intended to hurt anyone; she just had to do it. Had to get warm. But when flames destroyed half of the housing unit, Mom and Dad sent her away.

The train left Grand Central Station at 6:00 pm on Christmas Eve and Winnie watched through the window as her father walked away, hunched over as if carrying some awkward burden on his shoulders. He always walked like that when he was cold, but this was the first time Winnie wondered why. Snow fired out of the blackness and stuck to his navy-blue pea coat. He never looked back. Drops trickled like tears down the fogged window while Winnie's filthy finger drew a smiley face.

What would Dad tell her teacher? Winnie wondered. She's at boarding school? A madhouse? Maybe he would say that she died. There was a fire, and she did not survive. No one would question her disappearance because no one cared if Winifred Mudgett lived or died. The whistle screamed. Her heart hiccupped as the train lurched forward.

Christmas Eve alone on a train was exciting. There were two uniformed soldiers, one old man, and a young couple in the car. They all seemed to pity the freckle-faced little girl with the carrot-colored pixie traveling by herself on Christmas Eve. What awful parents the poor thing must have. Winnie noticed a hole in her coat pocket as the locomotive settled into a rhythmic motion. One of the soldiers came up the aisle and smiled at Winnie.

"Pardon me, sir, could you spare a nickel? I've lost the one my father gave me." Winnie poked her finger through the hole in her coat pocket to stoke her story. "And I'm so hungry it hurts." A tear rolled down her chubby red cheek like an exclamation mark.

Without hesitation, the soldier dug deep into his pants pocket. Scooped out his change and handed it over. "Merry Christmas, dear girl." She didn't need his ninety-two cents. Father had sent her away with a five-dollar bill tucked safely in her sock. It was her right to relieve a sucker of his money. Father had used the adage more than once but never mentioned how good it felt.

Spending Christmas Day alone on a train did not teach Winnie a lesson. It netted her six dollars and fifty-two cents before arriving at Union Station in Chicago that night. Families with too many kids slept on benches. Pathetic people curled up in dirty corners. Winnie found the café and bought a double-scoop of rocky road. She sat and licked and licked, then threw the cone in the trash while a girl in ragged clothes watched from outside the window.

A cold wind slapped Winnie's face when she stepped out to meet Thomas, Grandmother's driver, who was waving her over. He opened the back door of the cream-colored Buick, and Winnie dove in.

"I hear you're being somewhat of a shit," were the first words out of Grandma Bell's mouth. She grinned. "The apple never falls far, does it?"

"Yep." Winnie didn't understand but agreed anyway because just being in a car big and warm enough to live in made Winnie conform.

"It's a pleasure to finally meet you, Winifred." Grandma Bell patted Winnie's knee and inspected her. "My God, you are skin and bones." She shook her head—eyes never leaving Winnie. "And who in the world cut your hair?"

"I did," Winnie said proudly.

"I'll arrange to have it done. Now stop slouching. Sit up straight."

Winnie obeyed staring at the woman and her tremendous fur coat. There was nothing grandmotherly about her or her sweet smell, like cotton candy on an ocean breeze. Her thin red lips and ivory hair in a spectacular victory roll just like Lana Turner in *Somewhere I'll Find You*.

"My dad said you're rich."

"I am."

"If you're so rich, how come you won't give my mom and dad no money?"

"Money, dear. Just money. Not *no* money. Okay? Ask again using proper English."

"How come you won't give my mom and dad *moooneeey?*" Winnie dragged the word out low and slow.

Grandma Bell crossed her arms and looked out the window.

"Your father married a difficult and damaged woman. I warned him. He made his bed and now he can lie in it with your mother." She put her mink-coated arm around Winnie and squeezed a little too hard. "Let's get something straight, shall we?" Grandma Bell leaned her powdery white cheek against Winnie's and spoke. "You cause trouble for me, pull any shit, like lighting fires, I will not hesitate to send you straight to the orphanage. This is your one and only chance to lead a decent and comfortable life. If you fail, you will endure a lifetime of misery. Understand, *dear*?"

"Yes, ma'am." Something told Winnie Grandma Bell was not the type to make empty threats.

Grandma Bell came to Chicago from Norway in 1893 and later married Nicholas Howe, a lawyer who represented clients with murky reputations. After two years of marriage, Grandma Bell became a widow when Mr. Howe conveniently choked to death on a gumball. Grandma Bell inherited his Prairie Avenue mansion, a ten-thousand-dollar life insurance policy, and the ability to retrieve her only son—Winnie's father. She had given the boy up for adoption the year before marrying Howe. Having a child out of wedlock would have labeled Grandma Bell a tramp and made her marriage to Nicholas Howe Attorney at Law, impossible.

After receiving the life insurance check, Grandma Bell hired a detective to find the boy. It took three months and one thousand dollars to bring her six-year-old back from Boston. Grandma Bell changed the boy's name from William to Herman Webster Mudgett after his real father, better known by his alias as Dr. Henry Howard Holmes or H. H. Holmes. The newspapers labeled him the Beast of Chicago. Grandma Bell's one true love had confessed to twenty-seven murders and was hanged.

The house on Prairie Avenue was impressive. Elaborate.

Three stories of sturdy stone chiseled to perfection and protected from outsiders by a wrought iron fence. But any crook worth his salt could make short work of that fence by way of the Sycamore tree and the branch that reached into the yard. Maybe the fence was best suited for keeping people in. Arched windows and doors like a miniature castle. The street was paved and snow cleared away. No trash or old newspapers floating around like ghouls. No drunkards littering the neighborhood and chasing little girls home from school.

Inside stood a massive fireplace big enough to stand in. A wide walnut-colored staircase in the shape of a crescent moon tempted Winnie to float up into oblivion. She smacked the lion's head post and then slid her dirty palm along the perfectly polished banister all the way to the second floor.

The room was blue and smelled like rain on a hot day. Sky-blue tranquility and almost as big as any home Winnie had ever known. A writing desk sat in front of a stained-glass window. The wrought iron bed would never be shared with a stupid sister. When Winnie tossed her suitcase onto the mattress, the springs moaned as if in pain. They even moaned when Winnie opened her suitcase.

As she hung her only two dresses in the armoire, a strange chill almost like a cool breeze swept across her. The inkling someone was near turned into the potent sensation of being watched. Winnie spun around. Grandma Bell was there—sitting on the boisterous bed. She had arrived and somehow sat down without a sound.

"Do you approve of your bedroom?"

"Sure. It's great."

"Wonderful. Goodnight. Don't let the bedbugs bite."

Breakfast was on the table when Winnie sat down. Thick ham grilled to perfection and glazed with a brown sugar crust. It smelled like heaven and Winnie's mouth watered. She was hungry and unsure if paying her fair share, especially with a pocket full of money, was expected. She pulled out two quarters, tossed them on the table, stabbed the biggest slice of ham, and slapped it on her plate.

"What are you doing?" Grandma Bell asked as she poured coffee from a silver server.

"Paying my share." Winnie held a forkful of ham midpoint.

Granma Bell pushed the quarters back to Winnie. "I'd rather you owe me."

Winnie ate. And ate. She refused the scrambled eggs Grandma Bell offered, the toast, and even the fresh grapefruit. Ham was meat, and seconds of meat had never been an option.

"You must register for school." Grandma Bell sipped her coffee. "Thomas will take you."

At Barrette Elementary School, history, arithmetic, health science, and grammar were less challenging for Winnie than life with Grandma Bell. Grades were seldom less than As until it came to conduct. Being graded for conduct was unfair, not to mention biased, Winnie informed her teacher, hoping to raise her D to a B. This was the second time she'd received a D for conduct and Grandma Bell had rewarded the grade with a buggy whip to the back of Winnie's bare legs. Out of options, Winnie's D became a fat B with the help of a black pen stolen from her teacher's desk.

After a year in Chicago, Winnie still hadn't a single friend. Halloween was Winnie's favorite holiday, but trick-or-treating alone didn't sound like much fun—that's why Winnie stole a can of white shoe polish. While the shoe clerk was busy selling Grandma Bell loafers, Winnie shoved the can of polish down into the top of her boot. Cowboy boots were not only suited to riding horses—they were the bee's knees for hiding stolen goods. Adults always searched pockets when they had a suspect. They never looked in boots.

In her room, Winnie put the finishing touches on her ghost-white face and pulled a knit cap down over her hair. The plan was to ride her bike at full speed and snatch fat bags of candy from unsuspecting trick-or-treating fools. She was wiping the white from her fingers on the underside of her pillowcase when Grandma Bell screamed, "Winifred! Come here!" Winnie jumped and hurried down the stairs. "Winifred!"

"Coming!" Panic tingled Winnie as her heavy boots slapped each step on her way down.

"Raaar!" Something furry that reeked of cigarette smoke and lilac pounced on Winnie. "Happy tenth birthday!" Grandma Bell roared—dressed like a tigress in high heels—and swatted Winnie with her erect tail.

"It's not my birthday until tomorrow," Winnie said.

"Incorrect! I've changed it for you. Halloween is the best day for a birthday!" She pranced around the foyer like a rambunctious kitten. "Just think, celebrating your birthday on October thirty-first means there will always, always, always be parties to attend. Isn't that grand?"

Winnie wasn't sure if people could just go around changing their birthdays, but what difference did it make? November 1 had never been cause for celebration anyhow.

"Here." Grandma Bell lifted a box off the hall tree and handed it to Winnie. "Put this on." Winnie peeled off the lid and took out a black cowboy hat. A little leather holster held a silver six-shooter.

"I know how much you love those wild Westerns." Grandma looked sort of proud. "Hurry now, go wash your face, we're late."

The Lincoln Park Zoo was probably the best place in the world for a Halloween ball. It was like another world. A dark world with a million little balls of light circling the entire building. A man in a gorilla suit held hands with a chimp in a suit and tie.

"Howdy," Winnie said, and the monkey tipped his felt fedora at her.

Black silk tablecloths and giant glowing jack-o'-lanterns covered dozens of tall cocktail tables. At the bar, a cauldron bubbled. Tarzan offered Winnie a glass of blood-red punch. She took it. "Thanks."

Members of the Zoological Society and cigarette smoke filled the pavilion along with a swinging band that almost made Winnie want to dance as she bounced around the place. Instead, she came across the dessert table and filled her mouth then her pockets with candy corn. Trumpets screamed and shook the fake cobwebs that hung from the chandeliers as Winnie moved on with a gun belt swagger.

A brown man dressed in gold like King Tut stopped when Winnie pointed her six-shooter at him—a python draped around his shoulders like a shawl. "Give me all your dough." Winnie watched the snake's tongue flick in and out.

"This is all I have left." The man lifted the snake from around his neck and slowly lowered it around Winnie. "I am Mr. Armaan. And who is this cowboy stealing my best snake?"

"Winifred," she muttered, fascinated by the snake's cat-like eyes and the weight of the soft, smooth creature hanging on her. Hugging her. "Wow." Winnie stroked the scaled skin. "Is it a boy or a girl?"

"A boy. His name is Burney. He is a Burmese python."

"He's soft." Winnie stroked her index finger along Burney's triangular head. His tongue touched her, and she held her finger steady so he could do it again.

"You are not afraid. Girls rarely care for my snakes."

"You have more?" Winnie looked up at Mr. Armaan.

"Yes. I am in charge of the reptiles and snakes at the zoo." Mr. Armaan lifted Burney off Winnie and wound him around his arm. Winnie ignored the woman riding in on an elephant. The room gasped then erupted with applause, but Winnie was busy studying the end of Burney's pointed tail.

"Say, would you like to see our collection of ophidians?"

"Yes!" Winnie's eyes widened.

"You know what ophidians are?"

"Snakes."

"Come to the Snake House at two o'clock tomorrow and I will introduce you."

"Sure thing."

"Goodbye, Winifred."

"Bye." Winnie waved then climbed up onto the edge of the stage. Sat in front of the band's brass section for the rest of the night and watched Grandma Bell dance and drink with a man named Dick Perkins, the new zoo director.

For nearly a year, Mr. Dick Perkins visited Grandma Bell several nights a week. The affair was top secret since Mr. Dick was married and had a real family. He gave Winnie a VIP zoo pass and a tiny rifle that shot actual BBs for her eleventh birthday, but Winnie knew it was payment for her silence. In no time, she was out of BBs and the neighborhood was out of varmints. Especially cats.

Mr. Dick's kindness disappeared when Winnie shot and shattered the back window of his new Cadillac. His face turned red as he yelled, "Give me that damn gun! Right now," and held out his hand. "You're too old to play cowboy!"

Winnie crossed her arms while straddling her bike. "Your son Fred goes to my school. Did you know that?" She loved how fast his face morphed. Comprehension, shock, then frustrated compliance, in an instant. A smart man would never trade his family's happiness for a busted window, and Winnie knew it. She pulled the rifle off her shoulder and pointed the barrel at Mr. Dick's head. "I need more BBs."

Mr. Dick's jaw tightened as he raised his chin and wrung his hands. "I'll bring you some tomorrow. Just try to be careful...

please." He turned and walked away as Winnie drew a bead on his butt and pulled the trigger.

Summer vacation was only a day away, and Winnie was thrilled. She'd scored an A+ on her math exam and won a blue ribbon in the girl's long jump. It had truly been an exceptionally terrific day. Taking the stairs two at a time with the blue ribbon pinned to her plaid shirt, Winnie rushed to find Grandma Bell in her room.

"Howdy, Granny!" Winnie unpinned the ribbon and held it out. "Look what I won!"

Suitcases were stacked next to the door, and Grandma Bell was busy filling a trunk with formal gowns. The closet was open and empty, and Grandma Bell was crying. Winnie forgot about her terrific day. Her stomach tightened and churned. Panic banged inside her. "What the heck's going on?"

CHAPTER
THREE

Winnie

M r. Dick broke Grandma Bell's heart in half when he dumped her. It was the first and only time Winnie saw the old gal cry. Before Grandma Bell left Chicago for Paris, she hired a full-time housekeeper named Sylvia to look after things, including Winnie. Sylvia was like a mouse—always skittering around the house, tiny and quiet. There was nothing special or exciting about Sylvia.

For the first six months Winnie thought of Grandma Bell as soon as she walked in the house after school or went to bed at night or woke up in the morning. Her stomach ached every day and once during a thunderstorm Winnie cried under the covers. Maybe Winnie preferred having someone around. Someone smarter, prettier, and richer than anyone she'd ever known. Maybe she loved Grandma Bell.

For two years the house was bleak and had an abandoned feeling to it. Sure, Grandma Bell sent postcards from Paris and called Winnie once in a while, but it only made things worse.

Turning twelve and then thirteen with just Sylvia the mouse was worse than being alone.

Last year, Grandma Bell had promised she was coming home—until she met Pierre. Together they would travel the world. When Winnie's fourteenth Halloween birthday came, she didn't open the gift Grandma Bell had sent from Paris. Instead, she tossed it into the fireplace and drank gin from a bottle while the package and her throat burned.

The following year Winnie attended Wendell Phillips High School on the south side of Chicago. She was a freshman, as was Leonard Akins—for the third time. He was almost eighteen. A skinny, bucktoothed kid who sat behind Winnie in English. Her long red hair hung over the back of her chair and when Leonard stroked and patted it like a horse's mane, Winnie turned, and out of pure instinct, slapped his face—hard.

"Winfred Mudgett!" The teacher yelled from her desk as she stood.

"What?" Winnie screamed—all eyes on her. Students with open mouths gasped in unison. No one *ever* talked back to Miss Muller. She beat her ruler on her desk like a gavel while her face turned a vibrant pink.

Leonard's laugh was loud and obnoxious, like a howler monkey, but it pulled glaring faces off of Winnie. He was cocksure of himself, something she hadn't seen from anyone other than Grandma Bell. With a handprint blushing his cheek, Leonard grinned with his long stupid teeth just like the Big Bad Wolf. He eyed Winnie, then defiantly reached out and stroked her hair from top to bottom. He leaned forward and lifted his chin as if daring her to slap him again. She gave it to him. Same spot twice as hard.

"Office NOW, Winifred!"

Waiting in the school office was more exciting than Winnie had ever imagined. She sat along the back wall between two boys. A tall man in an overcoat and fedora walked in. He glared at the boy on Winnie's right, who'd been caught cheating on an arithmetic exam.

"Dad, I'm sorry!" The kid squealed like a piglet. Swore he would never, ever, ever do it again. With a disgusted look, his father walloped his kid upside the head before shoving him out the door.

A girl in a cheerleader uniform burst in, crying and holding her nose as it leaked red like a ruptured pipe. Blood trailed her all the way to the nurse's station. *Probably a pompom to the snout,* Winnie thought. What a crybaby.

Things quieted for nearly an hour until the boy on Winnie's left suddenly barfed. Vomit splashed across the floor like abstract art and reminded Winnie of Jackson Pollock. She'd seen his painting—*Alchemy*—at The Art Institute last year. The oil on canvas included sand, pebbles, fibers, and broken sticks.

What the hell has this kid been eating? Winnie wondered as a voice called her into the principal's office.

Principal Truman sat behind a metal desk and steepled his fingers. His chair whimpered when he leaned back. He pointed his little fingers like a pistol at the small chair in front of his desk. Winnie sat. Principal 'Not-a-True-Man', as the kids called him behind his back, was dainty and delicate in every manner including speech. Winnie knew what it was like to be different and had no opinion on the matter of Truman's feminine ways.

"Winifred, I'm afraid there isn't room for this type of behavior in high school. Mrs. Bramble has been trying to reach your grandmother for almost two hours."

"Good Luck. She lives Paris."

"Paris?"

"Yeah. It's in France."

"Why is she in Paris?"

"Because Mr. Dick Perkins broke her heart—she said Paris could fix it."

He crossed his arms, furrowed his brow, and waited a while. "When will she be back?"

"How should I know? Sylvia got a letter from her last month—said she has tuberculosis."

"Tuberculosis! That's terrible." Truman slapped his hand over his heart, then got up and sat on the corner of his desk—his tiny feet dangling like a child's as he faced Winnie. "Who's Sylvia?"

"The lady Grandma hired to take care of...the household."

"I see." He looked at his shoes. They were desperate for a polish. "I'm sorry to hear about your grandmother, but in accordance with school rules, I have to suspend you for fighting."

"Okay." Winnie stood to leave.

"Try to stay out of trouble, Miss Mudgett. You're an extremely intelligent young lady. And boys *do not* like roughneck girls. Remember that."

She glared at him, disappointed by his failure to understand the benefit of being different. *Him*, of all people. Her indifference for Truman chose sides and wanted to scratch his eyes out. "*Unlike* you, Mr. Not-a-True-Man, I don't care *what* boys like." Winnie walked out and slammed the door.

That night, Winnie woke to a knocking on her second-story window. She reached down between the mattress and box spring and grabbed the fireplace poker tucked away for just such an occasion. Ready and willing to bludgeon the intruder, Winnie pressed her bare feet along the frigid floor toward the window.

She adjusted her eyes against the dark. Knocks softened to a tap, tap, tap. With the poker, Winnie pulled the curtains back.

"Let me in," a shadow whispered desperately. "I'm freezing to death out here." The plea was familiar.

"Come on, Winnie. Please. It's me, Leonard. There's something I have to tell you."

Winnie unhooked the latch. Leonard lifted the window and crawled in.

"What the heck are you doing? How'd you get up here?" Winnie asked.

"The big sycamore. I'm a pretty good climber." He sat on the foot of her bed and rubbed his forehead. Winnie shut the window and stayed put with a firm grip on the poker.

"I can't sleep. I feel just awful about getting you suspended. Plus, I can't stop thinking about why you didn't rat me out today. Girls I know love tattling." He looked at Winnie like he expected a response.

She looked bored, but that was how she always looked. Every class photo since first grade confirmed it. The same somber, freckled-faced girl with the same orange hair that was just a little longer each year.

"Get out before I beat you with this." She raised the poker.

"I want to know why." Leonard walked over to Winnie. She raised the poker. "You like me, don't you?"

"Heck no!" She whacked him hard on the arm and he snatched it. Held it still as she struggled to pull it away from him. He twisted it out of her hand.

"I like you too, Win. A lot."

"I do *not* like you. Not one bit." Winnie crossed her arms. "What's to like?" The cold sent a chill, and she shivered as Leonard stared at her, wearing nothing but Grandma Bell's oversized nightgown. "How'd you know where I live?"

"Why, that's top-secret information."

"If you don't tell me I'll scream." Winnie knew no one would come. Thomas, the gofer chauffeur, was sauced and passed out by now and Sylvia had gone home.

"Okay. Okay. After school I went to the office. Told the secretary that Miss Muller wanted me to take you your work. You know, since you got suspended and all. I told her Miss Muller didn't want you to fail, but I needed your address so's I could drop off your work. She looked up the address and wrote it down for me. Even said what a nice boy I was." He lifted his chin and grinned.

"I don't think you're all that nice."

"That's 'cause you don't know me. You gotta give people a chance, Win. I know you think I'm dumb just 'cause I don't like school. But there's other kinds of smarts."

Winnie looked at him. Thought what he'd done was cunning. And he was right about there being more than one kind of smart. She didn't dislike him as much as she had only moments ago.

"You're cold. Get back in bed. I'll tuck you in and go. I just—" He shook his head and looked at the floor. "Thinkin' about you—I can't get no sleep. Thought maybe I ought to come tell you how I feel." He pulled the blankets back with the poker in his hand.

"Gimme that poker back." Winnie held out her hand.

"You gonna hit me with it?"

"Maybe."

Leonard set the poker down, then kicked it under the bed. "Now come on. Quit actin' like a little girlie girl and get in bed."

Winnie walked over, her little feet and legs numb with cold, and got into bed.

"Have you ever had a boyfriend?" He tucked the covers around her shoulders and up to her chin. No one had ever tucked Winnie in.

"Plenty," she lied. She'd never had a friend, let alone a boyfriend and no one other than Grandma Bell and Sylvia had ever been in her room. There was something nice about having him here. Tucking her in. Winnie noticed a warmth deep inside and liked it.

"Well, I ain't." He grinned. "Had girlfriends I mean. They usually act so dumb I can't stand to be around 'em." He sat on the bed next to Winnie. "But, not you. You're different. You're smart, but you don't let on that you're smart. And I think you're pretty. *Real* pretty."

His thin, chapped lips were on Winnie's before she could stop him. He had called her pretty and that consumed her thoughts at that moment. *Pretty.* Winnie had never considered or cared if she was pretty. He kissed her softly at first and she puckered, but when he turned his head sideways and pressed harder, Winnie felt his big buckteeth against hers and pulled back.

"Jeez, Winnie. You're one heck of a kisser. Look what you did." His goofy smile took up most of his face when he grabbed Winnie's hand and set it on his lap.

"What is it?" Winnie wondered what he was hiding in there. If, like her, he took things that didn't belong to him and knew better than to hide them in the obvious places like pockets. "Come on. What the heck is it?" Winnie asked and sat up while Leonard laughed.

"I thought you said you had plenty of boyfriends."

"Yeah, so?" Winnie grabbed at the goods between his legs. "You got the Crown Jewels in there?"

"Something like that." He squirmed. "Is anyone home?"

"Thomas, my bodyguard is here."

"You ain't got no bodyguard."

"Do too. He does whatever needs doing. So, if I need guarding—he'll do it."

"I best behave myself then."

"Yeah."

"Where's your mom and pop?"

"They died. I live here with my grandmother."

"Oh. Where's she?"

"In a sanatorium with tuberculosis."

"So, it's just you and this fella, Thomas?"

"No. Sylvia's usually here too, but she snuck home to see her kids. Thinks I don't know when she's gone at night. Now *come on*—show me!" Winnie insisted and slapped her hands twice into the mattress.

Leonard stood and unbuttoned his jeans. He was so skinny that the jeans fell without help. "Wanna go steady, Win?"

"Okay," she muttered—staring and stunned at poor Leonard's deformity. It looked exactly like the eyeless flesh-colored manaconda snake that had arrived at the zoo from the Amazon jungle just last week. Leonard looked ridiculous in his white T-shirt with that floppy snake trying to raise its head. It must get in his way, she thought. No wonder he acted like such an idiot so often. For the very first time, Winnie experienced a twinge of sympathy as Leonard stepped closer and let her get a good look.

"Touch it."

Winnie recoiled, but couldn't take her eyes off the hideous sprout.

"Please, Winnie, just touch it. That's what girlfriends do. Don't be a wet rag." The thing seemed to reach out for her. Could he move it around? How far would it stretch? With her index finger, she touched it as gently as she'd patted the manaconda. Leonard moaned.

"I love you, Winnie. I mean it."

She was sure she'd never heard *anyone* say those words, and from that moment on, Winnie let Leonard do what he wanted.

It took exactly four times before sex became enjoyable. After that Winnie had never looked forward to anything more. Leonard coming to her room at night was thrilling. And rather than examine the real reason she allowed him to so quickly consume her life, she chose the easy way and called it love. His warm flesh pressed against hers was better than ice cream on a hot day. Leo's hands and lips and arms and legs on her proved he loved her and being loved made all the difference in the world. Winifred Mudgett was no longer the unlovable outcast and kind of liked it.

It seemed Winnie had discovered the meaning of life and caught herself smiling and being kind for no reason—even fed the feral cats that hung around the baseball field. She stole an entire set of encyclopedias from the library—one at a time, of course—and left them outside the Chicago Orphanage Asylum, grateful she hadn't ended up there. Leonard had been coming to Winnie's room for nearly three months before she learned about reproduction in biology class and realized she was pregnant.

A million thoughts ran through Winnie's head in an instant. *My very own real family would prove Mom and Dad were wrong for sending me away. They were unfit parents— we would never be like them. I'd never abandon my kid for misbehaving. Never. I'll be a real mom and cook dinner every night. Make chicken soup when my kids are sick and rub their backs. First, there is a wedding to plan—and fast.*

She hadn't even met Leo's parents and hoped they were nice. He clammed up every time she asked about them. Tuberculosis would surely kill Granma Bell sooner than later, and that would leave Winnie with a big house in need of a big family and a dog. A furry collie like Lassie to play fetch with and help protect the children. Happiness guaranteed, but first she had to find Leo and share the good news.

The Winter Sock Hop was in full swing when Winnie found Leonard drinking beer with two gals in the parking lot. A light snow fell, dusting the Fords and Chevys while music seeped from the auditorium. A smile overtook Winnie's cold face and her irritation at Leonard's lie when she saw him. He'd told her he wasn't going to the dance—said he had to drive to Milwaukee to pick up parts for his dad's garage.

"Leo!" Her breath spewed in the freezing cold.

"Hey, kitty cat, what's the skinny?" He guzzled his bottle of beer while the two gals held hands and chuckled. Winnie had seen them before in the library. Brunette twins in pedal pusher pants and spotless saddle shoes. They even had matching red wool coats. Leo pitched the bottle like a fastball and it busted somewhere in the dark. "Ain't it past your bedtime?" He looked at Winnie. Her mittened hands grabbed his arm.

"I need to talk to you." This was not at all the way she'd imagined giving him the good news. He was going to be a father. A genuine smile took up Winnie's entire face.

"See you dolls later." Leo belched like a gurgling toad and wobbled away from his friends. Winnie followed.

"Leo. I have great news. Please stop." He stopped, faced her, and waited with his arms crossed. "You and me are going to have a baby." She smiled and stood on her toes. "I'm pregnant!"

Leo's face went blank. He stared at Winnie a long while, then looked around the parking lot. He even looked behind him. The place was empty.

"Jeez, Win. Hot dog." He kissed her cheek and Winnie could smell the whiskey on him. "Let's celebrate!" He took her hand and led her behind the auditorium, where Nat King Cole crooned from inside. It was perfect: her hand in his, her favorite song "Mona Lisa" and fat snowflakes meandering—when something suddenly cracked. Pain like a thousand needles hit Winnie's face from out of nowhere. Something hit her. *What?* Thoughts tangled in one muddled moment. *Where's Leo?*

He buried the next blow deep. Hard into her stomach. She stepped back—doubled over—dying for air. Leo was standing there. His face twisting like a maniac as he grunted out a one-two combination to Winnie's jaw. She dropped to her knees—hands up in surrender. Leo's work boot connected with her face. Pain kicked inside her head like her skull was caving in on itself. There was no way to see what was coming next as her eyes watered. Her nose felt smeared across her face. Blood, wet and warm. The world sank and down she went. On her back. Helpless and limp when Leo lifted his leg and stomped her belly. Over and over again until Winnie knew her baby, their baby, was dead. She refused to cry out. To give in to the pain. In the tilted stillness, she closed her eyes and bled onto the soft clean snow while Nat King Cole sang her to sleep.

CHAPTER
FOUR

Winnie

I n the first blue light of morning, a janitor dumping last night's trash nearly stumbled over Winnie. In the snow, her eyes frozen shut on a blue face. Blood covered the lower half of her mouth and chin like a crusty red beard.

Time and space moved backward in a peaceful, dark dimension before Winnie awoke in the hospital. The doctor explained that three days had passed, and that her miscarried fetus had been cremated. She wanted nothing more than to return to that dark place where the things that didn't make sense didn't matter. Unlike reality, where everything that mattered never made sense.

An icy rain pelted the window and woke Winnie sometime in the night. With one eye swollen shut, she half-opened the other and caught her monstrous reflection in the glass. Her heart hammered and her stomach knotted. She peeked at herself again. An undead mummy with its head wrapped in gauze. Slits for eyes and a nose like an overripe plum. Stitches ran diagonally from the side of her chin through her lips and up her nostril. A macabre Picasso, she thought. Shivering in the warm bed—she felt the pain of being kicked and wrapped her arms around her middle. An unwanted vision of Leo's work boot came at her face. She flinched.

She turned away from the window, shut her eye and tried to dive back into the deep dark. Sweat stung her stitches. "Feck eeou. Feck eww! Fuuuck ewww!" Every single fuck you was pathetic as she tried to scream through clenched teeth, stitched lips, and a wired jaw. A nurse rushed in and out. Moments later, she returned and stabbed Winnie with a syringe full of something wonderful.

The police officer believed Winnie when she whispered in his ear that she had no memory of the attack. He slapped his black leather notebook closed. Said he would be in touch with Grandma Bell and if he were unable to contact her, or a parent, he'd have to notify the authorities. "You are a minor," he reminded her like she might have forgotten.

The janitor was Winnie's first real visitor, but she had no recollection of him. He proudly explained in great detail how it was God's will he'd found her. How snow and blood had frozen on her face and "if truth be told" he'd saved her life. He must have expected Winnie to be grateful, and he leaned in when she mumbled to him. She tried in vain to tell him to get lost. She wished more than anything that he had left her there in the cold dark where pain had ended. Why bring her back to suffer? *Why?* With her arm resting along her side, Winnie mustered the strength to raise her middle finger. The janitor called her a vulgar and wicked sinner before leaving the room.

After two and a half weeks, Doctor Heinz removed the wires from Winnie's jaw. He explained with an extra dose of reassurance in his voice that she was healing extraordinarily fast and should make a full recovery—except for the scar that would forever pull at her upper lip and the *"very good chance"* she would never bear children. Winnie ignored him. Focused on the lightbulb hanging from the ceiling until her eyes burned, trying to justify her miserable existence.

"Winnie? Did you hear me, dear?"

Winnie eyed him.

"Your grandmother has finally been located, and it seems she's recovering from tuberculosis in a sanatorium. In France. Which means my dear, she can*not* care for you. I've contacted the police and they in turn have contacted the authorities. You won't have to be alone any longer." He looked like he was on the verge of solving some great riddle. Winnie deprived the doctor of any and all appreciation.

The next day, a nurse with an unnecessary smile brought Winnie's soup. "Good news, Winifred. You may not have to go to the orphanage after all. The police department contacted your father. He's on the telephone line." The nurse set a food tray down on an over-the-bed cart. Winnie looked down into a bowl of what looked like green *Creature from the Black Lagoon* shit. The smell hit and Winnie gave the tray a good shove. It rolled to the window.

"Not in the mood for food?" the nurse asked.

"Would you eat it?"

"Alrighty, then." The nurse lifted the receiver next to the bed—pressed a blinking red light and put the phone to her ear. "Mr. Mudgett?" She nodded a good while as if Mr. Mudgett could see her, then handed Winnie the phone and watched with an offensively cheerful face.

"Can I get a little privacy?" Winnie glared at the nurse until her smile dropped and she huffed out of the room. Just getting out of bed was an accomplishment. Every painful move was a slow, stiff effort. She pinched the receiver between her ear and shoulder. Her jaw still tender, she winced and took the phone with her hand instead.

"Dad?"

"Winifred! How are you doing? I hear you got hurt?"

"I'm fine." Winnie shook her pillow from its case.

"Well, why are you in the hos—" Winnie tossed the phone on the bed and smothered it with the pillow. She had to keep the line open. A red light on the switchboard at the nurse's station represented a connection. A connection meant Winnie was still in her room. She slid her hand under the mattress. Pulled out a pair of jeans and a sweater stolen from the hospital morgue a few days ago. No way she was going to live in the Chicago Orphanage Asylum. No way.

A stabbing pain caught in her back as she hurried to dress. The galoshes taken last night from the nurse's closet were a near perfect fit and hardly made a sound when Winnie left her room. Her head throbbed as she held tight to the handrail and stepped down the staircase to the cafeteria.

The thought of real chewable food made her mouth water and her stomach growl until she exited the stairwell and the aroma hit. Steaming fish sticks fought dank cafeteria air for dominance. The smell coated the back of her tongue and clogged her appetite. She never missed a stride, just lifted a lady's brown fur off the coat rack on her way out the exit.

It was warm for February, especially with that damn fur coat on. What little snow was left had turned to slush, and the windy city was justifying its name. Winnie watched and laughed as a hot dog vendor chased napkins that blew like confetti from his cart. Off pure instinct, she moved in. Snatched a dog and was halfway down the block before the vendor even turned back. It was the best meal she'd had in weeks. Chewing was a painful challenge. Teeny tiny juicy bites were savored all the way to the Lincoln Park Zoo.

Screaming kids echoed like savage beasts as a woman pushed a stroller through the zoo's open iron gates. Tiny bronze lion's heads roared silently at gorillas as elephants stared down rhinos from atop pillars lining a cement walkway. Winnie was trapped behind a family that moved like slugs. Mom in her stole and perfectly pressed dress. Dad in his Sunday suit and tie. Two sons with matching brown crew cuts jumped up and down, too excited to walk. Dad held Mom's hand as they hogged the entire walkway at sloth speed.

Contempt forced Winnie's hands into fists. It wasn't their speed that angered her. It was the unobtainable. She stopped walking. Took a breath and then another. Clouds churning and crawling. Unlocking her fists, she stretched her fingers and looked down at her palms. Pink lines like scars across her long fingers. She flipped her hands over and studied the veins. The knuckles. The right pinky nail retained a speck of dried blood under it. A lion roared and urged Winnie on.

The reptile house had always been humid and dimly lit the dozen or more times Winnie had visited. A heavy scent of rotten eggs and creeping creatures kept visitors to a minimum most of the time. Two teenage boys slapped and thumped the glass as Winnie walked in. She ordered them to "Knock it off and split or else."

"Yeah, who died and made you boss?" the smallest one said.

"I did." Winnie slipped between the boy and the glass. Uncomfortably close. "I'm leaving for hell soon and there's room for one more." Her jaw tight and the red scar pulling up her lip complemented her eerie appearance when she smiled.

"I'm not afraid of you!" The boy stepped back. "Take a long walk off a short pier why don't you?" He left, followed close behind by the other.

Winnie pressed her forehead against the glass, staring down at the long and slender green tree snake wrapped around a eucalyptus branch. Mr. Armaan, a kindred spirit since their meeting at the Halloween Ball years earlier, had let her hold the green snake when it arrived last summer. Mr. Armaan was an expert on every species of snakes, especially the venomous kinds, and had taught Winnie well. It never failed to fascinate her when he milked the cobras and vipers, but most impressive was feeding time. There was something spectacular in the life and death panic that filled the rodents' eyes a split second before the snake's lightning strike. Everything must have an end or there is no beginning. Winnie thought about her unborn and her own new beginning and grinned.

"*The bite of an Inland Taipan delivers a witch's brew of toxins,*" Mr. Armaan had said. "*First, you will become paralyzed. Then, soon, breathing is impossible. You die a thousand deaths.*" The words echoed in her head: *A thousand deaths. A thousand deaths. A thousand deaths*, as she sat on her fur coat in the snake house and waited for feeding time.

In less than an hour, an assistant appeared behind the glass—corralling the tree snake from his cage. Winnie recognized the young man from one of her many VIP zoo tours with Grandma Bell and Mr. Perkins. Gently, she tapped the glass and waved. Sam, written on his nametag, mouthed, "Hi," and removed the snake. After a moment, the side door opened.

"How are you, Wilma?"

"Peachy keen, Sam. Could I watch you feed the snakes?" Getting her name wrong was inconsiderate—now she wouldn't feel the least bit bad for doing what had to be done.

"Is Mr. Perkins with you?" Sam asked.

"Yes. But he had zoo business to take care of. Told me to wait here." Winnie put her big fur coat on.

Sam nodded. "Okay, great. Come in." He led Winnie inside.

A dozen glass containers sat in a row on the counter like extra-large cookie jars. Each one held a venomous snake. The one labeled *Oxyuranus Microlepidotus* held her favorite—an immature Inland Taipan only a foot long. A coral snake rose in its jar and watched her as if requesting release. Winnie touched the glass as the snake flicked its tongue at her.

At the end of the counter sat a wooden box lined with little metal squares like a miniature milk crate. It held small jars of golden venom worth thousands of dollars. Sam opened and reached into the "LIVE MICE" box. "Would you like to feed Burney?"

"I'll just watch this time."

Sam folded back the large wire roof on Burney's cage and was dangling the mouse by its tail when suddenly a sharp bang of breaking glass caused him to yelp and turn. Shards scattered the floor. "I'm sorry! I'm so, so sorry!" Winnie cried as the king cobra slithered over the broken glass.

"Oh, shit!" Sam stood. Tossed the mouse in front of the cobra, attempting to distract it. "Get out! Quick!" he screamed. While Sam fumbled with his long snake tong and the cobra, Winnie snatched the Inland Taipan jar and carried it out. A girl with a limp and a snake in a jar strutting along the path like she had every right to do so.

In the women's bathroom, Winnie locked the stall door and set the snake jar on the back of the toilet. She pulled the hospital pillowcase from her coat pocket and carefully worked the jar into the case. Few people seemed to notice or care about the scarred girl toting the sack like Santa all the way to the bus stop. That's when it hit her. For the first time, Winnie understood how easily she could achieve what her sister, Nell, had labeled *dastardly deeds*. She pondered the reasons she'd been granted the art of manipulating situations into her favor. As with any newly acquired skill, a twinge of pride arose. Remorse and empathy were as dead as her baby.

Sylvia was in her ususal dingy yellow apron and seemed genuinely glad to see Winnie when she walked into the kitchen. She even hugged the girl. "Let me make you dinner. How's fried chicken sound?"

"Swell."

"Phone's been ringing off the hook today." Sylvia washed her hands at the sink. "Your grandmother called—she's feeling much better." Sylvia set a deep cast-iron skillet on the stove. "She said some new treatment called chemotherapy is killing her tuberculosis."

"Great." Winnie would not be needing the house. Not now.

"Then, the hospital called looking for you. They said you left without being released. I told them I hadn't seen you because, well, I hadn't. Maybe tomorrow we should let them know you're okay?"

"Yeah. Sure."

Sylvia reached a chicken out of the icebox and set it in the sink. "Last but not least, your father called. He's coming to get you. He'll be here day after tomorrow and I guess I'll be out of a job." She pulled a butcher knife from the drawer and began quartering the chicken.

Winnie's stomach knotted. Herman wasn't coming all this way just to apologize and retrieve the daughter he'd abandoned. Nothing good could come from returning to New Jersey to a family who hated her.

Speculating about Herman's return spoiled Winnie's appetite and ruined her bubble bath. It was impossible to relax and think straight without Herman interrupting her thoughts. Legally, he was still her father and could force her to return home or do with her whatever he liked. Not a chance she'd wait around to find out. The bathroom mirror was fogged and Winnie left it that way. She didn't need to see her scarred upper lip while she bobbed off her long hair.

Tomorrow would be Valentine's Day. Tomorrow night—perfect for what Winnie had in mind. With the stolen snake and a full suitcase under her bed, she slept like she hadn't a care in the world.

Leo lived alone in a one-room shack a short distance from his parent's house. Winnie knew he would be out and drunk by the time he returned home because she had arranged it that way. A lovely Valentine's Day card and a bottle of scotch, taken from Grandma Bell's liquor cabinet, had been left in Leo's truck earlier that day. The card invited him to meet his secret Valentine at the Cosmic Bowling Lane's parking lot for a "good time." Winnie signed it "Love, Lorraine."

A dog barked outside the unlocked cabin as Winnie snuck in and hid in the closet. It was cold and reeked of Leo. Like sweaty cheese. With the door slightly ajar, Winnie could see a slice of the bed and kept a firm grip on a pointed shovel shortened by a busted handle in case things did not go as planned.

Winnie had dozed off and lost track of how long she'd been in the closet when Leo's truck finally rattled into the yard. The dog barked, then bayed. It seemed like forever before footsteps stumbled up the porch. When the door opened and slammed, Winnie's heart leaped into her throat.

A light popped on. The bedsprings groaned and Winnie watched Leo's hands untie and pull off his leather work boots—boots that had kicked and killed her baby. It was all she could do to keep from exploding out of the closet and pounding his skull to a pulp with the shovel.

He stood. Unbuttoned his plaid coat. Winnie gripped the shovel and squeezed her eyes to quell the rage roiling inside her. It had to look like an accident, she reminded herself. An accidental death would not raise the suspicion of murder. But if her plan went sideways, Winnie would use the shovel and accept the possibility of being caught. Leo peeled off his coat, left his white T-shirt on, then stood and undid his jeans—stepped out of them bare-assed, then disappeared. The light went out and the bed squealed.

Winnie waited.

He snored a long while before Winnie gathered her courage and stepped out of the closet. Her stiff legs tingled and ached as she moved soft and slow to the foot of the bed. She leaned the shovel against the wall, then carefully folded back the blankets, revealing Leo's enormous feet. The rhythm of his snoring never changed. Not even when she shook the snake against the glass jar to aggravate it. The dog barked. Winnie hadn't considered a dog when planning her escape, but she had the shovel to protect herself.

The metal lid scraped against the glass as she slowly twisted it off the jar. Then, without hesitation, she dumped the serpent onto Leo's legs. The wrathful snake raised its head and warped its upper body into a perfect question mark—an irrefutable *why*. The provoked snake hissed, ready to strike. Quickly, Winnie threw the covers over the snake and pinched Leo's foot. He kicked a little. Then kicked more. Harder and faster. He flew up and grabbed his leg. A low guttural groan of terror escaped him in the confusion, followed by a demon scream that rose from the depths of his soul and sent the dark room into a frenzy.

Winnie hoped the sickening scream would not wake Leo's parents next door as she wound the lid back onto the jar. Leo didn't even notice her. He was too busy thrashing. When the blankets fell away, Winnie saw it. The snake had sunk its fangs deep into Leo's calf and wasn't letting go. The sound of snake slapping skin and Leo's exaggerated mournful squalls reminded her of the last time they were in the sack. But this was so much better. So much more satisfying than she could have ever imagined. A smile stretched her scarred upper lip as she set the jar on the floor, then used the back of the shovel to shut him up.

The first blow to his belly knocked the air out of him. The metal rang out and she should have stopped there, but an uncontrollable urge took over. On the verge of exhilaration, something like an orgasm, she couldn't stop. The second and third blows to his torso might contradict the appearance of an accidental death. Leo's eyes bulged.

The snake released, fell, and slithered under the bed. Out of breath, Winnie went to the door with the shovel and waited. Surely, he would die, but she had to see it for herself. Watch the paralysis take hold. The pain.

Leo gripped his stomach with both hands and writhed on the bed. Winnie leaned against the door. "The snake bit you because *he* was afraid. Isn't that funny? *Him* afraid of you." Leo spewed all over himself and the yeasty smell of Scotch filled the tiny room. "The Taipan has these really neat toxins that help the poison spread faster, so pretty soon you're going to choke to death on your own blood. How do you like them apples?"

"I'll kwil..." His speech slurred. Paralysis plain and simple. "Hewwwppp." It was fantastically pathetic. He couldn't even scream and dropped his head to his chest.

"Guess what they like to eat," Winnie said. "Go ahead, guess." She waited as if he could answer. "Rats! Isn't that just the bee's knees?"

A light came through the curtain from somewhere outside, and Winnie sucked a breath. Pressed her back against the door. The dog barked louder as Leo shivered, then convulsed. It was an extravagant performance. The way his face contorted and turned beet-red as his entire body twitched then flopped around on the bed like a giant fish. A rotting good-for-nothing bucktoothed fish. Winnie smiled. Covered her mouth with her hand and felt the tender scar above her lip. She laughed when blood flew violently from Leo's kisser. "Happy Valentine's Day baby killer."

She cracked open the door and peeked outside. Where was that damn dog and why had he stopped barking? Winnie waited. Outside lights from the main house were on and lit the yard. Shit. If anyone was outside, she'd be seen.

Winnie shut the door and watched closely for the snake as she stepped to the small window beside the bathroom sink, hoping to escape. The window wouldn't open. Wouldn't budge. It could have been Winnie's lack of strength. Her mind raced—debated the probable outcomes. She had to get out—there was a very poisonous snake on the loose and she'd much rather be caught and jailed than bitten. She bent, kept the shovel low, ready to scoop and toss the snake as she made her way to the door, then opened it.

Outside, the big brown mutt stood growling at the bottom of the porch steps but was all bark and no bite the moment Winnie raised the shovel. She stepped off the porch hoping she wouldn't have to whack the dang dog. "Get out of here," she snarled. Adrenaline turned to ecstasy when he tucked tail and ran.

A man yelled, "Homer! Here! Leave that gal alone." The man, Leo's father Winnie assumed, waved and started toward her. Odds were good he pegged Winnie as a Valentine's Day floozy Leo had brought home. She kept her head down, walked fast, but he'd seen her—she was sure of it. Still stiff and sore from her injuries, Winnie ran the best she could using the shovel for support.

Through the woods, Winnie hurried until she reached the bridge that crossed the creek. Adrenaline masked some of the pain and she refused to stop until she reached the gully with the thick brush. Once there, she planted the shovel and leaned on it. Squeezed her side and worked hard to catch her breath.

Remembering the terror on Leo's face made her laugh out loud more than once as she hiked the narrow deer trail that led like a secret tunnel through the brush. She fought the slapping branches all the way to where her bike waited in the dead of night like a trusty steed. Winnie ditched the shovel in the brush, mounted, and pedaled home.

Though she'd been seen and was sure the police would try to find her, she didn't care. Not one bit. She held the power now and knew it. Felt like she could eat the world if she wanted to. Exterminating vermin like Leo was an achievement beyond compare.

The urge to yell—to pump her fist in triumph—was overwhelming once Winnie was safe in her room. In her bed, under the covers, she let loose a whooping holler that felt like it had been trapped since the day she was born. Nothing was better than passion for a new love. An undeniable consummation.

CHAPTER
FIVE

N ana's smile started on one side of her face, then slowly
slid into place.

"Killed a snake with a snake," she giggled. "Ironic, huh?"
Her giggles gained strength and turned into a cackle. "Guess I
was just born with the devil in me thanks to Grandpa Mudgett.
H.H. Holmes is what they used to call him. Boy oh boy, that man
was awful wicked. You know about him?"

"The name rings a bell, but."

"He was America's first *real* serial killer. Back before every
Tom, Dick, and Harry was branded a serial killer." Nana laughed.

I wondered if I too was geared toward the same homicidal
fury.

Nana's laugh caused a coughing fit. She gasped for air. I
grabbed a cup of water from her food tray and helped her drink.
After a few sips, she regained control.

"I'm not exaggerating one bit when I tell you that taking
Leo's life was wonderful. Physically pleasurable. Like when

you're freezing cold and you get near a fire—the warmth sinks in and sends those sweet chills through your body. It was just like that." Nana's wide eyes were awake—alive. And, as if on cue, thunder rattled the window and walls.

Some say you can feel darkness—that evil has a presence. For the first time, I felt it. Caught a glimpse of it and understood what she meant. Realized I should have been horrified—repulsed at the very least—but truth be told, killing Leonard had made the world a better place. He was never going to contribute anything good to the world.

I was perplexed. Nana had just confessed to murder. She'd *killed* another human being, plain and simple. I racked my memory, wondering how I'd missed it all these years. Living with her for most of my life, there had to be hints of something sinister. Had I overlooked it? Made excuses for wicked behavior because I loved her? No. I could not recall a single incident. True evil just wasn't there. My mind drifted without permission to a place I did not need to go right now.

I'm a murderer too. Shame and revulsion hit like a fist to my gut. My husband, Mark, convinced me to kill our unborn child—and like a fool, I obeyed. Only difference was my murder was perfectly legal and *not* at all pleasurable. Guilt comes and goes but never fails to maul my conscience every time I see a baby, hear one cry, or worse, get close to a five-year-old. Regret inevitably turns to wonder at what he or she would have looked like. How can I ache for a child I've never known? I always believed that women have the right to terminate an unwanted pregnancy and still do, but for me it was an awful mistake. A child to love would have offered an option to the unbearable loneliness devouring me little by little.

Nana's eyes looked heavy and I could see she was struggling to hold them open. Rain pecked and streamed down the window.

"You're a good girl, Jessica." She was wrong about that, but it was good to know she thought so. Nana always had my back even when I didn't deserve it.

I was twelve when I went to live with Nana on Blue Mountain. My real father left my mother while she was pregnant with me and according to Nana, that's when my mother became forever *"gloomy."* I was two years old when my mother married Raymond Peterson, who was sent straight from hell—where I'm certain he'll return. He never loved us kids but neither did my mother. She never showed me or my older brother Joey any sort of affection whatsoever. Not once do I recall her telling me she loved me. It made no difference what we did—good or bad, there was no reaction from her. When I was nine, my grades went from all As to mostly Fs and my mother had the same empty look she always had when she tossed my report card into the trash like junk mail.

I could have discovered the cure for cancer and it wouldn't have mattered. It was like having a dead mother who did nothing but cook and clean. I prayed each and every night that my real father would return to save us.

Mostly, Raymond picked on Joey, but when Joey ran away, I became Raymond's only option. His favorite saying after every fight was "Home is where the hate is." An ugly grin on his tobacco-stained lips. Lips like worms ripped from the earth, twisting and filthy.

One morning, before school, he called me a stupid-ass fat cunt for not replacing the toilet paper. My mother heard him say it. At the kitchen table, she stood next to him with his plate of crispy bacon and scrambled eggs in her hand. Slowly, like some sort of zombie she set it down in front of him and went back to the stove—emotionless. It was the last time I let her lack of love and concern hurt me.

I skipped school that day and called Nana. She said I should never allow anyone to drag me down into their custom-built shithole. Nana said she was *"damn glad"* to have me and for the first time in my life, I mattered. Nana never made me feel bad about myself. Not even a little—and to an overweight twelve-year-old, that made all the difference in the world. I went from waking up and wishing I'd died in the night to truly looking forward to the day ahead. All because of Nana.

"That's enough for now. You need to rest." I rubbed Nana's shoulder.

"I'm fine," Nana mumbled with closed eyes. "I have to..." She drifted off and I turned off the recorder.

It was damn near four o'clock. With all the storytelling and murder confession, I had lost track of time. Nana and I had both had enough for one day. I kissed her goodbye.

Daylight dwindled fast this time of year, and my mind raced as I flipped the windshield wipers onto high. The truck splashed along Blue Mountain Road and I swigged from a big bottle of Pepto Bismol. My guts hadn't stopped churning with worry since Mark disappeared. Plus, I honestly missed my cheating husband. Two lanes of busted asphalt twisted up the mountain until it turned to gravel and forked just ahead. I slowed for the turn and the deep puddle that followed. Fog coated thick pines and hid the hills and canyon below. How could Nana, a feeble old woman be a killer? And if she were, why? What motive could she possibly have? The relentless question forced a laugh. Not only was the notion speculation at this point—it was ludicrous, I decided, as my headlights lit the yellow police tape strung across Nana's front gate.

The light at dusk was grainy and with rain it was hard to tell if anyone was securing the property. I saw no one and stepped out. An aggravating rain pelted my face, forcing me to hurry while I tore the tape from the side. The Master lock and heavy chain that usually kept the gate closed lay in the mud just below the post. Someone had cut it.

Ever since I could remember, Nana's gate had been locked. Always. It was one of her rules you didn't break. Even if you were just dropping off groceries or salt blocks, didn't matter. You shut the gate and locked it. A total pain in the ass to be sure, but Nana swore it was the best way to *"keep the riffraff out."* That and a pack of good dogs.

There were only four people who had a key to the gate: Mark, myself, Nana, and Jim Kelly, who lived in a rusted singlewide on the ranch and did much of the work over the last twenty years. He and Nana were like oil and water. Constantly bickering worse than an old married couple, but I'm positive he loved her. A quiet man. Hardworking in spite of being an alcoholic. He'd left town without a word the day after the sheriff questioned him about Mark's disappearance, and I couldn't come up with a single reason why.

Mark and Jim were hunting buddies back before I married Mark fifteen years ago. According to my husband, a hunting buddy is the best kind of friend a man can have. So why would Jim have left the ranch? Where would he have gone? He didn't even own a vehicle. Sold it a few years back when he got his third DUI leaving the VFW hall. On his way home he ran a teenage girl off the road and she just missed hitting a tree. Jim wound up in a ditch with a busted nose from smacking the steering wheel. Just the thought of having almost killed that girl scarred Jim so badly he quit driving since quitting the booze wasn't an option. On summer nights he'd ride a horse into town, do his drinking, then ride back home.

Did Nana do something awful to Jim? I couldn't fathom it. None of it made any sense so I quit thinking and swung the gate open, got back in the truck shivering, and blasted the heater as I drove in without shutting the gate.

The stench of wet hog manure and muck lingered as I passed the empty pens. The swine had been removed and sent to auction days ago, but the aroma lingered.

Wendy, my favorite of Nana's mares, nickered when I slid open the barn door.

"Excuse me, ma'am?" I damn near jumped out of my skin.

A scream froze in my throat. I caught my breath. "Ho-ly shit." I bent with my hands on my weak knees to calm my heart.

A deputy, covered in a long black slicker with a hood, stepped up. "Sorry. Didn't mean to scare you."

"I'm just here to feed the animals." I straightened—raised my shaking hands in surrender.

"Well, no one's allowed in here. I have orders to arrest all trespassers," he said.

"I'm not trespassing. This is my grandmother's place and if I don't feed the animals, who will?" I crossed my arms. "They supposed to just starve to death?"

"Sheriff put in a request with animal control to pick them up."

"Christ. I'll come get them tomorrow. You let them know I'm coming." I filled the wheelbarrow with extra-large flakes of alfalfa. "They need to eat. So, arrest me after I feed."

"I know it seems silly, ma'am. I'm just doing my job." He stepped in front of me. "Here, I got it." He rolled the hay-filled wheelbarrow outside of the barn and followed me down the hill through the mud to the horse pens. I lifted the heavy flakes and pitched them over the fence into feeders we'd made from old tractor tires as the deputy pushed the wheelbarrow along the fence line.

"Thanks." I appreciated his help. "Just let me check the dogs and I'll get out of here."

"No need. Animal control removed them today." Thunder grumbled somewhere in the distance and I wanted to scream.

"How do I get them back?"

"Go in tomorrow—oh, wait, no, tomorrow's Sunday. They're closed. You can go in Monday. Shouldn't be a problem."

I nodded and took the empty wheelbarrow around the opposite side of the barn. That's when I saw it. Sitting atop the high hill like a monster in the disintegrating light. How had I missed it earlier? Had the rain obscured my view? Or was I just that out of it these days?

A yellow excavator replaced sow pens that had been made of heavy gauge hog wire welded to iron pipe in four-foot sections topped with a corrugated tin roof. Nana and I, but mostly Jim worked and sweated for weeks one summer to build those perfect pens. To see them mangled—bent and broken on the side hill like some sick modern art exhibit—was a reminder that life as I knew it was over.

Every year, as far back as I can remember, at least a dozen 4-H and FFA kids bought their Hampshire project pigs from Nana. Her pigs had the best show record in all of Calaveras County. Seeing this would kill her. It was like someone was stomping my chest as the realization that Nana was never coming home hit me. My hands turned to fists. "You guys confirm anything yet?"

"I'm not at liberty to—"

"Why the excavator?"

"I'm not at lib—"

"Yeah, yeah. Of course not." I left the barn and was heading for my truck when I noticed how decrepit Nana's farmhouse had become. How had I not noticed the peeling white paint? Its wet wooden underbelly was gray and weathered in the darkness. It was as if the place was withering away with Nana. "I'll be back tomorrow for the horses. Early." It would take two trips in my stock trailer to get all the horses picked up.

"Okay, sure." He walked back toward his SUV, parked on the muddy road below the excavator. Yellow police tape decorated the half-acre hill like party streamers. They had sectioned off some of the ranch and put up three blue canopy tents. I'd read that the California Conservation Corps had been recruited and were sifting the property for evidence on their hands and knees in a row of twelve. Any chance of a decent outcome was as destroyed as the hog pens.

Being home didn't offer the comfort I had craved, but a double dose of Pepto and the half-bottle of cheap Merlot along with the electric blanket set on high helped.

I hated that I missed Mark. He was my first love and the only man I'd ever been with. It was like part of me was missing. He'd been gone over a month and it killed me to think about him with her. I let the memories pull me all the way down into the rabbit hole of when we'd quit having sex. Mark called it "whiskey dick." Said it wasn't me and as soon as he sobered up, he'd prove it. Now I know it was me, because he chose to prove it to Gabby instead. The ignorant blind loyalty I gave never failed to sting and remind me that the wound was still there—wide open and bleeding.

Mark had been arrested for insurance fraud. The yearlong state investigation built a solid case against him. Thirteen horses killed by my veterinarian husband, most of them electrocuted, and then claimed as colic cases for their mortality insurance payment. The state had proof that Mark's involvement in the killings went as far back as four years. Convinced he was guilty, I left Mark and stayed at Nana's. That lasted about a week. Daily,

Mark begged for my forgiveness; reminded me how much he loved me and how we swore before God to stick together until death do us part.

After using our ranch as collateral, I bailed him out of jail and within six months we'd lost everything. Our veterinary practice and home were in foreclosure. Mark's attorney suggested he plead guilty. That same week, Mark's assistant, Gabby, came to my home and confessed, in *my* kitchen, that she was in love with *my* husband. And that he loved her too. She was young and skinny and had a sweet face that reminded me of someone famous. I wanted to kill them both. According to Mark, Gabby demanded he leave me and start divorce proceedings or she would turn on him—testify as a witness for the state. The next day Mark disappeared.

It softened my own sorrows to compare tragedies with others on the local TV news. *"A Lodi science teacher, Anthony Patterson, was arrested in Las Vegas, Nevada on statutory rape charges. Last month, Mr. Patterson fled the state with his fourteen-year-old student,"* a man with a lazy eye reported as I nursed my Merlot—let the bloody thickness tingle and linger on the back of my tongue before sending it to my bloodstream.

"An unidentified man was found frozen to death near the Mokelumne River." Rain hit the tin roof like pebbles and I speculated on my life once Wells Fargo finally took this place. No home, no warm bed, and no toilet. How would I survive? I wouldn't. I'd be the woman on the eleven o'clock news— unidentified and frozen to death. Mark's photo filled the flat screen.

"Police and the F.B.I. are still searching for Mark Williams, a prominent Calaveras County veterinarian who is suspected of being linked to the killing of dozens of racehorses. According to investigators, horse owners Lupita Contreras

Morales and Omar Vasquez collected over two million dollars in fraudulent insurance claims under multiple aliases. Anyone with information should contact the Calaveras County Sheriff's Department."

I wondered if they'd blame Nana for his disappearance or find his remains where they'd found his phone. Buried in the hog pens.

I swigged the last of my wine, tried hard to hold the door shut on my memories and turned the channel. *Finding Bigfoot* was on Animal Planet. It was Mark's favorite. We'd watched every episode—all nine seasons—together. The creature fascinated him and somehow watching it that night soothed my loneliness until the electricity went out. I stared at the dark ceiling desperate for sleep. Not the tidbits of rest I'd been getting over the last few months, but the deep nourishing sleep that pulls you into the depths of being, strips you of time and place and most of all who you are or ever have been.

CHAPTER
SIX

A t six a.m. I nursed a red wine headache with four Ibuprofen and more Pepto. The temperature in the house was cold enough for me to see my breath when I coughed because the fire in the woodstove had gone out sometime in the night. I stirred what was left of the coals with the poker, then went to the porch and gathered an armload of pine. After restarting the fire, I set the oven to five hundred degrees and made coffee on the propane stove. Two cups of Folgers helped bring me back to life. I opened the oven's hot jaw and let the heat engulf me.

With a second round of storms approaching from the west, there was no telling when the power would return My head felt less likely to explode after a shower with what little water was left in the tank. Mark knew how to crank up the old generator and get the water pump going. I hadn't taken the time to learn—another reason to miss him.

As I toweled off in the bathroom, my mind took flight. For no good reason I began contemplating why Mark never took time away from his practice to go on a vacation or a weekend cow horse competition with me. *"Can't do it,"* he'd say. *"Think how many sick and dying horses I treat each week. Now, what if I wasn't here?"* He'd wait for my response.

"They'd take them somewhere else. You're not the only vet in the world."

"Exactly. Then, I'd be out of business and you'd have to buy your own horses. Pay your own bills and entry fees."

I had no counter. He was right. He'd made good money and never complained about my addiction to showing reined cow horses or the ridiculous amount of money I spent to win a few silver buckles.

Looking back, I think there was a better than good chance that the real reason he encouraged me to go to the horse shows without him was so he could be with Gabby. The thought was like picking a scab I just had to keep going until I bled. Gabby had worked for Mark for three years and I had no idea when they'd started sleeping together.

My insides twisted as I worked a hooded sweatshirt over my head. A weak attempt to avoid eye contact with myself in the dim bathroom mirror failed. Mauve semicircles under my eyes matched my wine-stained lips. Pulling my ponytail through the back of my ball cap, I noticed something stuck in my hair at the temple. I leaned into the mirror, let the cap hang, and tried to scratch it off. Picking and pulling.

"No way."

Gray! God, help me I looked like shit.

Rain let up while I hooked the trailer to the truck, and soon the sun busted through the clouds. It looked like heaven and reminded me I'd have to miss church today. I'd been good and hadn't missed a service for five Sundays in a row. God could see the mess I was in and should cut me some slack. I doubted the parishioners would, but they'd at least pretend to understand my predicament.

In the truck, I clasped my hands above the steering wheel. "Lord, I've confessed my sins and pray for forgiveness. I walk with You as evil abounds and ask for strength in this time of terrible need. I repent from the depths of my soul and receive You into my heart as my savior and Lord of my life. Amen."

The curvy backroads to Nana's ranch ran sixteen miles but took forty minutes to travel dragging a trailer. I pulled up to the opened gate. The crime scene tape was down and lying on the ground next to the fence. Two Sheriff's Department SUVs sat on either side of the entrance. A seasoned deputy with a strong jaw and golden skin stepped out of his vehicle and walked over. I rolled the window down. "I'm here to pick up the horses."

He didn't say a word, just nodded, signaled me through, then pulled his walkie-talkie up to his mouth. As I drove toward the horse pens, a dozen or more investigators of some sort gathered under one of the blue canopies. Diesel smoke rose from a pipe on the excavator, but it hadn't moved since last night. I wanted to know what they were saying, what they were doing, and more than anything—what they'd found. Not knowing a single fact not only frustrated me, it caused the locals to create and share their own conclusions.

The serial killer of Calaveras was the topic of every Facebook post and I'm sure every conversation at the Cozy Cabin Café, the hardware store, Dollar General, and the post office. After Nana's arrest, I tortured myself with posts in her defense, then gave up and deleted my account. There were rumors that Nana was a witch who sacrificed babies she stole from orphanages in Peru. That was one accusation I knew was false since Nana never left the US and seldom the ranch.

I loaded four pregnant mares and one old mule into the trailer while keeping an eye on the excavator that idled and smoked in the dreary morning. A small group of men, maybe five or six, and two women stepped into what looked like white hazmat suits as I shut the trailer door and latched it. What would they find today I wondered? They must have found something because they wouldn't be tearing up the place unless they had a damn good reason. My stomach hurt.

Something I suspect was fear weakened my limbs as I flattened the clutch and cranked the steering wheel towards the front gate. It was all so unreal. Like having a vivid nightmare and knowing full well that I would never wake.

The gate was closed as I approached. The same two deputies now stood like soldiers inside the gate while a half-dozen news vans and SUVs from as far away as Sacramento and Reno set up camp along the gravel roadside.

"Holy shit," I said without meaning to.

A big camera balanced on a beefy man's shoulder as a woman in a raincoat stepped into the middle of the road. The deputy swung the gate open. I rolled through, offering him a thank-you wave. He saluted.

The reporter and her cameraman stood their ground in the middle of the road as I approached. They had to be filming me. A familiar-faced brunette with a KCRA cap and raincoat ran to my window as a second cameraman prevented me from moving forward. I floored the clutch and stomped the brake. A horse slammed against the aluminum divider. "Asshole!" I shouted. "Move!"

"Just a few questions?" she yelled.

"No thanks." I shook my head and tooted my horn at the man. This seemed to signal the pack. A swarm of cameras came at me from all directions and before I knew it the media had become a human roadblock. "Shit!"

"What can you tell us about the murder site?" someone yelled, then came a variety of voices from beyond.

"Do you know the suspect, Effie Hobbs?"

"They're calling her the 'Blue Mountain butcher.'"

"Why'd she do it?"

"Do you have any information at all?"

Time slowed the way it does sometimes in dreams—the bad ones anyway. I gripped the gearshift.

"How many bodies have they found?"

"Can you tell us anything?"

"NO!" I revved the engine, hoping they'd take me seriously. They didn't. A red-bearded cameraman adjusted the plastic cover over his camera and gave me the stink-eye. *What if I put the truck into gear? Floor the accelerator and watch them fly like a flock of ignorant turkeys. Bones and bodies breaking like sticks. The disrespectful pricks would run screaming with regret, and I'd be headlining the six o'clock news.*

I laid on the horn and drowned their shouts; hoped for the best as I inched forward. This should not be happening. I should be getting ready for church. Smiling. Hugging fellow believers. Singing hymns. Having my spirit lifted and soul redeemed. Someone hit the side of my truck. Why wouldn't the deputies tell them to back off, I wondered and drove home asking God to forgive my evil thoughts and foul language.

After offloading the first of the mares into my muddy pasture, I headed back to Nana's to pick up the last four horses. On the way, I stopped by the old Rail Road Flat store for more caffeine. Main Street was short and the two-lane had never seen so much traffic. For a quarter of a mile parked cars and news vans littered the curb. I pulled down a side road and parked the trailer at the old elementary school which had closed down a few years earlier due to budget cuts.

A crowd gathered around two plywood tables under the covered porch outside the store like someone was having a yard sale. A cameraman filmed the crowd then aimed his lens at the items on the tables: a dried white paintbrush, a worn pointed shovel with a wooden handle, rusted ear-notching pliers next to a muddy yellow ear-tag, busted hammer next to a handful of fence staples, a metal bucket bent to hell, and a foot-long section of heavy chain. *Who would buy that junk?* I went inside.

The small store smelled musty as usual, but swarmed with hungry press who had no other choice if they wanted grub since the nearest restaurant was an hour away. The dirty wood floor creaked as I walked to the coffee pot.

"That's her." It sounded like a girl and I could feel eyes on my back. The pot held just enough coffee to fill a cup. I took a sip.

"Someone should throw *her* to the hogs." That was definitely Carl, the bearded brute behind the counter. I've known him my whole life. Twenty years ago, Nana sold his oldest daughter her first 4-H hog. I say sold, but Carl never paid Nana. Not even when that champion hog sold for $6,700 at the county fair. Now that I knew Nana could be somewhat vengeful, I wondered why she'd let Carl get away with screwing her over like he did.

I waited in line, drank my coffee, and tried to ignore the woman asking if I was Effie Hobbs's daughter. "No," I said.

"Hey, Carl." I set the coffee on the counter.

"Two-fifty." He pulled on his long gray beard and eyed me as I held out my credit card. "No credit 'less you spend twenty bucks."

I could probably dig up two-fifty in change from my truck. Instead, I lifted the cup off the counter, gulped almost the entire cup, then set it back down. "Keep it." I walked out.

A crowd of about nine or ten was gathered around the makeshift sale table just outside the door.

"No way. Look!" A barefoot tweaker chick in short shorts and a Harley sweatshirt held up a pair of small black cowboy boots covered in muck. "I'm getting these." Heads turned her way.

"I wouldn't wear them if you paid me one million bucks." A woman still in her pajamas raised her overplucked eyebrows and shook her head. "She might a wore 'em when she was killin' them people, you don't know." Her head never stopped shaking. "Oh my gawd, she could a used this to bury someone." She raised a shovel off the table by its wooden handle with two fingers like a child might when they don't want to touch something.

"She didn't bury anyone, she fed them to her hogs." I said, recognizing Nana's boots, and the rest of the sale items from the ranch.

"Ughhh..." Pajama gal jacked her jaw then scratched at it.

"Know what this shit'll bring on eBay? Murder memorabilia baby." A fat man sucked his cigarette and rattled the piece of chain against the plywood.

Tweaker Girl set the boots on the ground and picked up a used 60 cc dosing syringe. "Wonder what she did with this?" She laughed like an old smoker.

I worked my way to the girl, picked up the boots, and tucked them under my arm.

"Hey! Those are mine," Tweaker Girl said.

"*No*, they're not," I growled, then grabbed the metal bucket and pushed my way through, filling it with most the items off the table. "Give it," I barked at Tweaker Girl, and she handed over the syringe without a word. I shoved it in the bucket and rested the shovel on my shoulder. Thought about cracking their ugly faces and skulls with the shovel, but hurried back to the truck instead.

Nana is not a serial killer, Nana is not a serial killer, Nana is not a serial killer.

I set Nana's things in the back of the truck as a cameraman and what I assume was a reporter approached. The camera followed me as I pulled away.

The road to Blue Mountain was clear, but news vans and media still lined the roadside. Four deputies stood outside Nana's gate as I pulled up and stopped. A boyish looking deputy checked my ID, then radioed someone on his walkie-talkie. After a minute he nodded and stepped aside as another deputy opened the gate and let me in. I loaded the last four mares with no trouble and no help from a female deputy who followed close behind and watched my every move.

As I pulled out and drove past the media circus, I thought about making a last-minute appearance at church—but decided Nana was more important. Just the thought of losing her brought tears. I wanted her to be innocent and prayed for it, but knowing the truth might set me free.

After the last of the mares were swishing their tails and pinning their ears at each other in my pasture, I hurried to the hospital. The trailer bounced and banged with no weight inside as I pulled into the parking lot and I regretted not taking an extra five minutes to unhook the thing at home. Winter was in full force. A mix of rain and hail showered me as I ran from the back of the parking lot to the hospital entrance as fast as I could.

Detective Rocha caught me in the hall on the way to Nana's room, and panic trickled down my spine like rain. He'd come to my home the day Nana was arrested and questioned me. We were well acquainted, since he had questioned me seven or eight times since Mark's disappearance. I knew he suspected I had something to do with it. He had to. Statistics prove that the spouse or lover is usually to blame. An obvious defense,

I reminded Rocha that I was wise enough to know I'd be the number one suspect.

"I could never hurt him," I'd cried the last time we spoke and very much doubted Rocha's smile when he greeted me.

I'd never noticed how round his dark eyes were or how compact his thin-lipped mouth was below his flat nose. Even his slick head was abnormally large for such a delicate neck and diminutive body. He could easily play the part of an alien creature with a little latex.

"Have a minute?" Rocha sipped from a Styrofoam coffee cup.

"No, I don't," I wanted to say, but instead forced a smiled and said, "Sure," and then followed him into an empty waiting room.

The Lysoled air felt sharp and full of teeth just waiting to chew me up. My disobedient stomach churned, then growled, and I grabbed it.

"We could talk in the cafeteria if you like?" Rocha offered as if he gave one shit about me or my hunger.

"That's okay. I need to see my grandmother." My wet coat groaned against the pleather chair as I leaned back.

"How are you doing?" He sat on the edge of the chair next to me, his knees too close.

He didn't care how I was doing. "Fine. I try not to think about it."

"Which? Your missing husband or your grandmother's victims?" He turned cold in an instant and his jaw flinched. His thin lips pressed into a straight line.

"I wasn't aware there were victims. Last I heard, nothing had been confirmed. It's impossible to get any information—"

"It's a tedious process since all that remains are bone fragments. But they're human. Bits of *undigested human bone.*"

That has been confirmed." He spread his long rubbery-looking fingers along his thighs. "I researched hogs, Jessica. You know much about them?"

"No," I lied, feeling guilty and waited to be struck by lightning.

"Did you know one lactating sow can consume a two-hundred-pound human in a week or less—bones included?" Rocha slapped his hands against the metal armrests. "Your grandmother had thirteen sows!" Spit flew from his mouth.

I stood and stepped aside.

"Soon as the weather cooperates, I'm certain we'll find more." He stood and leaned in so close I could smell the coffee and cigarettes on his breath. "Serial killers don't stop, Mrs. Williams. They kill until they're caught—or dead."

"Effie Hobbs is *not* a serial killer." I said it without the benefit of believing it, my cheeks burning as if I'd been slapped.

"Look, you don't want to be on the wrong side of this." He seemed to be waiting for me to agree, but I was still secretly digesting the word 'victims.' Plural. "You can help." His tone softened. "Offer the innocent families some closure."

I thought about the awfulness and suffering those poor people must be going through. Of course I wanted to stop their pain. Thank God my stomach was empty. I felt sick. Hot saliva filled my mouth. My hands sweated. I ripped my coat off. "I... I have to go."

"You can convince her to confess before she passes. It'd save the county and the families a massive amount of grief if she would identify the victims."

"I'll try." I blinked hard and fast, driving back burning tears and hoping to God Nana was not the murderous monster Rocha claimed. She was just Nana. I wiped my eyes with the back of my hand. "I'll talk to her."

A silent rage gleamed in his snarl as I opened the door and left the waiting room—regretting the promises I'd made to Nana and God to keep my mouth shut.

Pain looked intense, as Nana lay curled in a fetal position. She resembled a newborn and could not have weighed eighty pounds. Cancer had sunk its rotten teeth into her and was trying hard to swallow. Flesh clung to her bony arm like it was about to fall off as she reached for me.

"Jess." Her breath came in quick puffs between clenched teeth.

I bent down close to her. There was a stale stillness in the air, almost like rotting meat. It was hard to swallow, but I gathered what little saliva was in my mouth and forced it down.

"You want some pain medicine?" I asked.

"No. Makes me...sleepy...then can't talk," she muttered and used her whole face to close her eyes.

"Nana, the police have proof of human remains in the hog pens."

With a half-grin, she opened her eyes. "Press record."

CHAPTER
SEVEN

Jane Wayne

W innie woke, glad that the thrill of killing Leo hadn't deserted her in the night. The power of invincibility helped focus her thoughts on the next move. She had to leave before her father or the police showed up at the door. There was no cash in Grandma Bell's safe, but she had left behind six necklaces, two bracelets, and one hell of a pretentious cocktail ring that would easily fund Winnie's escape.

In Grandma Bell's bedroom, Winnie piled the jewelry on and sashayed to the cheval mirror. She ignored her awful bobbed hair and her scarred lip. She only saw how valuable she was now. Facing the large window was a small writing desk that held pens and Bell Howe's letterhead. Winnie took a seat. Chose a pen and dragged a page in front of her.

Dear Grandma Bell,

Thanks for giving me a place to stay and feeding me. I really liked it here. I wish you didn't have to go to

Paris and could have stuck around longer. I really liked going to museums and the zoo and even your dinner parties were okay. Sorry if I got on your nerves. I wish you were here now. You always know just what to do when things get knotted. I hope you don't die from tuberculosis.

SO LONG FOREVER,
Winnie

Winnie left the letter on the desk and walked out. She got halfway down the stairs before rushing back to Grandma Bell's bedroom. She snatched the letter off the desk. Ripped it into pieces and brushed them into the trash.

Downtown, Winnie hawked one of the diamond bracelets for eighty bucks and an autographed copy of Jack London's *The Sea-Wolf*. In the cab on the way to the train station, the driver shouted over slapping wipers. He rambled on about San Francisco and a fancy new train called the Zephyr that took high-class folks there in style. Winnie imagined herself on the top-notch train. Looking out the window from a luxurious leather seat this time and not seeing her father's back. Proof that she'd prospered since riding the train that had brought her here.

San Francisco sounded nice. Winnie had never even owned a bathing suit. Learning to swim would be exciting and lying on the beach in warm sand under continuous sunshine reading *The Sea-Wolf* was tempting, but it was a headline in the Sunday Times at the train station that distracted—then convinced her: "Sunshine Elevates Mood." She bought the paper and read the entire article. "San Francisco, here I come," she whispered.

The California Zephyr gleamed like a silver snake. It was the latest in luxury travel, and Winnie just had to ride that train. She had thirty minutes before the Zephyr would depart when the ticket agent explained how seats had been sold out for months. Winnie watched white ladies in white heels, white hats, and white gloves board the train with the help of a gentleman's hand on their backs.

Winnie wore boots, Levis, and a red and black plaid shirt with pearl snaps. She stood out like a raven among a flock of white doves. The thought of buying a ticket on the regular old boring train and riding it all the way to the West Coast irked her. With remnants of confidence, she walked around to the caboose.

An old black man in a black suit sat outside reading a *Life* magazine with John Wayne on the cover.

"You like him?" Winnie stopped at the steps. "John Wayne?"

The old man kept his finger in place, closed the magazine, and looked at the cover. "Sure. Who don't like cowboys?"

"I only like him cause he's my dad."

He inspected her a bit more closely. "Is not. You fibbin'."

"No. He sent me a ticket on this here fancy train so's I could go see him." Winnie conjured a cowboy drawl.

"Well, now." He stood. "I didn't think the Duke was married."

"Ain't no more." Winnie climbed the three steps onto the caboose and stood next to the man. "My mom lives here and I'm just going to visit him. My dad, John Wayne. Well, I was." Winnie teared up. "My mom's real mad about me leaving, but I miss my daddy—so darn much." Winnie drug her hands across her eyes and smeared the tears. "When he mailed me the ticket, I was so darn excited I packed a week ago. Anyhow, I had the ticket and all; it was right here in my back pocket." Winnie turned and showed the man her back pocket. "Now it's gone.

Don't know how I could've lost it." She unveiled her 'ugly face cry'. "I'll just *die* if I don't get to see my dad." Her sobs would have wowed the Academy.

"Aw, don't you worry none 'bout that." He patted her shoulder. "We got a passenger list."

"A passenger list?"

"Yes. If you got a ticket, your name on here."

"Shit." Winnie wiped her tears and jumped off the caboose. She plodded alongside the Zephyr as a girl looked out the window and smiled. Winnie reached down, filled her hand with gravel and threw it at the window on her way to board the dud train.

The assistant was shutting the door as Winnie jumped aboard. She looked out the windows while she slowly walked the aisle. Outside, a man in a faded navy-blue pea coat walked hunched over, just like her father. Her heart stopped as she stood still, focusing on the man. Something stung her eyes, and she blinked. Forgot to breathe until a harsh screech hit like nails on a chalkboard. The heavy locomotive backpedaled, and Winnie lost her balance. Grabbed the seat rail with both hands as the man disappeared into the crowd.

The plain train left Chicago and gained speed effortlessly. The last car was uncrowded and smelled like paste. Winnie flopped into the empty back row. The seats were hard worn brown leather. Every one of them cracked and stained. Winnie put her feet up and stretched out. Her eyes heavy with the train's rhythm as they chugged past the Chicago suburbs and lush farmlands of western Illinois.

After a nap, Winnie woke to bright light in her eyes. The fiery sun was setting blood-red on the murky Mississippi and reminded her of her dad. His face would burn as red hot as the sunset when he found he'd traveled all the way from New York to Chicago and Winnie was long gone. Glad to be heading west, she rested her head against the window and took it all in.

Two thousand miles of shining track threaded through the Rockies, then the Sierra Nevada Mountains, and eventually to the blue Pacific.

The West was bigger and more beautiful than Winnie had ever imagined. Artist Albert Bierstadt's paintings of the Rockies were spectacular but nowhere near as captivating as the real thing. Something about the way the mountains and canyons and rivers and trees as far as she could see held Winnie in awe. Made her feel good inside. Nearly as good as killing Leo had felt. Three days after leaving Chicago, Winnie stepped off the locomotive and onto the dark streets of San Francisco.

After a restless night's sleep in a motel next to the train station and a hearty breakfast, Winnie worked her way by cable car and city bus to the beach. There she bought a fancy bathing suit. A strapless red and white checkered one-piece with ruffles where Winnie's cleavage might be if she had any. She carried her clothes in a bag and wore her cowboy boots along with the new gingham suit out of the shop. She dashed through traffic and crossed the street pulling up the suit as it slid lower and lower. Her boots sunk in the deep sand. The Golden Gate loomed in the fog, and the stench of rotting kelp was not how Winnie had dreamed of the sunny West Coast.

The water was freezing, but she forced herself in anyway—farther and farther until she was waist deep. Being the only fool in the icy gray waves, tourists watched Winnie as if she were the entertainment. She acted tough, like the water wasn't cold as it splashed over her shoulders, but when something underwater brushed her leg, she bolted like a spooked horse. The suit fell to Winnie's waist as she made her escape. Being bare chested didn't slow her down one bit. She hit dry sand and never broke stride until she stole a towel and wrapped herself up in it. That ended Winnie's desire to ever step foot in the sea again.

After a few days, Winnie had hawked one of Grandma Bell's necklaces for three hundred bucks. She'd rented a room in a boarding house at Ocean Beach and learned where to purchase a fake driver's license from a man she'd met while dining at the Cliff House. At Kim's Kite Shop in Chinatown, she went from fifteen-year-old Winifred Mudgett to eighteen-year-old JANE WAYNE.

The upstairs room unlocked with a skeleton key. It was small but clean and had a bay window facing the street below. A sliver of ocean was visible whenever the fog lifted. Each floor had a shared bathroom, and meals were included for an extra ten dollars a week. On Jane's first night Miss Puente served her boarders clam chowder and warm sourdough at exactly seven o'clock.

It was quiet except for the sound of Spanky, Miss Puente's pug snoring under the table, and the odd slurp from one of the two brothers just in from Jersey. A well-coiffed fake redhead who'd introduced herself as Yolanda the minute she sat down, plucked a piece of bread with her pinky held high. Jane felt Miss Puente staring at her. She had the iron face of a woman who'd been stunning in her youth but hard living had caught up with her. "What the hell happened to your lip?" Miss Puente asked.

Jane never looked up. "Birth affect," she said between spoonfuls.

"You mean *defect*," Miss Puente said.

Jane looked at her. "No. I don't."

Miss Puente crossed her arms, accentuating the wrinkles between her heavy breasts. Her face became brittle as she narrowed her focus on Jane, who ladled a second helping of chowder into her bowl.

The two brothers from Jersey started arguing about Golden Gate Park Stables and the opportunity to rent a horse or take a riding lesson. They dunked their sourdough and debated the hourly rental rates of the horses in Central Park as Jane finished the last of the chowder. Miss Puente snatched the empty bowl and took it to the kitchen.

"I don't see how it could cost that much more out here," the brother who appeared older and was nearly a foot taller said around a mouthful.

"Yolanda wouldn't waste time *or* money on a stinking horse." The redhead spoke in third person and straightened in her chair. "Yolanda has much better things to do with her time and her money."

"Like what?" the younger Jersey boy smirked.

"Wouldn't you like to know?" She pursed her lips and rolled her eyes. "Forcing animals to carry you around on their backs is absolutely barbaric. We're *not* living in the 1800s anymore."

"Barbaric? Meaning unsophisticated and primitive or savagely cruel and brutal?" Jane Wayne said smiling like the devil himself. She wanted so badly to slap the woman just to see if her heavy powder would puff into a little cloud.

Yolanda put her chin in her hand and looked at the ceiling for the answer. "Both."

Jane burped as she reached over and sloshed her sourdough around in Yolanda's chowder. "How'd you get so darn smart? College?"

The Jersey boys laughed and when Yolanda left, Jane slid the woman's unfinished chowder to the pug under the table.

The thought of gliding along the trail atop a strong steed just like in the movies kept Jane up most of the night. She hadn't been this excited about anything since the night she killed Leo.

It was impossible to sleep, so Jane was at Golden Gate Park Stables by 8:00 am., two hours before they opened to the public. She walked around, watched an old bent man feed the horses, watched stalls and saddles being cleaned by black and white guys who looked like they'd had it rough. A tall palomino caught her eye and stole her heart when he leaned into her for a rub. An engraved wooden sign hung above his stall: *ROMEO*. Jane stayed and scratched his ears, rubbed his nose, and patted his neck. When she left to visit another horse, Romeo nickered, reared, and twisted his head like a wild stallion.

"Jeez, take it easy." Jane gave in and loved on him until a man in English riding britches and a fedora came by.

"He loves the girls that one." He sounded Irish.

"His name suits him." Winnie said.

"Are you here to ride?"

"Yes, sir."

"Well, let's get on with it, shall we?"

"Great."

"Have you ridden before?"

"A little," Jane lied. "Can I ride Romeo?"

The man twitched his gray mustache and twisted his head like Romeo had. "He can be a challenge, that one. Let's see how you do with Ricky, shall we?"

Jane Wayne slowly signed her new name for the first time. She handed back the release form and paid ten dollars for one hour of riding. Ricky, a big bay gelding, came to Jane saddled and bridled. She slipped her foot in the stirrup, jumped in the saddle, and gathered her reins the exact way she'd seen John Wayne do it so many times on the big screen. She kicked Ricky, but he did not take off the way the horses in Westerns did. He didn't leave at all. Just pinned his ears and swished his tail.

"Once you get him going, he'll be okay," the assistant who had brought the horse assured Jane, then gave Ricky a swat on his rump. The bay walked like he was stuck in slow motion and just might stop any minute. This was not the exciting high-speed gallop through the Wild West Jane had pictured.

The air was cool, and the sun had finally burned away the fog. The smell of warming eucalyptus made riding and breathing a pleasure. Although she could not convince Ricky to gallop or even trot, Jane caught herself grinning as she ducked under a low-hanging oak branch. There was something spectacular and soothing about the motion of the horse, as if his legs were her legs, his power was her power. It was nothing short of restorative. In those magical moments, Jane Wayne could leave the life she'd been stuck with and become the cowgirl she was meant to be. She rode ten miles and when she returned rented Wilma and rode another hour in spite of her stiff legs and sore rump.

Dust and dirt coated Jane's boots as she proudly hobbled like an old cowpoke the few blocks to the diner. After a patty melt and a chocolate malt, Jane went to the cinema, watched *Rio Grande* for the third time and wished she could live like they did in the Old West. Shoot people who did you wrong and ride fast to the next town.

In her room, Jane dumped the remaining cash from inside her boot onto the wood floor. She counted out one hundred and eighty-two bucks then tossed the spare change into her suitcase. She pressed and folded the bills, then placed them back inside her boot. After changing out of dirty clothes and into clean Levis and a new western shirt, Jane dug inside her suitcase. She uncovered a box of Kotex sanitary napkins. It was lighter than it should have been, and panic overwhelmed her as she opened it. Her heart seemed to stop beating when she opened the box and found Grandma Bell's necklaces gone, along with the cocktail ring. Something like a hot wave hit and then washed over Jane. She threw the box across the room and ran downstairs like she was on fire.

Miss Puente was in the kitchen placing a casserole dish in her new gas oven when Jane walked in trying to contain her anger. "Someone's been in my room!"

"Why would someone go into your room? How do you know this?" Miss Puente said it fast like she didn't appreciate the interruption and watched Spanky circle his bed next to the warm stove.

"Because some of my things are gone." Jane hitched her hands on her hips.

"Oh. Dear." Miss Puente began slicing onions with a butcher knife. "What things?"

"I had necklaces. Five, to be exact. And a ring worth a lot of *goddamn* money. They were in my suitcase and I want them back or I'll tear this place apart and everyone in it."

"Now Miss Wayne, you must remain calm." She put her arm on Jane's shoulder. The butcher knife uncomfortably close to Jane's face. "Not much happens here that I don't know about. What I cannot understand is how a young girl like you comes to own *so much* valuable jewelry." The smell of alcohol with her words.

"I inherited them," Jane said.

"Of course you did, dear. And now someone else has *inherited* them." Miss Puente went back to her onions with a wicked grin.

"I'll call the police."

"The telephone is in my office."

Jane walked out, battling the anger roiling inside of her.

She had kicked in two bedroom doors, searched inside, and was headed up the stairs to the third floor when the Jersey brothers grabbed her from behind. "Miss Puente says you gotta go," the taller brother grunted, sounding like an ape if apes could talk. With a brother on each arm, Jane Wayne was rushed down two flights of stairs and out the door. They tossed her and her suitcases out onto the sidewalk. "Miss Puente says don't come back, or she's callin' the cops!" The brothers turned and walked back into the house. On the third floor, Miss Puente looked down from behind laced curtains.

It was hard to think through the choking fog of anger. Jane sat on the cold sidewalk and watched the sunset like a tiny glowing ember in gray ash. *San Francisco isn't all that great. Too cold and dreary.* Jane carried her suitcases around town, bought the latest *Life* magazine, and read it over fish and chips. Cowboys and cowgirls riding along the high desert smiled at Jane from the glossy pages. "RENO, NEVADA: Divorce Capital of the World." The article explained how divorce seekers came from all over the United States and took up temporary residence at dozens of dude ranches in and around Reno. *Dude ranches.* Jane pictured herself there. Riding. Miles and miles of riding. Reno wasn't all that far. She'd leave tonight by bus or train just as soon as she made things right with Miss Puente.

CHAPTER
EIGHT

At noon, I asked Nana if she needed a break. "Hell no."
"Well, I could use some lunch." I was hollow inside, and
something on my stomach might help me digest whatever
dastardly deed had befallen Miss Puente.

"Did you ever speak to your family again?" I asked.

"Nope."

"Not even Grandma Bell?"

"Nope." Nana shook her head.

"Hello." A nurse in pink polka-dotted scrubs carrying a
gray plastic bag interrupted. "How are we feeling today Miss
Hobbs?" Her huge smile reminded me of Mick Jagger.

"Dandy," Nana said. "Now what?"

"Time to change your diaper, ma'am." She wiggled her
fingers into blue latex gloves.

"Diapers? I thought she had a catheter?" I asked.

"Doctor removed it this morning. And—" She lowered her
voice to me. "She had an accident."

"Accident?" I asked.

"I shit myself last night." Nana instantly went from spirited to deflated.

The nurse smiled sympathetically, set the bag alongside Nana, then pulled out an adult diaper and a box of baby wipes. Nana looked away.

"You'll have to step out of the room please," the nurse said sweetly.

The modest cafeteria was busy for such a small hospital on a Sunday afternoon. Maybe it was the lack of food choices in town. A precooked burger in a box seemed the quickest option, along with a bag of Doritos and a can of energizing Go Girl for a quick pick-me-up. I found a corner table next to a window and charged my phone and myself.

Nana had shared the darkest and ugliest parts of herself. But it still didn't feel right. I could not shake doubt from my mind and went back to the beginning, trying my damnedest to make sense of it all. Nana's extraordinary kindness whispered in the back of my mind. Like the summer day she refused to allow Jim to behead a rattler that had bitten his dog. Nana heard the dog yelping and saw Jim grab a shovel and run back toward the hay barn. I rode over and watched from my horse as Nana snatched the shovel from Jim then whacked him with it. Jim cursed, grabbed his arm, and bent in half. His brown tobacco shot across red dirt as Nana patiently worked that riled snake into an empty grain sack. Then she twisted the top and tied it shut with hay twine. Without a word, she set the sacked snake and the shovel in the back of her truck and drove thirty minutes to Forest Creek where she released it. At least I'd always thought she did. Now I'm not so sure.

The idea of nurture or nature came into play. Nana had never really stood a chance at a "normal" life. She was the granddaughter of H. H. Holmes. His name was vaguely familiar, but rather than torture my memory, I dug a pair of scratched readers from the bottom of my purse and Googled the name.

H. H. Holmes is notoriously known as one of America's first serial killers who lured victims into his hotel dubbed the "Murder Castle" in 1893. According to some claims, he killed up to 200 people inside his macabre hotel, which was outfitted with trapdoors, gas chambers, and a basement crematorium. Holmes was involved in a variety of fraud schemes, and it was actually his involvement in a horse swindle in Texas that led police to arrest him in Boston in 1894. Investigators soon began to suspect him of murdering his scammer associate Benjamin Pitezel in an insurance scheme, then murdering three of Pitezel's children—who were roughly seven to fourteen years old—in an attempt to cover it up.

There were dozens and dozens of books written about the killer: *Depraved, The Torture Doctor, Devil in the White City, The Beast of Chicago, Bloodstains, Inside the Murder Castle—* the list went on and on. *Ho-lee shit!* This inhumane monster was *my* great-great-grandfather. Could murder be as much a matter of blood as height and hair color?

A heaviness fell over me and I wondered how much wickedness had been handed down through the generations. Hunger and nausea fought for dominance in the pit of my stomach as I popped the pink, sweaty can of Go Girl and sipped.

A few tables away, a lady crumbled chicken tenders into bite-sized pieces for a toddler. The boy's ketchup-stained cheeks bulged like a chipmunk prepping for winter. Thoughts of what I'd done tangled my mind until, as if on cue, a very pregnant woman walked by outside the window. Refusing to agonize over my abortion, I agonized over Nana and recalled that she had said she could *not* have children after being beaten by Leo. Was she lying? It was possible. She was a world champion at deception. If she couldn't have kids, then where the hell did my mom come from? What about me?

There was only one way to know for sure. DNA. Everyone was doing it. Locating missing fathers and finding mothers who'd chosen adoption over abortion. Men and women discovering Daddy isn't their father and now they have new brothers and sisters. An episode of *Dr. Oz* explained how decades-old crimes were being solved with DNA evidence.

Before I could change my mind, I signed up for Family Tree, ordered two test kits with my over-the-limit Visa and hoped Nana would live long enough to spit in a plastic tube. More than anything I hoped she'd live long enough to complete her story. The narrative that was fast becoming my only way out of financial ruin and impending homelessness.

Two months ago, my medical insurance had expired, so I transferred my problems from expensive therapy with Maureen over to the sacrament of wine and church. I decided to give God a chance. He or she was always available and willing to forgive free of charge. I prayed. Long, hard, and silent for strength to get through this day; strength to accept the fact that Nana had killed someone—possibly a lot of someones.

God's love failed to soothe me or my trembling hands. My heart beat so hard my jugular throbbed. Could I self-combust at any moment, right here at this table in the hospital cafeteria? I needed someone to talk to other than Nana, God, or Maureen. Someone who would answer and advise in a clear and present manner and didn't charge by the hour. I stared at my lunch with no appetite.

When life got shitty, I always had Beth—I wanted to talk to her so badly, but could not forgive what she'd done. I stopped returning her calls, her text messages, and unfriended her when she admitted to knowing about Mark's affair with Gabby. Beth thought it best to not tell me. Said she only wanted to protect me. The betrayal of my best friend hurt almost as much as the betrayal of my husband. Maureen labeled me overly loyal and suggested Beth was untrustworthy. As did I after last Sunday's sermon when Father Garza preached Ephesians 4:25. It stuck with me like a good poem: *Therefore, having put away falsehood, let each one of you speak the truth with his neighbor, for we are members one of another.*

My burger was colder than my Go Girl and tasted like cardboard, so I peeled off the top bun, added Cool Ranch Doritos, then smashed the bun back in place. The chips breaking and cracking, just like me.

The guard had gone, but Detective Rocha was outside Nana's door when I returned. *Dear Lord, give me strength.*

"She ready to confess?" Rocha asked.

"She's not talking to you without her lawyer."

"Why make this difficult?" Rocha glared at me like he was assessing my value. "We've made significant discoveries at your grandmother's property."

"What's that mean?"

"Means we have DNA evidence confirming that at least ten individuals were disposed of. Human beings, Jessica. Why protect someone who could kill that many people?"

"I'm not protecting her. I'm listening to her. You can learn a lot by listening. And just because you found *evidence* or whatever on her ranch does *not* mean she had anything to do with it. She's an old woman. You have to *prove* she killed these people."

"Have you heard from your husband?"

"No."

"Think about it, Mrs. Williams. Mark was at your grandmother's—we found his cell phone there, and it was the last place he was seen alive. Jim Kelly confirmed it—before he too disappeared."

"You think my grandmother killed Mark and Jim?" I laughed. "She loved them both."

He didn't answer—just glared at me while I slipped past him into Nana's room.

"Where were we?" Nana asked.

"You don't waste any time, do you?" I smiled.

"Ain't got none to waste. We were talking about that thieving bitch, Puente. Nana sucked her teeth, wearing the sneer she always did when she didn't like something.

"You thought she stole the necklaces *you* stole from Grandma Bell?"

"Who the hell else? She was the only one had a key to my room."

I opened a fresh roll of antacids and popped a few in my mouth, then swapped the roll for the cell in my coat pocket. I smiled and tapped the red record button.

CHAPTER
NINE

Jane Wayne

The Victorian side door to the kitchen was locked. A breakable window sat eye-level and even in the dead of night would allow Jane to be seen should anyone happen to look her way. The stained glass would break easily, but the racket was too risky. A risk Jane would take if picking the lock didn't work.

Just last week, she'd read in a dime store pulp about how Jesse James had picked a jailhouse lock. He used a sharpened piece of chicken bone, but Jane used her metal nail file. She slid it into the keyhole—keeping the tip at an upward slant until it would go no further. Slowly she turned and pressed the file with her right hand as she turned the doorknob with her left. The tumblers inside obliged with an encouraging click, and the antique lock popped.

Jane left the door ajar and went in. She'd gone over and over the plan step by step in her mind earlier that evening. Getting her jewelry back was too risky, and odds were good that

Miss Puente had already hocked them. Jane weeded through her memories of the house, trying to recall something of value. Something easy to carry that would be worth the trouble when pawned. But Miss Puente was too smart to leave valuables in the vicinity of boarders with sticky fingers.

This was the next best thing. Jane went straight for the new gas stove. First, she scooped Spanky from his warm bed, hightailed it across the street, then set him safely in the neighbor's fenced yard. As she hurried back to the open door, she dug a pack of Pall Malls from her coat pocket, then tucked a single cigarette in behind her ear.

Next to the kitchen sink, Jane opened the bottom drawer. Four dishrags and one towel should do the trick. Jane folded a dishrag into fourths, slid it under the front corner of the stove, then repeated the process until each corner was well-padded.

Slowly she pulled one side of the stove away from the wall without making a sound. Behind the stove, she knelt and wrapped the dishtowel around the copper gas pipe. With all her strength she kicked at the pipe. The sound mimicked the old water pipes that knocked continuously throughout the house. Another kick and nothing. She sucked in a breath and gave it her all. The force broke the connection. Gas hissed like a snake.

She shoved the stove back in place, stepped away, and lit the candle on the kitchen table just in case. She pulled the cigarette from behind her ear and lit it as she went to the door. After a deep drag in, she blew, then turned and flicked the cigarette above the stove. It sparked off the wall and disappeared behind the stove as Jane stepped backward out the door. Resisting the urge to watch was impossible. One more moment and the gas should ignite. "Come on," Jane whispered.

Flames exploded up the wall and spread under the ceiling, turning it black in an instant. It knocked Jane backwards and out the door onto her ass. The heat was intense—on the verge of being painful. Jane felt the burn sting her face, but she couldn't go. Not yet. She stood, captivated. The fire sounded like it was applauding Jane's performance. She bowed and ran.

Two blocks behind the burning Victorian Jane gained the elevation she needed to appreciate her best work yet. Flames swayed and swirled in the breeze. Like sunshine, the glow lit the night sky. Sirens played background music as tendrils of smoke tried to rope the moon.

Reno in March may as well have been the Arctic compared to San Francisco. Jane had arrived in the Biggest Little City and found it abundant with opportunity. A newsstand on Virginia Street sold the *San Francisco Chronicle* and Jane scanned it daily for news on the Puente boarding house fire. At last, there it was. The obituary section confirmed Miss Puente's death. The others had escaped. A sense of accomplishment brought a smile to Jane's face. *Did the old battle-axe scream? Of course she did. They all did. Could they be heard above the roar of the fire?* Jane wished she knew. Wished she could have been there to hear it. Smell it. At least she had rid the world of another parasite. It was a gift—like Superman's power.

Her furnished studio apartment overlooked the Truckee River, but the view added to the cost of rent and Jane's funds were running low. Georgia, the prostitute next door who preferred to be called Miss Georgia on account of winning some ridiculous Peach Pageant when she was sixteen, both enticed and disgusted Jane. But for the first time in her life Jane had a friend.

Two weeks in Reno and Miss Georgia had taught Jane to use makeup, drive a car, and pick pockets. "A pretty gal is always the last suspect, regardless of the crime," she declared with ruby-red lips that stuck to her white teeth whenever she flashed her Peach Pageant smile.

Jane paid for dinner at the Cal Neva Casino and although money was tight, she tipped the waitress an extra quarter. On the way out the door, she helped herself to a caramel-colored cowboy hat from the rack. She'd just read the help wanted section of the *Reno Gazette:* "Washoe Pines Guest Ranch in Washoe Valley, Seeks Experienced Ranch Hand." A real cowgirl needed a good hat.

The next morning, Jane climbed through Miss Georgia's kitchen window and took her car keys. The working girl was never up before noon, and Jane could have the car back before then. A sleeping pill dissolved into Miss Georgia's water glass on the bedside table ensured Jane a few extra hours.

White dust tailed the baby blue Bel Air like smoke as Jane turned off the alkali desert road and pulled into the Washoe Pines Guest Ranch. Wind blew the stolen hat off her head the moment she stepped out of the car. It tumbled as if it were trying to get away. Jane waited for it to stop, but when it didn't she took after it. Sagebrush and a piece of rusted tin banged against a fat ponderosa pine as Jane chased her hat, then stomped the damn thing to capture it.

A lanky cowboy appeared out of nowhere. He stood by the car and watched Jane pick up her hat, punch it back into shape, brush it off a bit, then slam it back on her head. Jane held the oversized hat down as she walked toward the real cowboy, refusing to feel foolish.

"Hello." The dude looked to be in his late thirties and had to be six feet tall.

"Howdy, I'm here for the job."

"You?" He chewed the toothpick in his mouth.

"Yeah, me. What's wrong with that?" Jane pulled the hat off.

He was looking at her scarred lip. "Nothin'. I just...You gonna clean stalls? Brush and saddle horses all day?"

"Why not?"

"Cause most people 'round here don't like hard work. Worse is they ain't much fun to be around."

"What's new?"

"Well, I ain't the boss, but I know he's desperate. No one else wants the job—he might give you a shot. I'm Guy by the way." He took off his hat and smiled.

"Jane." She didn't smile.

"Jane." He laughed. "Like me Tarzan—you Jane?"

"Huh. Good one wise guy. I get to ride if I work here?"

"Why sure."

The long red barn housed a dozen horses with more penned up out back. Jane looked around and had visited a few of the horses by the time Guy returned. He assured Jane that he'd discussed it with the boss and she was hired. She could start by cleaning stalls. It took three hours to muck out a dozen stalls. Time was running out on returning Georgia's car without her missing it, and Jane promised Guy she'd be back by 7:00 am the next morning. The job paid two hundred dollars a month plus room and board.

Miss Georgia was furious when Jane pulled up and parked. "I got us donuts." Jane grabbed the pink box and jumped out of the car. "I wanted to surprise you. I know how much—"

"Aw, bullcrap!" Miss Georgia grabbed the box of donuts, and Jane followed her up the stairs. "What the hell were you doing with my car, Jane? And why do you smell so foul?" Miss Georgia stopped at the top of the stairs and looked down at Jane.

"I'm sorry. Truly I am." Tears welled up. "I didn't think you'd mind. Honest."

"Oh, go take a flying leap." Miss Georgia walked to her apartment door, opened it, and stepped in. "You don't get horse crap on your boots at the donut shop. Good luck!" She slammed the door.

"I don't need luck. I have skill and ability," Jane said.

Before starting her new life as a cowboy, Jane needed what she called "walking around money"—she was down to ten bucks and payday at the ranch wasn't for two weeks. A sunset stroll along Virginia Street usually proved profitable, but early evening snow flurries kept tourists bundled up for a damn blizzard. No way Jane could lift a wallet. She leaned against the *Biggest Little City in the World* sign as the yellow neon lights popped on. She lit a cigarette. Smoke billowed and hung in a heavy cloud while she buttoned her fur coat. Pigeons searched and pecked for scraps before roosting for the night.

Harold's Club was filled with gamblers, ringing slot machines, and once in a while, cheers. Jane worked her way past the crowded blackjack and roulette tables to the high-limit slots. A cocktail waitress eyed her as Jane removed her coat. A cigar-smoking man with three necks sat to her right tugging the handle on a dollar machine. Jane tossed a silver dollar on the red carpet as she took a seat at the machine next to Cigar Man.

"Got a light?" she asked and pinched a cigarette between her fingers. He dug in his shirt pocket for a light. "Hey, is that yours?" She pointed to the silver dollar on the red carpet.

"Oh hell, must be." He hefted himself off his chair and stepped away from his machine. Away from his bucket of silver, he grunted as he reached down and picked up the coin. Jane and the bucket of silver were gone before he stood up.

She strung her forearm through the bucket handle and covered it with her coat as she calmly hurried toward the front doors. "Stop!" someone yelled and Jane considered running, but didn't. She wished she had when two security guards blocked her exit.

"Excuse me ma'am. May we take a look under your coat?"

Before she could refuse, someone jerked the coat so hard that the bucket spilled silver tokens only two steps from the front doors. "That's her!" The fat man waddled over in a hurry. "That's her!" His face red and sweaty, chins quivering with every word. "That's my money, you little thief!" A thousand eyes bore holes into Jane as the two security guards escorted her away.

The men plunked Jane down onto a heavy metal chair in a cinderblock backroom filled with boxes. They snatched her purse from under her arm and dumped the contents onto the floor. One of the men opened Jane's wallet and removed her ID. They took the ID and left. The door locked from the outside and Jane's palms began to sweat. She fanned her fingers then gathered her items off the floor and put them back in her purse. She smoked. A rat, with his head smashed in a trap between boxes of Borax, looked prophetic, but Jane refused to be scared until noticing what looked like dried blood splattered along dirty gray linoleum in the corner.

She chewed on a hangnail when the lock clicked. An old man with a pencil-thin moustache walked in and looked at Jane too long without saying a word. Jane spit her hangnail and crossed her legs. She gripped the cold sides of her seat, leaned back, and tapped her fingers against the metal.

"Stand up," he hissed, and Jane stood.

"Can I have my fur coat back?"

"No." He leaned against the wall and scratched his black hair that looked too dark for his weathered face. "I'm Pappy.

I run this club and I don't appreciate thieves. It's not good for business."

"I'm sorry. Truly." Jane teared up. "I was desperate and—"

Pappy grabbed Jane's chin and squeezed. "Save the act." He turned her loose, then pulled her ID from his suit pocket and looked at it. "I hope you didn't pay good money for this." He handed it over.

Jane snatched her ID and shoved it in her purse. "You calling the cops or what?"

"That would be entirely up to you."

"How's that?"

"How old are you?"

"Eighteen." Jane took her seat back and crossed her arms.

"I did not get this far in life by playing the stooge, *understand?*" Pappy stepped to the trapped rat and released it. Held it up by its long gray tail for closer inspection and swung the thing back and forth. Jane suspected he'd enjoyed killing bugs with a magnifying glass as a kid.

"You have one second chance to tell the truth or my boys will take you for a ride. The Nevada desert can be brutal." When he heaved the rat across the room and into a metal trashcan it dinged like he'd won a prize at the fair.

Pappy stepped close to Jane. "Now." He cradled her face with his ratty fingers. "How old are you?"

"Sixteen."

A grin lifted the man's moustache. "It's your lucky day." He removed his hands and stepped toward the door. "I have a friend from out of town who will like you." He opened the door. "You don't smell good. Someone will escort you to a room where you can change and clean up." He left before Jane could think of a response.

Roy Robinson sat in a red half-circle booth, sipping a drink with an umbrella, and stood as Jane approached with Pappy.

"Mister R, this is Miss Jane Wayne."

"Howdy, Miss Wayne. I like your boots." Roy wasn't ugly, or fat, or bald, but he did have eyebrows like black caterpillars. He wore his dark hair in a buzzcut and was clean-shaven like the host from *The Twilight Zone* television show until he smiled. His big braying-donkey teeth triggered memories of Leo. Jane slid into the booth. The soft leather seat encircled her like a protective father.

Pappy clasped his hands "Enjoy your evening, Mister R. I've arranged front row seats in our cabaret. Please let me know if there's anything else I can do to make your time with us more pleasurable."

"Thank you, Pappy. I appreciate it." Roy shook Pappy's hand and sat. "Jane Wayne. That's some name. Hey, that rhymes. I'm a poet and I don't know it—"

Thank God the waiter interrupted and placed a drink on the table. "Another Blue Hawaiian for the gentleman, and what would the lady like?" He looked at Roy for the answer.

"I'll have what he's having," Jane said.

Roy winked at the waiter, and he left.

"You're a pistol, aren't you?"

Jane grinned and looked at the menu.

"Hope you're hungry." Roy looked over his menu and never seemed to notice or mind Jane's upper lip.

"I'm starving." Jane set the menu down.

"You've decided?" He seemed surprised.

"No need to look any further when there's ribeye."

Roy closed his menu and cocked his head at Jane. "Most girls couldn't make up their minds if they had all night."

"I ain't most girls."

Roy laughed until the waiter set Jane's Blue Hawaiian in front of her. She sucked half the drink down before coming up for air.

"Careful, those will catch up with you when you least expect it."

Jane dabbed her red lipstick with her cloth napkin and placed a cigarette between her fingers. Roy reached for a lighter inside his suit coat and lit the lady's cigarette. Flames danced in his dark blue eyes like a two-way mirror—he could see out, but you could not see in.

After three Blue Hawaiians, dinner, and a generous portion of bread pudding, Jane and Roy visited the showroom. Topless women dressed like peacocks kicked their long legs in the air and high-stepped in unison to a Latin jazz band. Trumpets blasted and Roy bobbed his head with the swinging beat. Jane bobbed her head too, but only because she couldn't keep her eyes open. She was exhausted and Roy noticed. "Come on." He held his hand out for hers and she took it. They exited and as the showroom doors closed behind them, the world quieted. "Looks like it's past your bedtime."

Jane nodded and covered her yawn. "It's been a long day. And I start a new job in the morning."

"Let's get your coat and I'll drive you home. What's the new job?"

Snow powdered the streets, adding a silent dazzle to the city and the night. A slice of moon hung like a sickle blade shrouded by eerie golden clouds. "That's some crazy moon, huh?" Roy said as he held Jane's arm and stepped her up the stairway. Snow crunched under their feet in perfect rhythm. "A spectacular moon, on a spectacular night, with a *spectacular* woman."

Jane let go a laugh.

"What? I'm serious," he said.

"Knock it off. You don't need to sweet-talk me."

"Oh no?"

"No," she said.

"Okay." They stood at Jane's door. "I certainly enjoyed meeting you, Miss Jane Wayne."

"Likewise, Mr. Robinson."

"Please call me, Roy. Mr. Robinson reminds me of my dad." He brushed snow from her hair, then kissed her cheek. He smelled like beef.

"Good night," he said, and headed down the steps, then turned back. "Hey, you like horses." He trotted back up. "I know you're starting your new job and all, but would you consider accompanying me tomorrow? I'm meeting a woman they call Wild Horse Annie, and—"

"Yes! I read all about her in the paper. She's trying to save the mustangs from being rounded up and slaughtered."

"I'd love it if you'd come."

"Boy, I'd like to, but if I don't show up for work—" Jane crossed her arms and bit her lower lip.

"Come work for me."

"Doing what?"

"Whatever you want." Roy raised one eyebrow, and Jane recognized the devil in him. She pulled the housekey out of her handbag and opened the door.

"Let's discuss it somewhere warm." Jane grinned, and Roy followed her inside.

That night, Jane learned that Roy Robinson was thirty-six years old, owned a lumber mill in Humboldt County, California, and had a peculiar attraction to Jane's feet. On the couch, he'd spent a good portion of the night massaging her aching arches. No one had ever rubbed Jane's feet and she liked it. The combination of a hard day's work, three Blue Hawaiians, and a massage put Jane to sleep until Roy began licking and sucking her big toe like a lollipop. It tickled, but Jane was too tired to mind. When he began masturbating against her foot, she almost stopped him.

In what barely passed as a kitchen, light slipped through the edges of closed drapes. "Last night," Jane said, setting a plate of scrambled eggs and ham in front of Roy, "we never got around to talking about me working for you."

Roy looked at his plate then grinned at Jane. "I have a better idea." He took a bite.

"Yeah?" Jane poured ketchup on her eggs.

"Yeah." He walked over and knelt next to Jane. Took her little hand in his. "You're not like anyone I've ever met."

"Other girls don't let you fuck their feet?"

Roy froze. Dropped his chin to his chest, then came up laughing. "You are really something! I tell you, Jane, you just say it like it is." He shook his head. "I don't want to hire you."

"Oh...well, can you give me a lift to work? Out to Washoe Valley?"

"No. How about instead—we get married?"

"Married!" Jane stood up and jerked her hand back. "What for?"

"Because I need you. I've had more damn fun with you than I've had in years."

Jane slammed her hands on her hips. People didn't often catch her off guard. "I can't have kids," she blurted.

"Great!" Roy laughed louder than was appropriate. "Let's do it. Meet with Velma about the mustangs then get married this afternoon. I want to take you home with me today."

"You said you have land. You have horses?"

"Of course, and I'm planning on having a small herd of mustangs relocated to graze off one of my properties. That's why I'm meeting with Velma."

"Who's Velma?"

"Wild Horse Annie. Her real name's Velma Johnston."

Jane ran the facts: Roy owned a mill, which meant he had money, and Jane could ride horses without having to work.

"Okay."

"Okay?" Roy took Jane's hand again. "Okay, you'll marry me?"

"Yeah, sure, why not?" Jane shrugged and Roy lifted her off the ground like he was about to throw her in the air.

Jane couldn't believe her luck. She'd met Wild Horse Annie and became Mrs. Jane Wayne Robinson, wife of a wealthy and decent looking timberman, all in the space of an afternoon. Her days of shoveling horseshit were over before they began. From here on out her time would be spent riding through the forest. She imagined the sweet solitude of wind in her hair as she and her trusty steed galloped along just like they did in the movies.

A new saddle rode on the backseat of the Mercury station wagon and scented the car with savory leather. Roy had let Jane go wild at the D Bar M Western store in downtown Reno as a wedding gift. Before they left, Mrs. Robinson had a new custom-shaped hat that fit her head perfectly plus a bag of the latest in cowgirl fashion. She almost meant it when she thanked him for the diamond wedding band.

The drive through Lassen National Park was so spectacular that Jane swore she could feel it. Mile-high mountains erupting in the distance—skirted in green and topped with white. Black volcanic rock sculpted like cloud animals. Caves. Even the sky was perfect. Like driving through a painting. This, Jane thought, is positively the best day of my life.

As the landscape lowered, a soft rain fell and Jane fought to hold her eyes open. "How much farther?"

"About an hour." Roy turned on the radio. Soon they would be home. Jane sang along with the radio to the Tennessee Waltz and smiled at Roy. He squeezed her hand, smiled back, and sang with confidence. He wasn't a terrible singer, and they held the last note until Nat King Cole began to croon "Mona Lisa." Jane's heart sank, and she turned off the radio. The song that played the night Leo had tried to kill her would not kill her happiness today.

"Don't like that song?" Roy asked.

"Hate it."

The sun set and lit portions of the western sky on fire. A few miles east of Arcata, a billboard flanked by two monumental Coast Redwoods advertised Robinson Lumber Company.

"Whoa!" Jane slapped the dash.

Roy stopped the car. "Pretty impressive billboard, huh?"

"Oh my God!" Jane stared up—out the window.

"The damn thing cost a pretty penny, but—"

Jane jumped out, never looking anywhere but up. Dark chocolate mud sucked at her boots as she went to one of the tallest trees. "Unreal." She set her palms against the soft wet bark—her head back as far as it would go. The redwoods in San Francisco were nothing compared to these. From the delicate greenery, rain like diamonds came through branches and filtered light. The majesty and strength of this ancient tree unleashed its power on Jane. It was love at first sight.

"Come on. You're getting drenched!" Roy yelled from the car.

Jane walked backwards, staring into the sky as if she'd found God, then turned and got in the car. "I've read about Coast Redwoods, but seeing them is really something. They're incredible."

"That tree right there's worth a lot of money." Roy turned right, over a concrete bridge pocked with black like weathered headstones. Below, the murky green waters of the Mad River roared. The station wagon sped and splashed and floated for a half mile on a muddy road. Roy Robinson's impressive mill sat idle at the base of a redwood mountain. Thousands of logs dark with wet like rolling hills. "Almost there, honey babe." Roy looked at Jane and smiled.

The two-story farmhouse looked desperate for help. Faded yellow paint shed like skin from graying salt-stained boards. The entire house leaned to the east. Two pieces of rusted tin on the roof and along the covered porch flapped like a bird that couldn't fly. An arched stained-glass window glared down at Jane from the attic as Roy lifted her from the car. Rain spit sideways in wind that carried the scent of freshly cut lumber. Roy almost dropped Jane twice while trying to open the front door. They laughed like honeymooners. A smiling boy, about seven, opened the door.

"Hi Pop!"

"Howdy, Billy," Roy said. "This is Jane—your new mom. Go get Ben and your sister."

CHAPTER
TEN

"That fucker!" I went and said it out loud then grabbed my potty mouth. Nana laughed. I never wanted to forget the sound. Unlike most, her laughter drew breath rather than expelling it. She sounded like a baby donkey and I loved it. "How many kids did Rotten Roy have?"

"Three. Ben was the oldest. Then Billy, he was seven or eight, and Betty." A grin grew as Nana said her name. "Betty was barely two."

"Where was their mother?"

"Died. The year before. Hanged herself at the mill."

"Jesus."

"I didn't buy it."

"Why?"

"Early on it was just a feeling." Nana eyed me. "But later..." Her words were weak, but that didn't change the fact that she had burned down Miss Puente's house and killed the woman. That was victim number two. Nana was encroaching on serial killer territory and I began to doubt everything I thought I knew.

"What made you think it was okay to kill that woman?" I said it as slowly and softly as I could—hoping Nana would miraculously produce some sort of reasonable response.

"She was a no-good thief!" Nana's chin quivered. "The world's better off without her." Anger jolted her back to life. I considered reminding Nana that she had stolen the jewelry first, but then I thought better of it. I wasn't going to fix Nana. It was odd and inexplicable, but I loved her just the way she was. I only wanted the truth. At least, I thought I did.

"You seem tired. Want to rest a while?"

"Rest when I'm dead. Get me some coffee. Please."

"Can you have coffee?"

"Oh...better not, might kill me." Nana let her head fall back against the pillow—shaking all over as she laughed and coughed.

"I'll be right back. Want something to eat?"

"A Baby Ruth."

"Oh, yeah," I said. As long as I could remember, Nana had always kept a box of Baby Ruth bars in her nightstand. Before I outgrew bedtime stories, Nana and I would munch them while she read to me.

I walked out of Nana's room hoping Rocha was gone. All clear, but I took the stairs, assuming that if he were around, he'd use the elevator.

"Nana is not a serial killer. Nana is not a serial killer. Nana *is not* a serial killer." Whispered affirmations echoed between floors.

The coffee smelled burnt and looked worse. There wasn't one bit of transparency in the thick blackness as I poured a cup. Expecting I'd soon need a pick-me-up I grabbed a can of Go Girl. Then, a brilliant idea grabbed me. I took a second pink can for Nana and poured it into a paper coffee cup. Then, I microwaved it for one minute to rid the drink of carbonation and make it safe for Nana's IV. Mark learned the trick at vet school and I'd watched him mainline an energy drink solution after a week of foaling out mares all night. I searched and searched to find coffee cup lids and pressed them on.

No Baby Ruth bars. I bought Snickers, a Reese's Peanut Butter Cup, and a Twix bar. "Twelve-eighty," the lady at the register said.

"*What?*" I said it too loud, thinking I'd been over charged.

"Twelve dollars and eighty cents." She wasn't smiling, or joking, and didn't seem to be in any mood to explain. I held out my over-the-limit Visa. She tapped the reader hidden next to a bowl of bananas with her pen.

"Oh, sorry." I slipped the chip in and hoped it wouldn't be declined.

"Want your receipt?"

"No. Thanks." I stuffed the goodies into the kangaroo pocket of my sweatshirt and filled each hand with a warm drink.

I stepped into the elevator and skillfully pressed the third-floor button with a drink in my hand. The doors started to close.

"Wait up." A woman's voice.

Then a hand pushed through, halting the closing doors followed by a foot wearing a black alligator boot. I pressed the open button and almost dropped my cup. The woman pushed through with her shoulder and the doors opened. She stepped in and looked at me. My stomach clinched and I got hot as hell. *Son-of-a-bitch.*

It was Gabby, and I could see she'd been crying. "Hi Jessica. I heard they found bodies at Blue Mountain. If Mark's dead I need to know."

The doors closed.

"Please tell me, did Effie say anything? Did she—" Gabby sobbed. "Did she kill him?"

"I hope so." The words snapped like wet on a fire. "He used both of us. Now get a grip and get the hell away from me." I'd done my best to stay calm but failed completely. Ignoring her perky nipples pointing through her Reno Rodeo jersey was impossible.

The elevator creaked and rattled as it worked its way up to the third floor. Finally, a ding and the doors opened. Gabby stood blocking my exit.

"Get out of my way." A cup in each hand, I tried to slip past her, but she grabbed my arm. I stopped and shoved my face uncomfortably close to hers. I thought about headbutting her like I'd seen in the movies and wondered if it really did work or if I would I knock myself out. Therapist Maureen said I was impulsive. She didn't actually say it. She asked me if *I thought* I was impulsive. I hadn't decided, but leaned toward no. I focused on my breath like Maureen had taught me. In. Out. In. Out. "Let go of me or I'm going to kill you," I said with a smile.

"Is that a *threat? Are* you seriously going to *fucking threaten me?*" Gabby's head cocked and she stuck her index finger in my face. "You could show a little empathy!"

Empathy? Anger sparked then grew into a raging fire as the elevator doors attempted to shut then opened again. I tried for deeper calming breaths. Unwanted memories floated up like garbage on water. Visions of her sucking and fucking *my* husband. Coming to *my* home like an old friend and drinking *my* expensive wine while I cooked them dinner. I went so far as to churn the bitch peach ice cream. Time slowed—seemed to crawl around on all fours. I let my head fall back. Caught in the grip of instinct, I filled my lungs then slammed my head into her face as fast and as hard as possible. It sounded the way a tree does when it cracks then falls. She dropped just like in the movies.

"Oh! Shit!" I did it. My grin went from momentary satisfaction to Whoa, I'm in big trouble now.

Inside the elevator, she lay crumpled in the fetal position. The doors shut behind us. Her nose started to bleed. *That could be considered impulsive. Holy God, Jesus! I'm becoming Nana.* Someone would be by soon. Deep breath in through my nose. Maureen was right. Long slow breath out through my mouth. With no floors selected the elevator didn't move and the doors opened.

As fast as I could, I set the drinks down and flipped Gabby onto her stomach. Next, I picked up the drinks, stepped over Gabby and hurried towards Nana's room. If I ever saw Maureen again, I'd admit—I *am* impulsive.

On the way to Nana's room, I changed my mind and stopped at the nurse's station. I explained about the poor gal who'd passed out in the elevator.

Two nurses followed me at a trot, one pushing a wheelchair as I caressed my crucifix and silently begged God to please, please, please, forgive me. Gabby was sitting up against the door. The elevator buzzed from the doors being forced open—or it could have been my ears ringing from the pain in my head. Blood smeared the floor and the lower half of Gabby's face. She looked like a drunk clown as the nurses went to her. "I came back from buying snacks and saw her go down hard. Guess she fainted. Looks like she cracked her face on the floor. I heard it hit. You probably want to check for a concussion. Poor thing." Guilt motivated my mouth while my forehead felt like I'd run into a brick wall.

The nurses lifted Gabby out of the elevator and into the wheelchair. "What the fuck? You—" She rubbed her forehead and looked like she didn't know what day it was. "You—" Her mouth hung open. "Hit me." The words garbled and confused as she was.

"No one hit you." I shook my head, feeling the sharp ache in my skull and hoped the knot that must be forming wasn't yet visible. "Why would I hit you?" I looked at one of nurses. "How could I hit her with a drink in each hand?"

Gabby's chin hit her chest and she squeezed her eyes tight. "Fuckin... murderer..."

"I think she's on something." I turned and walked away. Gabby cursed me as they wheeled her back onto the elevator.

Nana slept. I set the drinks and snacks on her food tray and pulled a silver pocketknife out of my jeans pocket. Mark had given it to me for our tenth wedding anniversary. Memories of him tended to sneak up and suck me down into a hopeless darkness that devoured every bit of goodness that ever was or ever will be. Our perfect Valentine's Day wedding at Ironstone Vineyard came to life. I tried to ignore the words *MY LOVE FOREVER* engraved on the knife as I pried open the blade.

A hard ache grew in my throat. I swallowed and swallowed but the betrayal was killing me. Tears broke as I cut a slit at the top of Nana's IV fluid bag and lifted the lid off the microwaved Go Girl. Carefully, I poured it in and sat. Waiting.

I waited for half an hour, then decided to wake Nana. At first, I tapped her shoulder. "Nana." She didn't respond. "Nana." I shook her shoulder. She slid sideways off her pillow. My heart stopped. I realized then her heart monitor wasn't beeping. "Jesus Christ! Nana! I shook her shoulders hard with both hands. "Nana, please, Nana." She didn't respond. *Did I kill her with an energy drink?* "No, no, no. HELP!" The nurses were gone. They were busy attending to Gabby and now Nana would die all because I couldn't control my temper. "Help!"

She opened one eye and grinned. I couldn't speak and pressed my hand to my hammering heart. Nana opened both eyes and straightened up, smiling. Proud of her prank.

I wanted to kill her. After a long moment I spoke. "I thought you were dead."

She laughed. "You needed schooling to understand that I could go at any minute. Now stop wasting time."

"Are you kidding me?" I pressed my palms into my closed eyes. Red and green diamonds filled the back of my eyelids like a kaleidoscope. My forehead throbbed and I wondered if I had a concussion. "You about gave me a heart attack. Nana, seriously, that's not funny." *Fuck.* I removed my hands from my eyes. "Why isn't your monitor beeping?"

"The dipshit doctor turned it down when he was yakking it up and forgot to turn it back on. You get my Baby Ruth?"

"Ugh!" I rubbed the knot on my forehead, then unwrapped a Snickers.

"That ain't a Baby Ruth."

"They didn't have them. This is a Snickers bar, or there's Reese's or Twix."

"I only like Baby Ruths."

"They didn't have Baby Ruths."

"Why?"

"I don't know why," I snapped.

"On my death bed—and no goddamn Baby Ruths." Nana's eyes widened. Anger brought the life up in her—put color back in her face. Or maybe it was the energy drink in her IV.

"Sorry."

"Don't apologize! Never apologize! Never. Understand?"

"Okay." I bit the Snickers bar. The Go Girl had definitely kicked in.

She leaned her head against the pillow and looked up. "You remember Miss Dendrola Tree?"

"Of course." A warmth wrapped around me at the thought of that half-dead old oak. Miss Dendrola Tree was the name I gave the tree when I was little and didn't want to go home. My mother would yell my name and search for me when it was time to leave. But I stayed silently perched. Spending hours cradled between branches, I'd watched ravens bark at Nana's dogs until I learned to imitate their clicks and clacks and caws. Sometimes they'd answer back and sometimes they'd get irritated and fly away.

Dendrolatry means to worship trees, but I only worshiped that one. An oak growing at such high elevation was odd. Sometime nature creates rarities.

"That old tree knows the truth." Nana tapped my arm. "You understand?"

"Yes." I didn't.

"Don't forget." She looked like it was a matter of life or death. "Remember the hole where you used to hide cigarettes?"

"What? How'd you know about my secret hiding place?" She'd never mentioned it. Or removed my stuff.

"On my ranch I'm the only one with secrets." She took my hand in hers and squeezed. Surprisingly, her grip was strong. "Now, you climb up that old sucker when I'm gone. Take a peek inside."

"Okay." I had read that sometimes before people die, they ramble, say things that make no sense, and I worried the end was near in spite of her shenanigans. I grabbed my cell and turned on the recorder.

"After you married Roy and found out he had three kids what'd you do?"

"Smiled and played along."

CHAPTER
ELEVEN

Jane Wayne

The mill sat along the north fork of the Mad River on a six-acre flat-bottom bowl. To the west lay the rugged California coastline. East of the blue Pacific, Roy Robinson owned ancient redwood groves farther than the eye could see. 24,000 acres of pristine lumber. Each square mile worth ten million dollars. Jane did the math one day while Roy was in the bathroom and had left his briefcase unlocked on the kitchen table. She was searching for the combination to Roy's safe, but instead found timber contracts worth three hundred and seventy-five million dollars. Money does grow on trees.

A parcel of that kind of money would set Jane up for a good life. A new life all her own. A ranch with horses where she was the boss. The possibilities were endless. Jane wasn't leaving Roy until she had a damn good plan and her fair share of the mill money. That's why she didn't fight or fuss when Roy brought home a Clairol hair coloring kit and asked Jane to bleach her hair. Jane smiled and said, "Guess we'll find out if blondes really do have more fun."

Jane wasn't crazy about the color; thought she looked like a troubled boy trying to impersonate Marilyn Monroe. But it was Ben, the oldest, who made her regret the compromise. Roy was out of town buying timber and Jane was on the couch watching *Search for Tomorrow* when Ben placed an eight-by-ten framed wedding photo of Roy and his wife atop the TV. Jane sat up. She looked closer then walked over. The undeniable resemblance took Jane's breath away. The bleached blonde hair, the height and weight, even the blank expression on her boyish face matched just about every photo Jane had ever seen of herself. The cuckoo clock on the wall struck twelve as if she needed help understanding. Jane laughed.

In late spring, a constant veil of Pacific fog hung wet and heavy in the river canyons. The meadow was surrounded by primal forests that covered the mountains. Jane followed a game trail into an ancient redwood grove. It was like entering a living breathing kingdom of giants. She sucked in the misted silence as a sudden and inexplicable fear came over her.

Long stringy moss hung like witches' hair on dead redwood branches. Jane walked faster, the woods whispering in hushed voices behind her. Sword ferns reached out and swung at her from every direction. She ran. Thick grass carpeted the trail, then spread out across the forest floor leaving no distinct path. Jane stopped. She leaned against a downed redwood, breathing hard, fast, and extraordinarily loud. For a moment this ancient place terrified her. For the first time, Jane contemplated her insignificance in this world and closed her eyes. This forest, the trees, the sunlight would remain long after she was gone. The certainty of Jane's own death had never crossed her mind until then.

Sun shafted in white like daggers that shattered the forest roof. A raven cawed. Then another. Caws and cackles forced

Jane to look up. An unkindness decorated the redwood above her and seemed to be laughing at the silly little girl. "Arrrr!" she screamed and threw her arms up—spooking her insignificance and the unkindness away.

Summer neared and warmth cracked the gloomy days. Six starving mustangs were added to the ranch. The small herd seemed to appreciate the tender grass glistening in the sprig of sun breaking through the early morning—perfect for grazing. Coming off the Nevada desert these ponies were thin and accustomed to scrounging for every blade of grass. They must think they've died and gone to heaven, Jane thought while deciding which horse she'd like to break as soon as she had some help.

In Reno, Roy hadn't been completely honest about having horses. He had an old club-footed mule named Milo who limped like a water pump when Jane tried to ride him. Ben and Billy rode Milo bareback and whipped him with a switch to make him trot. It was cruel, Jane thought, and refused to allow it when Roy was gone, which was often.

Wasting her life tending to someone else's brats was a constant struggle, but when Betty spouted her first complete sentence at the dinner table Jane seriously considered packing.

"I shit my pants!" Betty said it like she was as surprised as the rest of the family. Ben and Billy laughed. So did Jane.

Roy placed his elbows on the table then laced his fingers and looked at Jane.

Jane looked down at her plate and sawed at the steak she had overcooked. "No way in hell I'm cleaning her."

"Go to the bathroom, Betty. Jane, help her." Roy rested his chin on his laced fingers and smiled.

"She ain't my kid." Jane bit the steak off her fork and gnawed on it as Roy stared her down. Betty slid from her booster seat and disappeared down the hall.

"She ain't mine either," Roy said softly, then sent the back of his hand hard and fast into Jane's face almost knocking her over backwards. Her nose and lips tingled with pain. She could taste blood. Felt it dribbling down her chin. Ben and Billy ran to their room like they knew the drill. Jane grabbed the steak knife—held it up, ready to take on Roy— then thought better of it. Not now, she though, but soon you bastard. Very soon. She set the knife on her plate and walked to the bathroom.

After cleaning Betty and herself, Jane let Roy apologize and rub against her feet. This was her job, she decided. Taking care of Roy and the kids would be her job and she'd be paid for her dirty work just as soon as she figured out how.

In the meantime, the horses relieved some of the resentment. Jane spent hours and hours with the mustangs. Named them numbers in order of likability. One was the only mare in the bunch. Roy called her the bitch. Jane called her the boss.

Gaining One's trust so that Jane could touch her took nearly two weeks but was an accomplishment worthy of the time and effort. It quieted Jane's mind when she couldn't sleep to think of the skittish mare and how good it had felt the first time she stroked One's nose.

More often than not, Roy was gone buying up sections of timber, which was just how Jane liked it. She didn't have to clean between her toes or shave between her legs. Living was simple when Roy wasn't around. Jane never cooked or cleaned unless he was home. Dinners without Roy were either peanut butter and jelly sandwiches or salami and cheese. Sometimes crackers were involved.

Once, Jane made a tuna casserole, but the cats were the only ones who seemed to enjoy it. When the boys complained about meals or what was in their lunchboxes, they went hungry until the next day.

By late summer life at the mill was bearable—until the morning Dink showed up on the front porch waving a pistol at Roy.

"I want my daughter." He was big, dark, and drunk. "Give her to me." He swayed in and out like the ocean waves. "My people will show her the way."

"Go back to the rez, Dink. Before I call the sheriff," Roy said.

"I don't live on the rez no more." Dink looked down at the gun in his hand and Roy made his move. He rushed Dink and jerked the gun out of his hand without the slightest struggle, then handed it to Jane. "Hide this." Jane had never held a real gun. The cold weight felt good as she lifted and carried it to the pantry. The top shelf was the first place she thought to hide the thing. Somewhere the kids couldn't get to it. The man yelled and Jane hurried back to the porch in time to see Roy headed for his new black Cadillac.

"I mean it. Now get!" Roy sounded like he was yelling at a stray dog. Dink looked at Jane as she stood in the doorway while Roy got in his car.

"Roy!" she yelled. "Don't leave me here with this drunk Hoopa."

"You've got the gun. Shoot his ass!"

"Roy!"

"Go inside and call the sheriff." Roy slammed the car door and left for Oregon.

"Gyppo!" Dink yelled at Roy. "He's a gyppo logger." He turned to Jane. "Ruins everything. The trees. The river." He stumbled backwards and almost fell off the steps. "The fish.

Carol." He dropped his head. "Carol." He started to weep. "Carol, Carol, Carol."

Carol was Roy's wife's name. "What about Carol?" Jane asked, ready to shut the door and lock it if he made a move.

"He ruined her. My Carol." He sobbed. "Hung her up like an elk." The big man's body sunk onto the steps and allowed the morning sun to enlighten Jane. Slumped with his head in his hands, Dink confessed, "I was gonna marry her and he ruined it."

"How do you mean? How did he ruin it?"

Dink lifted his arm and swept his big hand in a circle while mumbling. "I want my daughter."

"Where is she?"

"You have her."

"I don't have her."

"You do." He looked into Jane eyes. The pain on his face was undeniable.

"Betty?" Jane considered the possibility. The toddler did not resemble her brothers nor Roy. She was not pale like they were and she had big dark eyes. Exactly like Dink's. It suddenly became clear as hell. Carol had been having an affair with Dink. Betty was a product of that affair as was Carol's death.

Dink stood himself up using the railing as a brace. "Her name is Na-da' ay. Tree Stands. Not *Betty*." He walked over to Jane. "He will ruin her too. And you." Dink turned and stumbled down the steps. He walked away then stopped—looked at the sky and screamed, "Please!" Billy and Ben were at school, but Betty woke up wailing like never before. "Please!" Their cries joined the wind as Dink stumbled away down the dirt driveway.

Jane didn't carry, coddle, or comfort Betty when she cried. Most of the time a Hershey's chocolate bar did the trick. Half for

Betty and half for Jane. They sat on the sofa watching Woody Woodpecker eating a Hershey bar. Jane studied Betty's two-year-old face. She had no freckles like the rest. But it was her big brown eyes that confirmed it. Roy, Ben, and Billy all had the same troubled blue eyes. And Jane knew it was true. All the things the drunken Indian had said were true.

The revolver felt awkward and heavy in Jane's hands compared to her old BB gun. The cylinder held six bullets and Jane used them all to shoot cans off redwood stumps in a clear-cut. She hit three out of the six—nowhere good enough for what she had in mind.

Jane stole two boxes of bullets from the hardware store and she and Betty set up a tin can shooting range along the Mad River. Jane practiced turning around and leveling the gun on the tin can bad guy the way John Wayne did. "Big mouth don't make a big man." Jane fired. The can jumped and fell dead.

After shooting all but six bullets, Jane was on target more often than not. Betty was happy to help pick up each and every spent shell and put them back into their box. The girls walked to the river's edge and threw the boxes of spent shells and shot-up cans into the current. Proof floated away and sank into the murky depths of the Mad River.

Two days later Dink's brother rode up to the house on a shiny black horse. It was just getting dark and Roy wasn't home yet. Jane peeked through the open window and the kids followed.

"Hello? I'm Isaak Farmer. My brother Dink said he was coming here," the Indian cowboy hollered and stepped off his horse. He moved toward the porch. "Now, no one can find him. Please, ma'am, have you seen him?"

Jane opened the door. "Get back inside." Jane growled at

the kids and they stopped. "I mean it. Stay!" She shoved Billy back and shut the door, then stepped off the porch. The black horse enchanted Jane and she rubbed his velvety neck. "He was here a few days ago." Jane wondered if this Isaak knew about his brother's affair with Carol.

"I think something bad happened," Isaak said. "No one has seen him since he left to come here."

Roy's call came to mind like a spark. He had called last night and told Jane not to worry about Dink. "He won't be bothering anyone anymore," Roy had said. There was little doubt she had married a murderer. How ironic, Jane thought. How utterly ironic. "I haven't seen him since he left here. My husband will be home tomorrow. You should talk to him. Come by around eight. He's usually in a decent mood by then."

"I will." He turned to mount the black.

"You know much about training horses?"

"Yes."

"If you're interested, I have a mustang that needs to be broke. I'll pay you."

"Which one is it?"

"She's the mouse-colored thing with black legs."

"The grulla. I saw her. She has good bone."

"Yeah, she tried to kick me yesterday."

"Fifty dollars. No check."

"Sure." Jane didn't have cash or access to Roy's bank accounts. She hadn't even figured out the combination to the damn safe yet. But she had an idea. "What if I let you pick whichever mustang you like and you can keep it. In exchange for training the mare. That's probably worth more than fifty bucks, don't you think?"

He snickered. "Mustangs ain't worth shit unless they're fat."

Jane crossed her arms and kicked at the dirt. "Alright then, wait right here." She ran inside. The kids were piled around the window trying to eavesdrop. In the bedroom, Jane shut the door and opened a carved wooden box on the bureau. Roy's trinkets and treasures were inside. She found the gold pocket watch Carol had given him for his thirtieth birthday and went back outside.

Standing next to the horse with her back to the window, Jane slipped the pocket watch over to Isaak. He held it in his palm and looked at it.

"That watch and a horse. Deal?" Jane asked.

"Good trade. I'll take the horses now and start them tomorrow." He mounted his horse and rode away. "Tell your husband I will be back tomorrow night," he said as he rode away.

Jane grinned and went inside. "Good trade. Very good trade." She went to the telephone and dialed.

"Operator."

"Sheriff's office, please."

It rang three times. "Yello, this is Deputy Baker. What can I do you for?"

"This is Mrs. Roy Robinson out at the Robinson Mill. There was a man here prowling around and my husband isn't home." Jane played up the panic. "I don't know what to do. I have three small children here and we're all alone."

"Don't worry ma'am I'll dispatch a car immediately."

"Thank you."

"Ma'am stay on the line please."

"Okay." Jane could hear the deputy sending a car through the radio. It didn't take long.

"Ma'am?"

"Yes?"

"Did you get a look at the intruder?"

"Not very well—only from behind. He was big and had a cowboy hat on. Then a few seconds later I heard a horse. Sounded like he was trotting away."

"Okay. A deputy should be there soon."

"Please, hurry." Jane hung up and went out onto the porch as the children followed. Three scared children would add an undeniable authenticity to her story.

8:29. Twelve minutes after she'd made the call. Lights but no siren came up the graveled drive. As the sheriff pulled up, Jane lifted Betty into her arms and ordered the boys to keep quiet or else. Her plan just might work.

They found Dink the next day. Bloated in the Mad River and wedged in a logjam. A log driver found him but it took four of them to maneuver the logs with their pike poles and dislodge the corpse. Jane heard the sirens just before lunch and drove the truck to the mill. Some of the truck drivers overheard the call on their CB radio and gathered at the scene. Bad news traveled faster than the ambulance on its return via the two-lane.

Roy arrived home just in time for his favorite supper. Elk steaks with mashed potatoes and gravy. "How come you cook for Dad but not us?" Billy asked. Jane answered with a kick to his shin and he shut up. The children sat quietly and ate until Jane broke the silence. "Dink's dead."

"Who's Dink?" Billy asked and sat up in his chair.

"A troublemaker." Roy cut a hunk of meat. "And troublemakers don't last long around here." He filled his mouth. "You get your report card, Billy?" he asked around a mouthful.

"Yes, sir."

"He got two Ds and one F!" Ben interrupted with a smile and Billy lowered his head. He knew what was coming next.

Roy shook his head. "Unacceptable, William Henry Robinson. Absolutely unacceptable. Go to your room. Now!" Roy slammed his fists on the table and bounced every plate.

Jane knew the use of all three names meant the belt for Billy, and her inkling of doubt about Roy's involvement in Dink's death had been washed clean away when he failed to ask what had happened to the man. Why should he? Jane thought. He knew. He probably paid for it. She was glad the pistol was loaded inside her boot.

By eight that night, Billy had cried himself to sleep after a good beating with the belt and Jane had put Ben and Betty to bed with a double-dose of cough medicine. Roy was sitting on the couch working on his third vodka tonic when Jane walked in and handed him another. She turned the television off.

"Let's sit outside. It's such a nice night," Jane said.

"Jack Benny's coming on in a minute," he slurred. "I love that show." He reached for the remote and almost fell off the couch.

"Come on. I have a surprise for you. You're gonna love it." She pulled his hand and smiled her best smile. "Come on."

Roy was on the porch swing—about halfway through his drink when Isaak rode out of the dark. "Now what?" Roy stood and staggered forward. Jane stayed put on the swing—crossed her leg and removed the gun while Roy watched Isaak dismount from the black horse. Jane slipped the gun into the back of her jeans as Isaak wrapped the reins around the saddle horn. The horse didn't move when the Indian cowboy walked away and approached Roy.

"What the hell do you want?" Roy looked down at him from the porch.

"Justice. Only simple justice." Isaak took the stairs two at a time, the veins and tendons in his neck bulging like a charging bull. Roy stepped back. "Jane, call the sheriff."

"I will." Jane held the gun behind her as she stepped off the porch swing. She backed away from the men who were now uncomfortably close.

"I know you paid Swifty to murder Dink. Swifty asked God to forgive him before he died but he wouldn't tell me how much you paid him. How much, Roy?"

Roy downed the last of his drink and grinned. "Not much."

Isaak punched Roy in the face and he stumbled backward, dropped his empty glass, then landed on his ass against the swing. It bounced back and forth against him as blood gushed heavy from his nose.

"Stop!" Jane held the gun tight on Isaak with both hands.

"Shoot him!" Roy barked squeezing his nose. "Shoot him! It'll be okay. I promise." He looked comfortable with his back against the swing and legs out in front of him.

Isaak put his hands up in surrender and stepped back as Jane stepped forward. She stood in front of him—so close she could smell the Fab used to launder his clothes. Isaak backed up until he had one foot off the step. "Look, I'm leaving. I'm leaving right now, okay!"

"You might want stay. And watch." Jane spun toward Roy and pulled the trigger. The first shot clipped his shoulder and sent him sideways so that the second shot bit his jugular. Blood spewed out of him and painted the wood porch a sweet red.

The look on Roy's face was utter disbelief as he held the hole in his neck and coughed and choked then gurgled like a clogged drain. He kicked and kicked his pointed boots, heels hammering the porch. Jane stepped closer and shot over and over until Roy and the gun were useless. Bullets had twisted and cocked his head at a peculiar angle. His eyes and mouth hung wide open like he was dumbstruck.

"OH!! SHIT!!" Isaak ripped off his hat. "What the fuck are you doing?"

"Go home." Jane waited until Isaak rode away before calling the sheriff and screaming that Isaak Farmer had just killed her husband.

CHAPTER
TWELVE

Jane Wayne

In the pantry, Jane buried the gun in the flour tin, then shoved the tin to the very back of the top shelf. Lined up jars of peaches and pears in front of it. Tomorrow night she would throw it into the middle of the Mad River where no one would ever find it. Jane stepped from the pantry into the kitchen, slapping the flour dust from her hands, and caught Billy watching.

"What was that noise?" Billy rubbed his red and swollen eyes.

"Your dad's drunk and if you don't get your ass back in bed, he'll tan your hide again!"

Billy looked doubtful. "It sounded like shooting."

"You hungry? You didn't get to finish your supper, you poor thing." Jane grabbed two cookies from the jar while Billy headed for the front door. "Want milk?"

Billy ignored her as he neared the window. The curtains closed, he reached for them.

"Billy!"

The boy turned, and Jane grabbed his arm. She forced him back to his bedroom. "No milk and cookies for you. You just don't listen!" She shoved him into his room and slammed the door. Sirens howled.

By midnight, a deputy had shot photos of the crime scene. Statements were given by Jane and then Billy, who said he'd heard the shots but seen nothing. Ben and Betty, who had slept through their father's murder, were awoken and questioned. Reports were written while Roy rode in a silent ambulance to the morgue in Eureka. A few hours of hassle were all it took to rid the world of rotten Roy Robinson. Good trade, Jane thought as she hosed his cold blood from the porch. Very good trade.

The phone rang, and Jane tossed the hose into the rosebushes and went inside.

"Hello?"

"Sorry to call so late, Mrs. Robinson." It was the Sheriff. "I just thought it might help you and the kids rest easier knowing we've captured Mr. Farmer."

"Oh. Thank the Lord." Jane grabbed an oatmeal cookie from the jar. "Did he confess?"

"Not exactly. He raised his hands and swore to God that you shot your husband."

"*I* shot my husband?" Jane bit into her cookie.

"He run off into the forest, but my men tracked him down. He was hole up in an old hollow redwood. When Mr. Farmer attacked...well, my deputy shot him."

"Dead?" Jane shoved the rest of the cookie in her mouth.

"Afraid so."

Jane smiled, "Why did he do it? What did he have against Roy?"

"We'll be looking into that. Now try and get some sleep."

"Thank you, Sheriff and good night." Jane hung up the phone. Lit a cigarette and stepped out onto the porch.

The night was quiet. Peaceful and perfect. Through the treetops a waning moon with an odd ring that glowed like a halo. The smell of freshly milled lumber mingled with wet porch wood and blood. She let the water run on the roses while she lit the cigarette and rocked on the porch swing. Tapping and splashing her bare feet in the shallow pink puddle below. Happiness is never ever having to scrub semen from between my toes again, Jane thought and took a deep pull on her cigarette.

Early the next morning, Jane called Roy's mother, Arlene, and explained her son's tragic death, then concluded with how the children would be much better off with real relatives like a loving grandmother or an aunt. As far as Jane knew, Roy hadn't spoken to his family in years.

Grandma Arlene agreed to take the children and arrived two days later with Roy's big sister, Fran. Aunt Fran pulled Ben and Billy into her bulk and promised everything was going to be okay. Judging by the size of her, Jane believed that at the very least the kids would be well fed. Aunt Fran lifted the boys belongs into the trunk while Ben and Billy climbed in the backseat ready to go.

Betty stepped out of the house with fresh braids bowed at the bottom. Dressed in her favorite yellow jumper, the girl had her doll in one hand and a little blue suitcase in the other. Jane lifted, then carried her down the steps. "This is Betty." Jane walked to the car.

Arlene and Fran looked at each other like the devil had just asked them for a ride.

"What is it?" Jane asked and put Betty down.

"May I have a word—in private?" Aunt Fran asked with arms crossed.

Jane sensed trouble. "Wait here Betty."

Inside the house, Jane shut the door. Aunt Fran again crossed her arms, then lifted her chins, ready for battle. "We're not taking Betty. I know the truth. People talk and word travels."

Grandma Arlene looked out the window. "She is not Roy's child therefore she is *not* my grandchild. And after all that's happened, I think it's for the best."

Aunt Fran stuck a plump thumb at the door. "It's not our responsibility to raise an illegitimate child."

Jane opened the door. Walked out and grabbed Betty and her suitcase. She carried the child back to the house without a word as she passed Arlene and Fran on the steps. "I go bye-bye," Betty said, and Jane went inside and slammed the door. She sat Betty on the kitchen counter. "I go bye-bye."

"No. You don't want to go to that stinky old witch's house."

"Wike Wiz Oz?"

"Yep. Just like Wizard of Oz. She's the Wicked Witch of the West and you *do not* want to go her house. Remember how bad the flying monkeys scared you?"

Betty nodded with wide eyes. "Scawey me."

"You'd have to eat toads for supper." Jane grabbed a cookie from the jar and gave it to Betty. A two-year-old mind is easily distracted. "Let's go to the beach! You, me, and Dolly can have a picnic. And make a sandcastle. Okay?"

"Kay." Betty looked unsure and hugged her little dolly. Jane thought about hugging little Betty.

A week after his death, Roy was sent back home to Oregon. He'd been raised in Gilchrist, a mill town in northern Klamath County, where his mother and sister and now his two sons lived. Jane and Betty drove to the funeral in Roy's new Cadillac in just under six hours. That Caddy hugged the curves along the Pacific

Coast at ninety miles an hour while Jane smoked and sang with the radio. Betty slept in the backseat and was still asleep when Jane parked in front of the Deschutes Memorial Chapel. She flicked her cigarette out the window and stepped out of the car, smoothing out her new black dress. She crushed the burning butt with the toe of her black cowboy boot. With Betty half asleep on her shoulder, she went inside.

The casket was closed of course, but for a reason Jane couldn't put her finger on, something scared her. Maybe it was her conscience. More likely, the mix of formaldehyde and candle smoke set her nerves on fire. She took Betty to the ladies' room to pee. In the last stall Betty tinkled as two women walked in.

"This entire thing stinks to high heaven if you ask me." She sounded old.

"Did you see the widow? My God, Irene, she looks like a boy. And cowboy boots with a dress, I mean have you ever? What was Roy thinking?" The second voice pulled into the stall next to Jane and Betty. "Bet she'll have quite a payday when Roy's life insurance arrives." The woman cackled.

"The only life insurance policy Roy had was on me," Jane said as she and Betty exited the stall and for once she wasn't lying. The bastard had no life insurance but had taken a one-hundred-thousand-dollar policy out on Jane a month after their wedding. "I'm sure it was just in case I had an accident, like poor Carol." A woman with a face like rotting fruit looked surprised.

"Who's that?" the other woman asked from behind the stall door.

"The widow," said Fruit Face. "I'm sorry, I didn't mean—"

"Of course you didn't. No apology necessary." Jane punched the soap dispenser. "Cunt." She half-filled one hand with pink powdered soap.

"*Excuse* me?" Fruit Face's grin was as fake as her apology. The other woman exited the stall and pulled up to the sink next to Jane.

"I'm sorry for your loss." The woman washed her hands and smiled.

"I don't know what I'll do without him. I miss him terribly." Jane tried so hard to cry. She squeezed every muscle in her face, even her eyes. Nowhere near tears, she tried weeping sounds, but couldn't contain the irony and laughed instead. Jane walked out with Betty and a bit of pink powdered soap in her hand.

In the first pew, tears refused to come no matter how hard Jane tried. With each eulogy came more and more crying from somewhere in the back. Sobs came from all sides, and Jane knew it had to be done. She lowered her head and rubbed her eyes with her soapy fingers. It stung, and Jane finally cried like a grieving widow should.

By July, logging was in full swing while Jane waited out the lengthy probate process. She had colored her hair back to its naturally faded red. Thought about leaving town the minute Isaak Farmer's widow went to the sheriff and reported that Isaak had come home that night and told her that Jane had shot Roy. The sheriff questioned Jane, but called it a technicality. Said that he did not believe a word of it and wouldn't bother Jane again with such trivial matters. But people lied, and that included sheriffs. Just in case she had to leave in a hurry,

Jane packed a suitcase for herself and Betty and kept it in the Caddy's trunk.

Grandma Arlene filed a lawsuit, claiming that neither Jane nor Betty was entitled to any portion of Roy's estate. Benjamin Franklin Robinson and William Edward Robinson were his only true heirs, according to the statements filed. This would take months in court, maybe more, Jane's attorney advised. She couldn't just sit around waiting for funds that were rightly hers, so she made the best of it by keeping busy.

The mill, constantly cloaked in a cloud of dust, buzzed from dawn 'til dark. Harvest crews and mill workers filled the surrounding makeshift houses. Trucks hauled massive redwoods into the mill while trucks loaded with cut lumber headed out. Despite the hustle and bustle at the mill, business was less than half of what it had been the year before, according to Roy's accountant. Jane paid closer attention to the books after One, her favorite mustang mare, kicked and broke Jane's femur in two places. That put an end to all summer riding plans, but offered plenty of time to study and learn the ins and outs of the timber industry.

With a heavy cast on her leg, Jane studied how to sort and grade logs, work the scale and estimate value. She even kept a notebook of the entire operation and what every man did there. It would help prove how much the mill meant to her when they went to court.

Bull chain operators: pull logs into the mill. Work the conveyor belt that moves the logs into a chute that enters the mill.
Barker operator: runs the machine that strips the bark off the logs.
Deck workers: roll the logs onto a movable platform or carriage.
Block setters: arrange the logs in position—

On and on until Jane had filled journals with detailed explanations of each position and the secrets to running a mill. Her personal journals held the real secrets and were buried two feet deep in a metal box behind the house. Winifred Mudgett was long gone now and would stay that way unless someone were to find the journals. Then Winnie would live again only to suffer the prospect of a long and tragic prison sentence.

Probate court was worse than Jane had imagined. The minute she hobbled in on crutches, the hairs on the back of her neck tingled. The place felt harsh. Draconian. Intimidating looks on everyone's face were threatening and suffocating as Jane walked in. It could be guilt, but this was not the time or the place to birth a conscience. She forced a mask of bravery to cover the terror eating at her as she wiped her sweaty hands on her skirt, gripped her crutches, and worked her way to her seat.

"The petition claiming rights to Roy's estate is without merit." Paul Haley, Jane's attorney, sat next to her and put an extra dose of reassurance in his voice as he rubbed her good thigh. But the one life lesson Edgar Allan Poe had taught Jane was to never trust the living and believe only half of what you see and none of what you hear.

Jane leaned into Mr. Haley. "Is it necessary for me to be here? I'm not at all feeling well." Jane wiped her brow.

Mr. Haley removed his hand from Jane's thigh. "You don't look well, dear. What is it?"

"Morning sickness, I'm afraid." Jane covered her mouth like she might be ill at any moment.

"Oh. You poor thing. Go. I'll explain everything to the judge." He helped Jane with her crutches and escorted her to the heavy wood doors. As he opened a door, he leaned in and whispered, "This will no doubt help your case. No judge in his right mind will deny a pregnant widow." Mr. Haley looked like he had already won as Jane headed for the restroom.

She pressed her eyes closed and splashed water on her face. In the mirror, ashen skin and sagging dark eyes convinced her she was ill. Not with morning sickness. Jane knew that was a first-rate fabrication, but being here in this law-abiding hell was like holding Satan prisoner in heaven.

Probate court decided in just over a week. Robinson's Lumber Mill was to be sold, and the proceeds split equally among the three children and Jane. Also to be split equally were all assets and accounts. After Mr. Haley's fees, this would leave Jane and Betty each somewhere around three hundred to four hundred thousand dollars.

It was well into fall and Jane celebrated turning seventeen by having her cast removed then limping straight to the bakery. She was in the throes of deciding between the chocolate cake and the strawberry pie when Mr. Haley walked in. Jane went with the chocolate and hurried outside, but Mr. Haley followed. Jane explained her devastating miscarriage and the sympathetic attorney wrapped his pudgy arms around her. He hugged her too long and said he'd pray for her.

Jane pulled away and stepped back. "Roy's mother told me it was for the best," Jane lied and wiped a tear that came without the sting of pink powdered soap.

"Goodness. Seems insensitive. I'm certain she meant well. Mrs. Robinson, I give you my word, no one will keep assets that are rightfully yours." Mr. Haley went in for a second hug, but Jane exited just in time.

The mill just wouldn't sell in spite of reducing the price by fifty thousand dollars. Environmentalist had put a stop to cutting down old growth timber, and the logging industry was at war. No one was interested in investing in a mill they might not have logs for. Jane's portion of Roy's estate atrophied faster than her leg, which ached so badly it kept her up most every night.

Whiskey helped, and sometimes Betty rubbed the hurt for Jane while they practiced counting to ten or reciting the alphabet.

On occasion, when Jane slept, Roy intruded. She'd wake to find the heavy quilt pulled up or sometimes down, exposing her feet to the cold. It went on this way for a few weeks until the night she woke to her foot being squeezed so hard it hurt. She sat straight up. Pulled her knees to her chest. Covered her feet with the pillow. "Stop it, Roy! Get back to hell where you belong!"

Static suddenly blared from the living room. Jane rushed in to find the TV on. The screen glowing with black and white dots in the dark. She jerked the electrical cord from the wall. "Betty?" She rushed upstairs. Betty was sound asleep in her room. Jane watched the peaceful toddler, then crawled into bed with her. Cracks and pops and something like footsteps kept Jane up all night. From then on, Jane went to bed wearing her boots and wanted out of Roy's house as soon as possible.

Jane planted three candles in Betty's pink birthday cake. Aunt Fran had dropped Ben and Billy off outside the house in the rain after a phone call from Jane. She'd explained how poorly it would look to the court if the boys didn't attend their own sister's birthday party. "They have exactly one hour," Aunt Fran told Jane before driving away.

A rainbow of streamers and balloons decorated the dining room. A dozen or so kids, most of whose folks worked at the mill, lined up to play pin the tail on the donkey. "No cheating now," Jane said as she blindfolded Ben, then spun him three times. He held his arm straight and walked. Pinned the tail just below the donkey's ass. Kids and even a few parents laughed when Ben's face turned red and he threw the blindfold at Billy. Jane picked it up and was about to tie it on Billy when the boy looked scared—began breathing hard out of his mouth.

"Don't kill me. Stay away." He bolted out the front door.

"Okay, who's next?" Jane asked. It was all she could think to do in the moment.

"Me!" A girl of about five or six raised her hand.

Jane blindfolded and spun the girl while wondering what had gotten into Billy. What the hell was he so afraid of? The fright on the boy's face was not an act. He said, *"Don't kill me."*

Jane spun and spun the girl. Billy had refused the cough medicine that would have put him into a deep slumber, Jane remembered. He was too busy bawling after Roy beat him with his belt. Jane spun the girl again. Billy could have heard the shots, but so what? Did he see what happened? Jane stopped spinning the girl and released her in the donkey's direction, but like a drunk at closing time, the girl side-stepped twice before falling.

"Time for cake!" Jane said, and all the kids ran screaming into the dining room while Betty was blindfolding herself. Jane handed Betty a paper tail with a pin, then secured the blindfold and pointed her in the right direction. She guided the birthday girl's hand until the tail was pinned into perfect position. "Jackpot!" Jane yelled and lifted Betty in the air.

Billy refused to come in for cake and ice cream. He sat out on the porch swing and stared at the road.

Jane stepped out of the house and shut the door behind her. "What is it, Billy? Why would you say, 'Don't kill me?'"

Rain was loud on the tin roof and tried to drown Jane's words. Billy ignored her and kept staring down the road. The second Jane sat next to him, the boy up and ran. He stopped just past the porch and yelled, "You lied about Mr. Farmer! He didn't kill my dad! Liar!" He turned and ran down the muddy driveway toward the two-lane.

Well, shit. This was too serious to ignore. Something had to be done, and Jane stepped off the porch. With her bad leg, catching him was going to be painful, but there was no way around it. Before breaking her leg, she could have caught Billy with her hands tied behind her back. Now she wasn't so sure. Her cowboy boots gave Billy a definite advantage. The pain in her right thigh was like a knife, and Jane gritted her teeth and ran as if her life depended on it.

"Stop or else!" Anger always gave her strength.

Billy's chin came up as he tired. He pumped his arms for more, then looked back and saw Jane gaining on him. Rain had ruined Jane's hairdo, and that aggravated her to no end after spending the night in curlers. He was just within reach, but instead of grabbing the boy, she kicked his foot. An old playground trick she'd learned in second grade which always worked and was easily labeled an accident. Billy's feet tangled. He hit hard on his hands and knees. Mud freckled his face.

"Leave me alone!" It looked like he was crying, but she couldn't be sure. He was soaked. "I just wanna leave!"

"Then why'd you come today?" Billy didn't answer, so Jane stomped his fingers. "I'll break your fingers if you don't answer me!" She huffed like a freight train and bent to catch her breath.

"I love my sister and I don't want you to kill her."

"Why in the world would I hurt Betty? What is wrong with you?"

"You lied! I saw you!" His eyes were red. He was definitely crying.

"Here's the thing, Bill. You're confused. Maybe you miss your dad. But—maybe you don't. Odds are good you don't miss being whipped. Part of you is real glad your dad's gone and you feel kind of bad about that."

He lowered his head. Rain hid his tears, but not his sobs.

Jane pressed her foot down harder on his hand. "Did you mention this bullshit to anyone else?"

"No."

"Why not?"

"I wasn't sure." He sniveled, "I thought maybe it was a dream, until today. Back in the house, I remembered all of it."

"Boy oh boy, you have lost your ever-loving mind, kid. They're gonna lock you up and throw away the key. Can't even tell a dream from reality." In order to survive, it had to be done and Jane dug deep into the darkest part of her evil. She took a deep breath and chuckled. "Insanity is hereditary—you know that, right? I mean with your crazy mother and all her troubles, it'll be the loony bin for you, kiddo. No one is *ever* going to believe your cockamamie story." Jane let him soak up her scenario a while. "You know what they do to kids in asylums? *Do you?*"

He didn't answer through tears—just shook his wet head.

"First, you spend a few months in a straitjacket. Shit in a bucket and they hose you off because you can't use your hands to wipe your own ass. Next comes electroshock therapy. They hook electrodes to your brain and flip the switch. It's like being struck by lightning over and over *and over* until all you can do is drool and piss yourself."

Jane took her foot off his hand and knelt in front of him. His eyes met hers, and she softened her tone. "After all that, they release you into a dormitory with all the other crazies. That's when real hell comes knockin'. Men in there do awful things to boys. They'll gang up on you. Hold you down and pull off your drawers. You can't scream or cry for help 'cause they shove a filthy sock in your mouth. Then they'll ram their peckers so far up your bun hole you'll feel it in your guts. One after another until they've all had a turn at you. You want that? Do you, Billy boy?"

Headlights broke through the rain and headed toward them. It was Aunt Fran's car. Exactly one hour from when she'd dropped them off.

"Straighten up." Jane helped Billy to his feet and squeezed his arm. "Think about it, Bill. Think about it long and hard before you expect anyone to believe your bullshit. It'll ruin your life long before it ruins mine."

Billy stood sobbing in the rain and watched Jane limp up the muddy road toward home.

CHAPTER
THIRTEEN

Jane Wayne

L iving in fear of nine-year-old Billy spilling the truth was not an option for Jane. Though fairly certain she'd terrified the boy, counting on his silence was too risky. A boy's mind can change like the weather, and the urge to leave gnawed at her more and more every day.

It wasn't just Billy anymore. It was Roy's tormenting presence from out of the blue. Since Jane had threatened little Billy, Roy'd started leaving the toilet seat up. When Roy was amongst the living, it was one of the few things Jane had asked him not to do. Now he did it every night to spite her.

Going to bed with her boots on prevented Roy from molesting Jane's feet, but lack of sleep, night after night, allowed too much time to think. Too much time to analyze. Jane regretted the way she'd scared Billy and it caused her to finally break. She packed up the Cadillac in the middle of the night and by daylight the next morning, she and Betty were on Highway 101, headed south to San Francisco.

At a cafe in Ukiah, Betty ate three pancakes, and Jane had more refills of coffee than she could count. Next to the ladies' room, Jane dropped a dime in the payphone and called Mr. Haley to let him know she was on her way to San Francisco to take care of her terminally ill grandmother. "She raised me right. It's the least I can do. I love her so much and with Roy and the baby gone—" Jane pretended to contain her emotion.

Mr. Haley apologized about still not having a buyer for the mill and wished her and her grandmother the best.

"Thank you." Jane lit a cigarette and watched Betty bounce back and forth along a corner booth.

Just before the Golden Gate Bridge, Jane's leg throbbed so badly she could no longer take the pain and pulled over. An afternoon sun and a steady breeze worked in unison to scatter the fog. Jane helped Betty out of the car and held her hand as they walked along the spectacular Golden Gate. Walking improved the circulation in Jane's healing femur and eased some of the pain.

Sunshine and blue skies shoved away the fog. Kelp and eucalyptus mingled in the salty air, along with sparks off the bay. It reminded Jane of the last time she'd been here. The fire. The way hypnotic flames had sparkled and danced. Instantly, Jane felt better—good, really good—optimistic even.

"Boat!" Betty pointed to a cargo ship crawling out from under the bridge.

"Yes, boat. Big boat."

"Go bye-bye?"

"Bye-bye." Jane waved at the passing ship and Betty copied her.

Going out of her way to take a trip down memory lane, Jane drove past the old Puente boarding house. Remnants of the fire had been disposed of and a new wood frame stood like a skeleton in the fog. Jane made a quick u-turn and parked the Cadillac across the street from the framed house.

In the glove box, Jane grabbed Roy's Minolta camera that he'd forbidden her to touch. She squinted and focused the lens on the wood frame, then pressed the top button. The camera clicked, and Jane wound the film forward. She pressed and clicked two more times before pulling away from the curb and reminiscing about the fire that night. The hiss and then the boom that woke the entire neighborhood. The way the blown-out windows flickered with orange and yellow light, like the whole house had short-circuited. Smoke that slithered into the night sky. *Spectacular.* She stopped the car and looked back.

The Caddy idled down the street, but Jane could not take her eyes off the side mirror, still imagining the flames that grew and consumed the old Victorian. A pang of regret for not having had a camera that night smoldered as Jane drove away.

Holy Cross Catholic Cemetery was spooky even during the day. Gray headstones pocked with black mold made most names and dates impossible to read. Jane needed a girl, close to her own age, who had died before being issued a Social Security number. It was like looking for a needle in a haystack; Jane knew it would be, which was why she allowed herself plenty of time. She'd find her new identity, and when the mill money came, Jane would cash out and disappear forever. An ancient oak shook its gnarled branches at her like judgmental fingers.

There were hundreds, maybe a thousand graves, and Jane guessed they hadn't even seen half. Maria Consuelo Batista— born in 1934—died in 1946, but redheaded, blue-eyed Jane did not need the scrutiny of a Spanish heritage. Jane and Betty walked on.

They climbed a grassy knoll—looked down on a casket being carried by six uniformed men. An American flag masked the coffin. Betty ran down the knoll the way they had just come, but Jane narrowed her focus on the crowd below, dressed in black that circled the open grave. Pallbearers set the casket on a stand and stepped away in unison with a white-gloved salute. Betty screamed. Jane turned and ran downhill after her.

"What happened?" Jane knelt.

"Owie!" Betty was on her behind with her hands pressing her knee. "Owie!" Jane wiped away a trickle of blood. "Daddy did to me."

"What do you mean Daddy did?" Jane wiped her bloody finger in the grass.

"Bad, Daddy hold my foot." Betty pouted. "Make me fall down." She sobbed.

Chills crawled up and down Jane. She didn't know what to make of the possibility that Roy might have followed them. She'd thought she'd rid herself of him for good when she shot him. How the hell do you kill a ghost? she wondered.

"You're okay." She wiped the girl's tears. Gunshots exploded all around them. Jane threw herself over the girl like a bulletproof blanket. Her heart beating like something sharp had caught between her ribs. Bugles echoed "Taps", and Jane realized that the shots fired were a formal gun-salute from the funeral below.

Before Jane had had time to reconsider, she had willingly offered her life to save this girl. She sat up. Left Betty lying on her back crying and thought hard about what just happened. There on the cool grass, among the dead, Jane snatched Betty up and hugged her hard for the very first time. Something shifted in Jane and she cried. The world tilted a little as Jane cradled Betty and "Taps" rang in the background. It was not only the first time Jane wanted to hug another human; it was the first time she could recall really crying. Surrounded by headstones and crosses and praying statues, Betty clung to Jane's neck. It felt good. The world had given Jane a chance to save a little girl who, like her, no one loved or wanted.

"Stop crying okay." Jane lifted Betty's chin. Looked into her eyes and waited a while for them both to stop sniveling. "From now on—I'm going to be good," Jane promised herself as much as Betty. "I'll be your mommy. Okay?"

"Good mommy."

"Yes. A very good mommy. The best." Jane hugged Betty again.

The girls followed a gravel path that zigzagged along the terraced plots for nearly two hours. Then there it was. *EFFIE MAY HOBBS 1931–1946.* "Bingo!" Only fifteen when she died and very unlikely to have been employed and issued a Social Security number. Becoming Effie Hobbs would age seventeen-year-old Jane by four years. "Twenty-one's a good number." Perfect age for a young widow with a three-year-old daughter. Changing a three-year-old's identity would be easy once Effie explained she'd birthed the child at home and was now a widow. Jane pulled a pencil and a small notepad from her back pocket and wrote the name and birthdate.

"Can you say Effie?" Jane asked as she slid the notepad back into her pocket and tucked the pencil behind her ear.

"Afee," said Betty.

"Good enough." Jane took Betty's hand, then carried her to the car when she cried about being too hungry to walk.

After burgers and shakes at the new McDonald's, Jane bathed Betty in a motel room. Soon as the mill money came through, they'd go to Kim's Kite Shop in Chinatown and ask for the "new girl." Jane Wayne would become Effie May Hobbs, and eventually Betty would be...Betty needed a new name. "Okay, out of the tub." Jane held out a towel.

"No!" Betty rolled onto her tummy and ignored Jane.

"Fine with me, shrivel up like a prune. See if I care." Jane walked to the bed and flopped on her back. She stared at the brown water stains on the ceiling and listened to the couple next door, arguing about Bob's use of foul language and his lack of appreciation for Sheila's cooking. "Jesus Christ." Jane pounded the wall with her fist. Rolled onto her side and yawned, grateful it was just her and Betty now.

She opened the drawer in the nightstand and found a Bible. "Marvelous." She opened it. "I adore fiction." Jane flipped through the pages until a red circle on a black and white page caught her eye. She looked closer. Circled repeatedly in red ink was the name Ruth. "Ruth." Jane ripped out the page and set it on the nightstand. "Hey, Ruth." Jane walked to the tub. "You like the name Ruth?"

"Baby Ruff." Betty smiled.

"Okay then, get your ass out of the tub, Baby Ruth." Jane wrapped Ruth in a dry towel and hugged her for the second time.

CHAPTER
FOURTEEN

"Whoa! Wait up!" I held my palms out to stop her. Nana's story had rolled out of her like a familiar song, but I needed to slow down. "Stop."

My thoughts were tangled. She'd pulled the trigger and brutally murdered Roy Robinson. That made number three. Hell yes, he was an asshole and a murderer, maybe, but she could have left him. Called the police. No. Roy probably had the police in his pocket. *Was it her responsibility to stop Roy?* I could justify it if I tried. I squeezed the sides of my throbbing head trying to hold it together and closed my eyes. The image of Nana's little finger pulling the trigger was as clear and undeniable as if it were carved on the insides of my eyelids. I opened my eyes to rid myself of the awful vision and though to slow down my heavy breathing before I hyperventilated. I dropped my arms and relaxed my shoulders.

"Ruth was my mother's name." My hands were full of sweat. I swallowed hard. "You're saying Betty became *Ruth?*"

Pressure built inside until I was on the verge of coming apart at the seams. "My mother, Ruth, was really little Betty?"

Nana made a face as if the truth had left a bitter taste in her mouth. The lie hung in the air a long while before she nodded, then grinned like she had just shared the meaning of life with me.

"But Betty wasn't really yours. Ruth, my mother, was *not* your child and—" It was like being choked. I couldn't get my next breath or the words out. Time stalled. Lack of oxygen made me dizzy. I sucked a breath. Then deep breaths over and over until I could think. "You're not my real grandmother." Chills scratched up my spine with the words as tears filled my eyes and blurred Nana.

"Blood is nothing." The venom in her voice crushed me. "Doesn't mean shit."

Maybe not to her, but it sure as hell mattered to me. This was it. The proverbial final straw that would break me.

I wrapped my arms around my body and squeezed as if preparing for my inevitable straitjacket. *Who am I? What am I? Would the spit sample I sent to Family Tree reveal my roots?*

Thoughts raced and crashed. Murder might not be carved into my DNA after all. Not being genetically predisposed to killing people was somewhat comforting.

Nana shut her eyes, and that's when I saw it. A tear snuck out from the corner, ran along her temple, and hid in her hair. "I love you, Jess."

"Why?" The lump in my throat turned to stone.

Nana opened her eyes and looked at me. "Because you're good. Good and innocence since the day you were born, just like your mom."

A short round doctor with blond hair curled around her face like a helmet suspended my impending doom. "Hello, I'm Doctor Marshall."

"I'm Jessica. Her granddaughter." A sarcastic grunt escaped. "Or maybe not."

Dr. Marshall stepped next to Nana and raised her voice. "Hello, Miss Hobbs. How are you today?"

"Not good." Nana looked about as approachable as a pit viper. "What do you want?"

"To make certain you're comfortable."

Nana seemed suddenly exasperated. Breathing became an effort and slowed. Her eyes fell shut. Something changed, but I couldn't put my finger on it—she looked like she was dying. I forgot about her not being my grandmother. Losing Nana scared the hell out of me.

"Nana?"

"Miss Hobbs, if you're in pain I can increase your medication."

"That's not a bad idea, Nana. It's late and you should rest." I needed to make my getaway. Escape somewhere—anywhere but here.

"No." Nana's head shook as if in slow motion. "If—I—die..." Words crawled out of her dry mouth. "The oak."

"You've had enough for today." I'd had enough for a lifetime. My maternal grandmother had hanged herself. A Native American named Dink was really my grandfather—who was ultimately murdered thanks to Roy Robinson, the man who was not my grandfather and was shot to death by my sweet Nana. I had two uncles if they hadn't been shot, or hanged, or God knows what.

How the hell could I write Nana's story when I myself couldn't make sense of it?

"I'll come back in the morning." I leaned over and kissed her cheek. "No matter what you're still my Nana." Relief lifted her wrinkled face, but I was numb.

Her skeletal hand pressed against my head and pulled my ear to her mouth. She whispered, "I kept—my promise—to—Ruth." I didn't move—just waited for no real reason. Breathed in her stale scent.

"You didn't kill *anyone* after Roy?" The doctor must have heard me and snapped her head around, looking wide-eyed at me, but I didn't care. "*Nana?*" She didn't answer. "*Nana.*" I shook her shoulder.

"I'll send a nurse to increase her morphine. It will help her through the night." Dr. Marshall left the room.

I had to be sure I understood if she meant what she said. "Nana? This is important." I shook her shoulder a little too hard.

"Damn it, Roy," she mumbled without moving or opening her eyes. After all these years, Roy was still haunting her. Then, it hit me. *No.* It was never a ghost tormenting Nana. It was her own conscience. It had to be. It was comforting to think she had one.

"Nana. Did you say you did *not* kill the people they found on your ranch?"

"Mm—hmm."

"You're *innocent?*" Hope caused me to say it too loud.

Nana shook her head. "Not innocent." Her eyes cracked open. "Did it—for—you." Her eyes closed.

"For *me?* Did what for me?" She didn't answer. "Nana?" I waited for a response that wouldn't come, then kissed her cheek and left.

Dr. Marshall stood at the nurse's station filling out paperwork. "Excuse me, Doctor. Do you have a minute?"

"Sure."

"Any idea how much longer she has?"

The doctor shook her head and offered a sympathetic smile. "I've had patients worse than her last for weeks without food or water, and I've had patients in better condition who didn't survive but a few days. There are too many variables. She seems *very* strong-willed. Those types usually hang on the longest." She patted my shoulder.

Did it for you. A thousand thoughts scratched at my mind as I drove. No matter how I worked it out nothing made sense. Nana claimed she had kept her promise to Ruth and never killed anyone after Roy. But killing Roy made three murders. Did that qualify Nana as a serial killer? If so, I could shitcan the daily affirmations. Nana swore she didn't kill again, but then who the hell did? Maybe it was all just rambling lies spewed from a dying old woman.

Fact or fiction? The harder I tried to work it out, the more insanity knocked. I couldn't wait to get home and have a drink or two or three. But first, I had to talk to my mother. She might be able to shed light on Nana's story. *God help me.* Conversations with Ruth were like trying to run through a pasture full of thistles with shorts on.

My evil stepfather Raymond was on the tractor alongside the road, dumping brush onto a smoldering burn pile. He was an ugly forge of a man, always smoldering like that burn pile until the wind changed and he flared up. My mother Ruth was the exact opposite—empty and cold. I swallowed down the handful of antacids I'd been chewing, pulled up next to him, and rolled my window down. The pinched expression on his face hadn't changed in the seven years since I'd seen him. He turned off the tractor and looked at me with the same disgust as always. "What the hell you want?"

"I need to talk to Ruth."

"She ain't here. Moved into some old folk's home. Goin' around actin' like she's got the dementia. Lemme tell you, she ain't got no goddamn dementia. She's fakin' just so she ain't gotta live here with me," he snickered.

If my mother had dementia or was faking it to escape Raymond, she was either brilliant or damn lucky. I couldn't speculate one way or the other, but leaned toward luck over brilliance. I should at the very least feel sad or bad about my mother being in a home, but I didn't. Anything was better than living with Raymond and it was good to know she was being taken care of.

"What's the name of the place?" I asked.

"I don't know! Paradise somethin'."

I rolled up the window and turned the truck around on the narrow road while Raymond glared at me like the asshole he is as I passed. I took a deep breath. Focused on forgiveness and stopped the truck. One more extra-deep breath and I backed up. Rolled the passenger window down. "Thanks, Raymond. I'll say a prayer for you." It was the first time in my life I saw an actual miracle. Right there on the side of the road in the rain, Raymond's face softened. "Paradise Ranch. In San Andreas. But you won't make it in time. Visiting hours are from nine to five."

"Okay. Thanks." *Holy shit, forgiveness is divine.*

My house was dark and cold since the power was still out. I'd thrown Nana's mares and mule two bales of alfalfa that morning, so they didn't need to be fed tonight. It was strange, but nice not having an hour's worth of chores every evening. Especially on a stormy night like tonight when the number one priority was to get a fire going in the woodstove, light candles, and pour a generous glass of wine. Ibuprofen hadn't remedied my pounding headache one bit and I almost wished I hadn't headbutted Gabby. I pulled a sack of semi-frozen corn from the freezer and held it to my forehead.

Candlelight lit Mark's half-full bottle of Pendleton whiskey. It stared at me from the counter where he'd left it after we'd argued about him spending what little money we had on expensive whiskey. He finally slammed his fists on the counter and confessed it was a gift. I didn't have to ask from whom. I knew.

Maureen had helped me understand why I'd continually compromised my integrity for Mark. It took her the better part of our last visit to explain how my real father abandoning us before I was born had left an empty hole. I'd tried to fill that hole by any means possible. A Harvard study done over a twenty-year span showed that girls raised without fathers become so desperate for the love of a male they subject themselves to all sorts of abuse. Mark never hit me. I wished he had. Maybe then I would have left.

I tossed the bag of corn on the table and pulled the cork on the Pendleton. Took two big swigs straight from the bottle. The burn warmed me and I forced down another. With my eyes squeezed shut, I freed the fire in my breath. "Fuuuck!"

It took a good hour and most of the whiskey before the woodstove put out any meaningful heat. With all that had happened today, Mark shouldn't have disrupted my thinking. There wasn't time to ruminate on what he'd done and he wasn't worthy of my concern, but I couldn't stop myself. How could someone who was gone weigh me down so much? I was living in a house full of reminders. His mud-caked elk skin boots were on the hearth where he had taken them off. I opened the woodstove and tossed them in. I hated myself for loving Mark.

After his boots burned, I went to the bedroom. The dresser. Grabbed an armful of T-shirts and socks—no underwear because he never wore any. On the way to the woodstove, I stumbled and nearly fell when I tripped over the Bigfoot T-shirt I'd bought him for his birthday last year. *Hide and Seek World Champion,* the shirt read above a Bigfoot peeking out from behind a tree. The tag hung from the label. Mark refused to wear it. Said Bigfoot was not a fucking joke. *Yes, he is! And so are you for being obsessed with him.* He was a well-educated veterinarian, for Christ's sake. It was easy to rewrite the scene in my head—create better dialogue, stronger character, instead of what I really did, which was to apologize like a pathetic good little wife. The Bigfoot shirt along with the others went into the woodstove in two loads.

Next, I gathered our wedding album and removed every single framed photo with Mark in it from the wall. Thin glass busted easily when I bashed it with the empty whiskey bottle over the garbage can. I ripped out the pictures. They melted more than burned. His pillow, dress shirts, jeans, baseball caps, dirty cowboy hats—even his good fifteen-hundred-dollar black Resistol cowboy hat—all into the woodstove.

By midnight Mark's things were nothing but ash and I felt like I had stretched fence all day. I was hungry. There wasn't much left in the house to eat and most of the food in the fridge was bad. I grabbed a cast iron skillet, set it on the wood stove. and dumped the corn in. With a spoonful of butter, some salt and pepper, I fried the corn. After eating the entire thing, my stomach churned like an old Maytag, but at least my head didn't hurt. I chugged a half bottle of Pepto, curled up with a wool blanket on the couch, and cried my drunken self to sleep.

Monday morning hit like a sledgehammer. My head felt like a balloon wrapped in barbed wire—one wrong move and BAM! Daylight bled through the window shade. The digital clock flashed 12:00 am, but I was lost in time. At least the power was back on. My bowels growled. I sat up and immediately grabbed my head to keep my brain from exploding out of my ears.

"Dear God help me."

My mouth watered and a hot wave of nausea hit. I ran for the bathroom, bounced off the walls like a drunk and didn't make it to the toilet before my stomach turned inside out. Last night's whiskey with Pepto Bismol chasers left pink all over the bank-owned hall carpeting.

My cell was dead. I turned my computer on to see what time it was, but the numbers were nothing but a blue blur. So much of my life was wasted trying to find my damn glasses. I'd trade a valuable body part to have my vision back. A cheap pair of dust-covered readers looked at me from the bookshelf. I wiped them with my shirt. 7:45am.

All I wanted to do was crawl back into bed and sleep my life away, but there wasn't time to wallow in a puddle of pity. I needed to get to Nana, but first the well pump needed resetting so I could get water and a shower.

It was only 8:30 in the morning, but Mark Twain Hospital was bustling. Maybe because it was Monday or maybe decent weather created patients. The elevator was full and rather than wait for the next ride I made the mistake of taking the stairs. The exercise worked like detox. Mostly I dry-heaved, but was grateful to rid myself of last night's fall from grace. *Please forgive me dear, Lord. I*—my stomach heaved and sent a monstrous racket echoing the stairwell. *I'll never do it again.*

In the women's bathroom I rinsed my mouth and splashed my face. A blue bruise bulged along the top of my forehead and I wished I'd worn a ball cap. I pulled my bangs down over the knot and rushed to Nana's room. There was no longer a deputy at her door, and a deep sinking feeling pulled at me. I held my breath and walked in. She was sleeping. *Thank you, God.*

Or maybe she's dead. I looked up at the heart monitor. It beeped steadily with a comforting monotony. The little dot tracing beautiful peaks and valleys meant more time. I groaned with relief and flopped into a chair.

I watched Nana sleep. She looked peaceful. Too peaceful and kind to be a killer. But she had killed Leo. And burned that woman in San Francisco. Then there was Roy. *Three.* I found my readers in my purse and Googled *serial killer definition* on my phone.

According to the FBI website, a serial killer is someone who commits at least three murders over more than a month with an emotional cooling-off period in between. *That confirms it.* My heart sank. It also stated that female serial killers are extremely rare. I had never considered that and typed in *female serial killers.*

Psychology Today went into great detail about how female serial killers are *not* motivated by sexual gratification, like most male serial killers, but rather by a twisted sense of love, sympathy, or altruism. A stereotypical example of a female serial killer is a nurse who kills her patients because she wants to end their suffering.

Dear God help me. Nana was all of these things! *She did it.* She was convinced that ridding the world of these awful people made it a better place and to be honest, in the deepest darkest part of myself, I secretly agreed.

I looked at Nana—watched her a long while and just knew she wouldn't lie to me after all she'd confessed. If she was responsible for the human remains in her hog pens, she'd be proud of what she'd done. She'd want the whole damn world to know and she'd reveal exactly how and why she'd put those people down.

The Mick Jagger lookalike nurse walked in with an armful of charts. "Oh. Hello."

"Hi." I perched my readers on top of my head.

"Visiting hours aren't until nine." She looked at her watch.

I looked at my phone. It was 8:45am.

"Okay. You really want me to leave?"

"If it were up to me, I'd say stay. It's no big deal. But you know how these things go." Her smile seemed to beg: *Please don't give me any shit—I'm not in the mood today.*

"Is the cafeteria open?" *I could use some Gatorade.*

"Yes." She was definitely relieved I was cooperating.

In the cafeteria I grabbed a red Gatorade and went to the register. I was hospitably greeted by a cute cashier with honey-brown eyes, who looked like she had Down Syndrome. I noticed an open sliding door under her register and boxes of candy bars: Snickers, Twix, Reese's Peanut Butter Cups. There on the very bottom shelf sat a box of Baby Ruth bars. "Are those Baby Ruths down there?"

"Yes, ma'am." She smiled. "You want one?"

"Yes, please. Two."

She got two bars out, scanned them, and pressed a button on the register. "Three dollars and ten cents please."

I handed over my card, then opened the Gatorade and took a tiny sip. *Shit.* She hadn't charged me for it. My conscience reared up and I prepared for battle until I remembered God was watching.

"I don't think you got this." I handed over the drink.

"Oh. Thank you." She scanned the drink. "Seven dollars and eighty-five cents, please."

We both stared at the register until it made that beautiful grinding calculator noise and spit out my receipt. *Thank you, God.*

On my way back to Nana's room, I stepped into the elevator and my cell phone rang like an obnoxious alarm. No one called other than spammers these days, but I tucked the candy bars under my arm and dug into my coat pocket. I could just make out the caller without my glasses: *Calaveras County Sheriff Dept.* No way I was answering it. I pressed silent as the elevator door dinged open and I stepped out, checking my phone for the voicemail icon.

Outside Nana's door, I took one last glance at the screen. Up popped the voice message icon. My heart tensed as I pressed play. "Mrs. Williams, this is Detective Rocha. We need to talk. I'd appreciate it if you could come in this morning. Please get back to me as soon as possible." He'd hung up without saying thank you or goodbye. *Rude.* I wished he'd have been more specific about what exactly he wanted to discuss. I didn't do well when he caught me off guard.

Nana was awake and took notice when I walked in. "What took you so long?"

"These." I presented the Baby Ruth bars and Nana's face lit up like a naughty kid who's gotten exactly what they wanted for Christmas. I unwrapped a bar for her. "Hope it's okay for you to eat this."

"Come on, get with it." She was bright-eyed and opened her mouth like a baby bird. I broke off a small corner and fed it to her. She chewed and smiled as chocolate gathered between her teeth. "If you eat these, there's an entire box in the cafeteria."

"Finally, a reason to live," she scoffed, then opened her mouth for more and I was happy to oblige.

"Need some water?" I poured her a cup and she shook her head no. "Nana, yesterday you told me you didn't kill those people they found on the ranch. Do you remember that?"

"Why the hell wouldn't I remember? Give me some more."

"Not 'til you explain why there are human remains in your hog pens. I know you know."

Nana glared at me with a mix of shock and anger like I'd never seen. I took a huge bite of her candy bar. "This is soooo good. Mmm-mmm-mmm."

Nana just shook her head. A smile reddened the scar on her upper lip, which made me wonder how different her life might have been minus Leo's cruelty that night. What if instead of beating her, he'd loved her back and they raised their child?

"How'd human bone fragments get in your hog pens? Huh? How?"

"Ask the oak."

"Come on, Nana. I don't have time to mess around today. I have to get your dogs from the pound, go see Ruth and—"

"What! My dogs are at the pound?"

"Aww shit," I whispered, wishing I could take it back. "Animal Control had to take them so they wouldn't disrupt the investigation."

"Dirty, rotten, no-good rat bastards! They have no right—"

"It's okay." I busted a bit of Baby Ruth and held it in front of her like a peace offering. "I'm going to get them today and keep them at my place."

"Get 'em now! Get old Duke. Please. He's probably scared to death. Poor old fella. Damn those fuckers!"

"Nana! Don't say that." I poked a bit of bar into her mouth. "They don't open until ten," I said, and waited for her to calm down. Duke had always been special since the day she found him tucked under a rotting cedar and growling. Someone had dumped a liter of Pitbull mix pups where the ranch met the road. Two were dead and the remaining three were near starved to death. Jim gave one to a bar buddy and Nana kept the other two. The brindle she named Duke and the black female Pancho, after

Pancho Barnes the infamous stunt pilot and all-around wild woman. Pancho tore after a mountain lion one night and never returned. For fifteen years, Duke slept at the foot of Nana's bed and was at her side every moment of every day.

As soon as Nana swallowed, I was ready with a piece of Baby Ruth.

"He needs his medicine. Are they giving it to him?"

"I'm sure," I lied.

"Water," she said in a calmer tone and I helped her sip. She sipped and sipped and soon as she was done took my hand.

"You're gonna see Ruth?"

"Yes. She's in a care facility."

"What's wrong with her?"

"I'm not sure."

Nana squeezed my hand with the strength of a baby. "I loved Ruth more than anything in the world."

I reached into my coat pocket, pulled out my phone, and started recording.

CHAPTER
FIFTEEN

Effie

J ane couldn't wait any longer. The urge to start her new life as Effie May Hobbs was too strong. First, she needed her share of the mill money. The plan was good. Solid. She couldn't chance Roy's Cadillac being seen and sold it for fifteen hundred dollars, exactly half of what Roy had paid for it. Now she and baby Ruth had enough cash to live on for at least a few months.

With the child in tow, Jane took a bus south from San Francisco to Monterey. The *Chronicle* had advertised a used Ford pickup for four hundred dollars.

Jane dickered with the pickup's owner and after a rousing rendition of how her dear departed husband had been brutally murdered by a drunk Indian the strawberry farmer sold Effie the pickup for three hundred and threw in two boxes of fresh strawberries.

They left Monterey and drove north feasting on sweet strawberries. Two new five-gallon fuel cans filled with diesel rode in the back of the truck, covered by a heavy canvas tarpaulin. Jane had carefully researched the weather by phoning the Humboldt County newspaper. A slight chance of rain in the forecast for the next few days, but a storm bringing possible flooding from the north could arrive as soon as the weekend. It was Wednesday and Jane was done waiting.

In Eureka, Jane and Ruth had dinner, then killed time at the drive-in watching *The Story of Robin Hood and His Merrie Men*. With a precautionary dose of cough syrup, Ruth had no trouble sleeping on the cozy little bed Jane had made for her on the passenger seat.

At two in the morning, Jane parked the truck off the Forest Service road that ran behind Robinson's Lumber Mill. She reached for the Minolta camera off the dash and slung the cord across her shoulder like a rucksack. With Ruth asleep inside, she slipped out and locked the doors. Tucked the keys deep into her jeans pocket, then opened the tailgate as quietly as she could. Slowly, she slid the two five-gallon metal cans of diesel out of the back of the truck. Before starting off, she tugged on the carpeting glued to the bottom of her boots just to be sure no trace of a footprint would ever be found. She gripped the heavy cans as her heart raced.

"Shit," she whispered and set the cans down. She'd almost forgotten the extra-large aerosol hairspray in the glove compartment and went through the passenger side to retrieve it. Jane stuffed the hairspray down the front of her coat.

Like a ghost in the darkness, Jane limped along the high side of the muddy road. A rush of excitement freed adrenaline and quickly masked the pain in her leg as fuel sloshed inside the cans and diesel fumes complemented the night air. Every now and then wind moaned through the trees. She stopped.

Jane froze in place when something dark moved in the redwoods to her right. Her breathing and heartbeat like a freight train leaving town. She stood, not making a sound. Branches broke and footsteps came closer. What the hell would someone be doing out here at this time of night? Jane wondered. The security guard had been laid off indefinitely along with the workers. Had someone followed her? She had broken no laws yet and set the cans down, then turned around. Ready to forego her plan. She headed back toward the truck when something big stepped out into the road behind her. She could feel it and turned.

A Roosevelt elk eyed her. His massive antlers at least four feet across. "Oh shit!" Jane slowly lifted her camera, but the bull bolted back into the black forest.

Jane splashed and soaked the timbers inside the mill with diesel. Doused the big pile of sawdust and shavings pushed up against the back of the mill and only a few feet from the roof. In minutes, she'd spent both cans. The sweet scent of diesel filled the night. Jane took a moment and a deep breath before reaching out the hairspray from inside her coat. With a flick of her lighter, she worked the hairspray like a blowtorch. Whoosh. The pile exploded into flames. Heat hit Jane like a wave, but she wasted no time and ran to a corner beam—ignited it with her hairspray blowtorch. Before setting fire to the stack of timbers waiting to be milled, Jane snapped as many photos as she could. The fire grew arms that seemed to be reaching out for her. It was a thing of beauty and Jane caught herself smiling.

With the empty cans hidden back in the truck, Jane unlocked the cab. Ruth sat up.

"Hey Baby Ruth." Jane climbed in and started the ignition.

Ruth rubbed her eyes and held her dolly.

"Go night-night, baby." They sped along the back road. Ruth plopped her head onto the cloud of pillows and went back to sleep as the truck tore onto the two-lane blacktop. Not one set of headlights, not one fire truck, or the sound of sirens. Jane lit a cigarette and turned south onto Highway 101.

Insurance would not only cover the replacement value of the mill, but all the equipment as well. Jane estimated her and Baby Ruth's share of the payment could be more than the three-hundred thousand she would have received if the mill had sold. What would she do with all that money? Soon, she and Baby Ruth would be able to go anywhere and do anything they wanted.

In San Francisco, Jane waited a few days before calling Mr. Haley, her attorney. From a payphone she explained that her grandmother had passed and she would be returning home after the funeral next week.

"Mrs. Robinson, I've been trying to locate you. I called the phone number you gave me and the woman there said I had the wrong number. I—"

"I'm so sorry, Mr. Haley. I must have transposed the numbers. I do it all the time."

"Well, I'm afraid I have some terrible news." No one spoke for a moment. "There was a fire at the mill."

"Oh my God. Is anyone hurt?"

"No, but—oh this pains me to tell you—but the entire mill was lost."

"What do you mean lost?"

"Fire consumed the entire structure and all the equipment."

"What about the horses?"

"They're fine as well as the house."

"Oh, thank God." Jane paused waiting for the man to fill

the silence. When he didn't Jane cried then finally spoke. "Mr. Haley, I'd like to donate the mustangs to the Hoopa Tribe."

"Oh. Okay. Certainly, I can take care of that. You're an extraordinarily kind woman, Mrs. Robinson. Just send a letter confirming your wishes."

"I'll mail it today. What do we do now?"

"Well, between you, me, and the fence post, this may be the best thing that could have happened."

"How can that be?"

"You see, the insurance company will have to pay on replacement value, not current market value. Which, trust me Mrs. Robinson, will be much more profitable for all involved. Except the insurance company, of course." He snorted a laugh.

"Oh my. I hadn't thought of it that way." Jane grabbed her smile to keep from laughing.

"Of course not, why would you? Anyway, I've already proceeded with the claim adjuster and preliminary investigations are inconclusive. They have thirty days before I summon them."

"This is just awful. First Roy, then my grandmother, and now this," Jane sniveled. "Mr. Haley, please, can you handle this? I just don't think I'm up to it."

"Yes. Of course. Don't you worry about a thing. Give me your mailing address for the claim check."

"Oh. I don't have one and I'm not sure where I'll be staying."

"Understood. Yes, I will arrange to have the funds wired to an account."

Jane knew the numbers by heart. "Got a pen?"

Night after night Jane woke to Roy choking her. The vindictive prick must have been furious about his mill burning down. In the little motel Jane sat up in bed gasping and screaming without making a sound as he laughed. She knew it was crazy. Knew her mind was just tormenting her but couldn't make it stop. For nearly a month he haunted her until she dreaded sleep.

Benson Insurance could not prove the fire was arson, but were delaying payment on the claim. Mr. Haley threatened to take the tragic story of the evil insurance company and the orphaned children, the penniless widow, to the press. Finally, Jane took matters into her own hands and called Frank Souza, the head of the insurance investigation. Before making the call, Jane had wired him five hundred dollars as bait and he bit. Now that he had accepted her bribe and authorities could prove it, Jane explained to Mr. Souza that he would be a complete idiot not to accept ten percent of the claim proceeds she was offering. A week later, the funds were wired to Jane Wayne's account. Three hundred and eighty-two thousand dollars. None of which would ever be paid to a crooked arson investigator.

Betty's funds were placed in a trust. Retrieving Betty's funds would be challenging, especially since the girl would soon be known as Ruth, but Jane loved a challenge and was over the moon with the small fortune tucked in her account.

To celebrate their wealth, Jane took Ruth to the San Francisco Museum of Modern Art. Exhibits by Jackson Pollock and Henri Matisse held Ruth's eye, but they both agreed that Frida Kahlo's *The Wounded Deer* was the day's favorite. In the gift shop Jane bought Ruth a print of it and promised she'd soon have her very own room to hang it in. They visited the zoo, bought new cowboy boots at OK Corral Western Wear, then ate ice cream and lobster for dinner.

Chinatown was bustling by ten the next morning. Jane had no trouble finding Kim's Kite Shop.

"Pew wee." Ruth pinched her nose and scrunched her face. That rotten-egg smell reminded Jane to keep an eye out on her left for the narrow stone staircase that led down to a heavy teak door shaped like a kite.

Inside the shop, Chinese kites of every size and color hung from the ceiling. An old woman sat on a stool behind a glass counter. Last time Jane was here, it was an old man with few teeth who sat in the old woman's place. Ruth couldn't be controlled and grabbed at a dragon kite. "No, Ruth." Jane lifted her onto her hip and looked at the old woman. "I'm here to see the new girl."

"No new girl." The old woman stood up and leaned her forearms on the counter. She had to have weighed three hundred pounds.

"I've already seen her, a while back, and I need to see her again. Please." Jane cocked her head.

"No."

"Look God damn it." Jane set Ruth down on the counter and pulled two hundred dollars out of her front pocket. "Here." She slapped it down in front of the woman. "New girl. Now."

The old woman smiled—she too was lacking a few teeth. "Go new girl." She pointed to a door that Jane knew led down into a dank basement where a teenage girl would write down your new name, new date of birth, and take your picture. As soon as Effie May Hobbs opened a bank account, Jane Wayne would withdraw her funds and no longer exist.

Lack of sleep prevented Effie from thinking straight. She wanted out of San Francisco. Jane Wayne's money had been withdrawn and deposited into Effie May Hobbs' bank account. There was not one good reason to stay, but Effie couldn't decide where to go or what to do. Planning was like trying to breathe underwater. It was impossible.

Effie and Ruth walked on the beach most every day until the afternoon a business card tumbled up the beach toward them. Ruth picked it up and handed it to Effie. "Golden Dragon

Fortunes. Let us guide you to good fortune," Effie read aloud. The address was only a few blocks north. "What the hell. Let's go Baby Ruth."

A bell jingled when Effie opened the door and walked in with Ruth. A man stood like he'd been waiting there for them. He locked the door. "Welcome. I Wanugee. So nice you finally come. Please, follow me." His black silk robe was tied at the waist with a wide red belt and swung like a pendulum when he walked.

They followed him to a sitting area with three red velvet chairs that looked more like thrones, with carved wood handles and feet that looked like hooves. Wanugee tucked his hands deep into his sleeves and sat. "Hello little one." He smiled at Ruth.

"Hi." She was more interested in his red slippers and the shiny gold flowers embellished on them. Ruth touched one with her finger and looked at the man.

"You like flowers?" He stood, walked over to a vase, and plucked out a white orchid. "You like?"

Ruth held out her hand and Wanugee gave her the flower, followed by a courteous bow.

"You know why I'm here?" Effie asked.

"The question is—do you know why you are here?"

He's good, Effie thought. "Yeah. I need some goddamn sleep."

"Yes. I can see darkness in your eyes. Perhaps..." He stroked the silver hair that hung from his chin. "My method based upon four pillars of destiny. Year of birth, then month, day, and also hour." He pulled a leather notebook and a pen from a pocket in his robe. "Dates and elements transcend matrix of metaphysical knowledge. What is year for your birth?" Wanugee set his pen to paper.

"Shit." Effie rubbed her brow; should she give him Effie's date of birth or her own? She needed a moment to recall either. "Ughh, I...I'm so tired. 1935." Her own. "November first. But my grandmother changed it October thirty-first, Halloween. Does that matter?" Christ, did the fact that she'd changed her birthday more times than she could recall matter?

Wanugee wrote without looking up. "What is hour?"

"I have no idea." That was the truth. She didn't know if she was born in the morning, afternoon, or night.

"Now elements." He seemed to be doing math in Chinese. Writing symbols vertically instead of horizontally. "Fire!" He looked like he knew what she had done and spoke slowly. "You are fire. You create ash." He slid the notebook back into his robe. "Every element has element that creates it and finally element to control it. Only water control fire and therefore harmony only obtained when water drown fire." He stood and walked toward the door. Effie lifted Ruth off the floor and carried her to the door.

"I don't know what the hell you just said. What am I supposed to do with water? Drown myself? Live on a boat? What?"

"The answer will come in the rain." Wanugee unlocked the door, bowed, and held out his palm.

"Jesus Christ." She pulled a five-dollar bill out of her jeans and slapped it into his hand. "Thanks for nothin'."

That night, while Ruth slept, Effie lay in the bathtub hoping to control her fire and find a way to rid herself of Roy once and for all.

"Rain." She set her head against the back of the tub. "How's rain the answer?" She closed her eyes. "Rain, rain don't go away, come right back this very day." She was asleep before she knew it.

Effie awoke to the feeling that something was crawling in her hair. "Damn you, Roy!" The tub water had turned cold long ago, and Effie shivered as Ruth rolled and rubbed the little motel soap in her hands. "Wash you haiw," Ruth said as her tiny fingers wiggled around under Effie's hair.

With her big toe, Effie pulled the stopper out of the drain and wondered how long she'd slept and if it was morning or night. "Thanks for washing my hair, I gotta rinse it now, okay?" Effie turned the shower on and waited for hot water. "What time is it?" She pulled the shower curtain shut.

"Eat time," said Ruth.

Effie had slept six miraculous hours in a row without Roy and was famished. A block from the motel was a small coffee shop. With sleep and a good breakfast came a clear head and a plan. Sort of. Effie checked out of the motel, loaded the suitcases in the back of the truck and Ruth in the front, then started driving north. Wanugee had promised the answer would come with the next rain, but Effie was sick of waiting. If the rain wouldn't come to her, she would go to the storm.

Before she knew it, they were crossing the San Francisco-Oakland Bay Bridge. Sunlight threw sparks across the water all the way to Alcatraz Island. The pale prison grew like a monolith from the gray rock below, and Effie thought of the attempted escapes—the prisoners who'd drowned trying to swim to freedom. She pictured herself treading the frigid dark water. The sharks.

"Find us a song, baby."

Ruth turned on the radio and pressed the buttons with her thumb until Hank Williams sang about a wooden Indian.

"Which way?" Effie asked, and Ruth just smiled. "Come on. I'm letting you set the direction from here on out. We've got no place to be and I don't know how to get *there*. North, south, east, or west?"

From the bridge, Ruth had guided them into Stockton. Outside the little town of Lockeford, Ruth pointed left onto Highway 88 and they gained in elevation and scenery. The two-lane was flanked by rolling green hills dotted with oaks and cattle as far as the eye could see. Clouds gathered overhead and Effie's leg ached.

They stopped in Jackson, a historic gold rush town in the Sierra foothills, and filled the truck with twenty-nine-cents-a-gallon gasoline, then filled their bellies with nickel cokes and twenty-five-cent burgers from Mel and Fay's Diner.

A half hour out of Jackson, Ruth said, "Turrrn," and Effie did. Right up Highway 26. The road climbed and curved, then narrowed at the bridge that hung over the north fork of the roaring Mokelumne River. They crossed the Calaveras County line. Through the tiny town of West Point—population two hundred and sixteen.

"Turrrn!" Ruth ordered and pointed left as they approached the bridge over the south fork of the Mokelumne River. The mountain road was steep and curvier than anything Effie had ever driven.

"Christ. Maybe we should go back."

"Nooo." Ruth seemed sure.

"Who the hell died and made you boss? Oh yeah—never mind." The road climbed and snaked through the mountains. Twice it seemed to turn back into itself. "Whoever built this son-of-a-bitch must have one sick sense of humor." They'd not seen another vehicle or human being since crossing the bridge over the Mokelumne an hour ago.

After ten long miles of forested and fractured blacktop, the road narrowed. "This is the worst excuse for a road ever. Son-of-a-bi...gun." Branches reached out and scratched the sides of the truck like nails on a chalkboard, then what little pavement was left disappeared. The rough dirt road contorted and rumbled their insides.

"This is stupid." Effie pulled the truck to the right of where the washboard road forked and got out to pee. She walked to the edge of the dense forest, then ducked beneath the sagging boughs of a hundred-foot-tall Douglas fir. Pulled down her pants as rain dropped on her bare thighs amid fat trees covered in moss. She inhaled the spice of wet pine and realized how much she'd missed the smell while pulling up her jeans and walking toward the truck. Clouds churned and tree tops swayed like hands beckoning her this way—whispering: *Come here, come here.*

"Out!" Ruth demanded, and Effie obliged. "Go home!" As soon as Effie set Ruth down, the girl took off at a run down the side road. Effie let her, figuring the girl had been in the truck for hours and a run would do her good.

The sky darkened and spit as she remembered all that Wanugee had said and decided it was bullshit, a scam that was just a way to make a buck, and her desperation had allowed him to play her.

"That's far enough," Effie yelled, but the girl kept going. Running, even when Effie started after her. "Ruth! Stop!"

Ruth was out of sight as Effie followed a bend in the road. Sprinkles turned to rain. "Ruth! Stop damn it!" Effie forced her bad leg to trot and the toddler came into view up the dirt road. She looked like a wet doll standing there with her chubby arms at her sides, staring at a large pond surround by a meadow. Thunder boomed in the distance. A dark blue wall of trees crowded around the far side of the meadow. It was the definition of natural beauty, Effie thought, but doubted the mesmerized three-year-old could possibly appreciate it. Ruth sure seemed in awe of the view. Effie got closer and stumbled over something. Hidden there at her feet amongst the dead thistle and needlegrass was a *FOR SALE BY OWNER* sign that must have blown off the fence. Rain came down hard.

CHAPTER
SIXTEEN

N ana looked so far away. So happy. I hated to drag her back
to reality when my cell phone rang like an alarm. Caller
ID read: *Calaveras Co Sheriff's Dept.* Rocha again.

I silenced the call hard and fast and knew I couldn't keep
ignoring him much longer. A ding let me know he'd left another
message.

"You let Betty, I mean Ruth, lead you to Blue Mountain?"

"That's exactly how it happened."

I shook my head in amazement. "That's wild. I doubt
readers will buy it."

"Who gives a shit? Write the truth and call it fiction."

"Ha! Yes, ma'am."

"What time is it?" Nana asked.

I looked at my phone. "Ten twenty."

"Go get my dogs, damn it." Her face went from angry to
desperate in less than a second. "Please."

"Okay. I'll be back in a few hours. You rest up." I kissed
her cheek and hugged her extra long. That's when I noticed

the undeniable smell of stale urine followed up by that familiar stench of the women's bathroom at Walmart. "When's the last time they changed you?" I rubbed Nana's boney shoulder.

She barely shook her head. "I don't know. Last night, I guess. Now get the dogs."

"Last night!" I brushed her hair back. "You need to be cleaned up." My blood boiled at the thought of Nana lying in her own urine and feces for God knows how long. I stabbed the call button over and over until a nurse arrived.

"Do you need something?" She stood in the doorway.

"My grandmother needs her diaper changed." I said with wide eyes and very matter-of-factly.

Nana shook her head. "I'm not a goddamn baby."

"Get her cleaned up *now*." No longer suppressing my irritation.

"Certainly." She left in a hurry.

"I'm ready," said Nana, staring at the ceiling, a glint in the corner of her eye, tears welling that she tried to blink away.

"Nana, no. It's okay." I rubbed up and down her arm, but she just shook her head.

"When someone has to clean my ass..." She shook her head and looked as pitiful as I'd ever seen. "I'm better off dead, Jess."

"Don't say that. Don't you dare say that. This is no big deal. Really. They do it all the time." But I couldn't think of anything more demeaning for someone as strong as Nana, and it broke my heart to see her like this. Vulnerability was worse than death to Nana. I kissed her hand, then her forehead. "I'm gonna get the dogs. I'll be back as quick as I can. I love you."

The hospital doors slid open. Two deputies marched in and inspected me as I started to exit.

"Ms. Williams?" a gravelly voice behind me said. My heart sped and sputtered and for no good reason I wanted to run. Far, far away. Forever.

"Yes?" I turned but didn't smile.

"I'm Deputy Figueroa. This is Deputy Hanson. You're wanted for questioning. Would you come with us, please?" said the gravelly-voice guy. He looked like the same cop that was at Nana's gate the morning I'd picked up the mares.

"What for?"

"Ma'am, the detectives will explain everything. We're only here to bring you in." Figueroa moved in and was even better looking up close. Perfectly fit for maintaining peace.

"Am I being arrested? Should I get my lawyer?"

Deputy Hanson's pale face finally spoke. "You're needed for questioning, ma'am. You're not under arrest."

"I was just on my way to Animal Control to get my grandmother's dogs. Can I come by in about an hour—two at the most?"

"I'm afraid not." Figueroa shook his head.

"Ma'am, please follow me." Pale Face stepped forward and Figueroa followed close behind me, I guess in case I made a run for it. The patrol car sat parked curbside. Figueroa opened the back door. "I have to ride in back? Like a prisoner?"

"Sorry, ma'am—policy." Figueroa seemed sorry, but not as sorry as I was. Nothing good could come of this. My nerves were combusting and my legs shook as I dropped into the backseat and hoped no one I knew would see me.

Pale Face escorted me into a tight, windowless room in the Calaveras County Sheriff's Department. The heavy steel door shut with a clang and there I sat. All alone on a cold metal folding chair at a table pressed into a corner. Awaiting my fate.

If I had to guess, this had something to do with headbutting Gabby. I pulled my long bangs down over my bruise. Were they watching me, I wondered? I looked up for a camera and there it was—a black bulbous eye in the sky placed directly overhead.

Looking down on me like God. Waiting to analyze every move I made. Judging. Don't borrow trouble—another one of Nana's pearls of wisdom and perfect for the occasion. *Don't borrow trouble.*

Detective Rocha opened the door and held it for a slender black woman in beige slacks and a blue blazer. She had an air of importance that Rocha lacked, and she smelled nice. They sat on the same side of the table, like two against one under lights bright enough to perform surgery, and opened their files. Mint-colored cinderblock walls radiated a frothy green hue, accentuating Rocha's alien-like features.

"Mrs. Williams, this is agent Tracy Lee. She's with the Federal Bureau of Investigation and the lead investigator on the Blue Mountain case."

"Hello, Mrs. Williams." She made it a point to look me in the eye.

"Hello." *Holy hell, the FBI.* This was much worse than headbutting Gabby. I straightened in my seat and tried to look innocent. Tried to act like things were just fine, but the knot in the pit of my stomach knew better. The momentary silence got louder and louder. Almost ringing in my ears. It was odd, I know, but I let Agent Lee's plump pearl earrings distract me; the way the light played with the iridescent colors. The slightest movement of her head made the shimmer swirl and change from light blue to pale pink. I wanted to be like her. Wanted her stiff-backed dignity. Her distinct take-no-shit aura. She was beautiful and, more than likely, smart. I'd bet she paid her own bills on time and had never been dependent on anyone.

I straightened again in my chair. Laced my fingers on my lap and squeezed, but couldn't overcome the feeling that I was slouching. "What's this about? I have to get my grandma's dogs—" My throat was suddenly so dry that my voice cracked and I knew I was in trouble.

"Mrs. Williams," Agent Lee opened a manila envelope and dragged out several 8"x10" photos and slid them in front of me. "This was discovered on your grandmother's farm. Located where the swine enclosures stood," she said.

It was a blurry Rorschach test until I slid the glasses off my head and into place. Examined the extreme close-up photos of a long flat piece of silver-colored metal about the size of a Popsicle stick with seven holes in it. An inch ruler at the bottom of one photo showed that the part was exactly six inches long. I shuffled the photos. The last was a close-up of scratches and gashes in the metal plate.

"What is it?" I looked up at Agent Tracy Lee, then back at the close-up. My brain racing but going nowhere.

"Our forensics lab has identified this as a plate commonly used in surgical reconstruction of fractured bones. Typically, there would be a serial number stamped into the metal, but as you can see, the numbers are missing." She leaned forward on her elbows. "Mrs. Williams, the item in this photograph was discovered buried in Miss Hobbs's swine enclosure. We have your husband's medical records and in 1999 he fractured his left radius and his ulna. The injury was severe enough to require the surgical implant of two plates and ten screws, one of which we believe is the same item in these photographs."

Rocha took over. "This new evidence strongly suggests probable homicide."

First astonishment, then a heaviness clutched my chest. I grabbed my mouth with both hands and squeezed my face. I was being wound tighter and tighter until tears burst and I stood. Blood rushed from my head. I was dizzy as hell.

"Mark always complained about that plate. Said it ached. Sometimes for no good reason he'd get stabbing pains up his arm from it."

Visions of my husband being thrown to the hogs. Their hungry teeth biting and tearing out chunks of flesh and bone until there was nothing left of him but metal and screws!

I felt faint and bent over. My glasses fell when I dropped my head to my knees.

"Oh my God. Oh my God."

"I'm sorry. I know this is not the outcome you were hoping for. None of us were," Agent Lee said.

"Can I get you some water?" Rocha offered as he picked up my glasses and set them in front of me.

I didn't answer. Just wondered why the hell I was having a visceral reaction to the news of Mark's death. Why the hell should I care? I sat back down, crying like a brokenhearted widow. Swiping my tears with my sleeves. I sniffed my runny nose.

"Did you hurt Mark?" Rocha asked.

"No." I looked to Lee for help. The agent softened and even appeared sympathetic.

"Was it an accident?" Lee asked.

"Stop it. Want me to take a polygraph? I will." I said through a flood of tears.

"Can you think of anyone who would want to harm your husband?" Lee asked.

"Yes! I've already been over *all* of this with him!" I eyed Rocha, hoping he'd help me. "There's a waiting list of people pissed at him. Including me! He was working for the cartel or something. People that paid to have their losing race horses electrocuted so they could cash in. They knew Mark would talk if it'd reduce his sentence."

"Why would they leave his remains in a pigpen on your grandmother's farm?" Tracy Lee asked with a blatant head tilt.

"Why not?" *Dickless Tracy!* "Seems like an easy diversion."

"What was the relationship like between you and your husband?" Lee asked.

I ran my sweaty palms down my thighs, then squeezed at my knees. "Awful. And I've already been through the whole thing with him. *Twice.*" I pointed at Rocha. He only crossed his arms and leaned back in his chair. "I'm not doing this again. Read the report if you want to know about me and my husband." We all shut up for a moment. "You think I killed Mark and fed him to Nana's hogs?"

"We're just trying to do our jobs, Mrs. Williams," Lee said.

I nodded and nodded. Rocha left the room.

Agent Lee leaned on the table and laced her fingers. "I know this is difficult. I really appreciate any help you can offer."

"I did not kill anyone."

"What was the relationship like between Mr. Williams and your grandmother?"

"Great. They were close. Talked on the phone every day. Until she found out he was killing horses."

They didn't need to know it was the maddest I'd ever seen Nana. "Jim drove her over to our house. Mark was still in jail." Thank God, because Nana had a long electric livestock prod in her hand and no doubt intended to use it on Mark. Said she was *"gonna give him a taste of his own goddamn medicine."*

"When you say Jim, you are referring to James Kelly, correct?"

"Yes."

"And Mr. Kelly drove your grandmother, Effie Hobbs, to your home?"

"Yes."

"What happened when Miss Hobbs and Mr. Kelly arrived?"

"Nana, *Effie,* had read about Mark being arrested for killing horses in the paper. She was disappointed that I hadn't come to her." Disgusted was a much better word. "She asked if I knew about the killings and the insurance fraud. I told her I had no idea and was struggling to believe it myself." She'd pressed the business end of that hotshot against my heart, but I kept that part to myself. At the time I never thought for a split second she'd electrocute me. It would have killed me, but now I'm not so sure. "She asked me if he did it." With her finger on that big red trigger that would jolt me into oblivion. "I said yes. I was pretty sure he did."

"Did your grandmother, Effie Hobbs, speak to Mark after his arrest?"

"Not that I know of. Maybe."

Rocha came in and set a bottle of water in front of me.

"Thank you." I opened it and chugged down half the bottle.

"Have you had any contact whatsoever with Mr. James Kelly?" Lee asked.

"Jim? No. Not since he left." I wanted a real drink more than my next breath and started to cry again. "Can I go? I really need to get some air." I stood.

"There is the matter of battery charges being filed against you from a Gabriela Hernandez. She also filed a restraining order. But, under the circumstances, I think it can wait until tomorrow." Lee looked at Rocha, who raised a brow. "Will you come in early tomorrow morning? Nine o'clock?" she asked.

"Yes, of course. No problem, I'm always up early anyway." I turned and pulled on the door, but it wouldn't open until Rocha got up and pressed the intercom.

"Okay Hanson," he said with his alien mouth. The door buzzed, and Officer Pale Face opened it from the other side.

"Follow me please, ma'am," Pale Face, said.

His shoes squeaked along the beige flooring as I followed him down the hall and through a second set of exit doors. "I'll drive you back to the hospital," he said.

"I'll walk."

CHAPTER
SEVENTEEN

D eep breath in through my nose, then out through my mouth. Over and over. "Nana is not a serial killer. Nana is not a serial killer anymore." *Anymore. She did not kill Mark. Or the people in the pens.* I chewed the last of a roll of antacids between breaths and talked to myself. "No way she killed Mark. No way."

It was a two-block walk from the Sheriff's Department to the hospital. Figuring out my next move, ahead of putting one foot in front of the other was impossible. The photos of Mark's surgical plate and the notion of him being gnawed down to nothing but a piece of metal made me sick. I shouldn't feel bad, or sad, not after what he'd put me through, but I loved him and being Catholic comes with oppressive amounts of guilt.

Mark was dead. Jim Kelly was a suspect. Nana was definitely a suspect. I know I was. What about Gabby? Boy, I hoped so. I reached the hospital parking lot, unlocked my truck, and would have beaten Danica Patrick to the corner market. The credit card blessed me with a cheap box of red wine and a twenty-five-cent large Styrofoam cup and straw.

In the truck I dumped wine into the cup, secured the lid, and stabbed the straw through the perforated hole. I sucked down the sweetness as if I were dying of thirst. Felt it trickle in and warm my soul. I wondered if I might be an alcoholic while tucking the half-empty wine box under the seat. *Maybe. Probably. No, because I could get through the day without wine if I had to. But I didn't have to, so why should I?* I started the truck, nursing the straw all the way to the other end of town.

Barks echoed from the Calaveras County Animal Shelter as my boots crunched across the gravel lot. Inside, yelps and bays and yaps reverberated off the dark wood-paneled walls and agitated my skull.

"Hi. I'm here to pick up the dogs from Blue Mountain Ranch." I tried not to yell, but still be heard by the big-boned brunette at the counter.

"What's the name? The owner?" She gave every impression of being incredibly inconvenienced by my arrival.

"Effie Hobbs." I clinched my jaw as the woman inspected me and scratched her raised brow. *Toughen up and get used to it.*

It took a moment for her brain to recognize the name. "Effie Hobbs? Isn't she in prison or something?"

"Or something. She's my grandmother." I unbridled my best wine-buzz grin.

"I can only release the animals to the owner. Unless you have written permission approved by a notary." She didn't bother to sound sympathetic.

I bit my lower lip and faked a smile. "Besides being under arrest, the owner is in the hospital busy dying. She asked me to get her dogs. I didn't know about a permission slip."

"It's not a permission slip." She rolled her chair back and spun around to a short filing cabinet. Bent over in her chair, she exposed a florescent pink thong while opening the bottom drawer. "This form needs to be filled out and..." She pulled the form from the drawer, kicked it closed, and rolled back to the counter like she'd done it a million times before. "...notarized." She slapped the paper on the counter. "Fees will be in accordance with time spent at the facility."

Crying seemed like the next best option, but what I really wanted to do was curl up in the kennel with Nana's dogs until there were no tears left. *Toughen up.* God help me, I had to go see Ruth. I took the form, folded it into fourths, and slid it into my back pocket. The Ibuprofen and cup of wine waiting in the truck pulled at me like a magnet. Too bad memories don't respond to time the way wine does.

Paradise Ranch was no paradise. Ignoring the stale greasy smell took tremendous effort and mouth breathing. An elderly woman with a walker and a severe gaze stood idle while an old man in a wheelchair counted his toes.

"Nine." The poor thing whimpered, slapped his forehead, and started counting again.

"I'm here to see Ruth Peterson," I told the woman at the counter who looked like she could be a resident.

"And you are?" She lifted a pair of glasses hanging from a jeweled chain around her neck and placed them on her face.

"Jessica Williams. Her daughter."

"Oh." The white-haired woman quickly looked me up and down, then smiled. "I'll let her know. Please, have a seat."

After a few minutes, the woman returned and motioned for me to follow her. An almost unbearable nervousness struck with the thought of being in the presence of my mother after seven years. I stopped and considered leaving as my palms sweated. How I wished I'd taken the time to pour a second super-size cup of wine.

The white walls were bare except for a long, wide print that hung in a gold frame above a twin bed. Heavy sky-blue drapes slid open contradicting the dark gray outside.

"Ruth, your visitor is here," the woman sang. Slowly the bathroom door clicked, the handle turned, and the door cracked just enough for a shadow to peek out at me. I turned, pulled off my coat, and sat in a rocker tucked against the corner like it wasn't allowed to rock.

"Hello, Ruth." I worked the rocker away from the wall and rode it back and forth and back and forth waiting for my mother to exit the bathroom.

"I'll leave you two alone." The woman shut the door behind her and Ruth stepped out of the bathroom, bent and gray and pathetic.

"Who are you?" Her voice was weak, unlike like Ruth's as she balled up a ragged tissue.

"Jessica. Your daughter. You don't know me?" I stood and stepped toward her. "Jessica. I'm Jessica."

Ruth's head shook and tears filled her saggy dark eyes. I recognized the look. The guilt. The ache caused by a lifetime of bad decisions. She played with the tissue in her hand and I knew damn well she knew me. She glanced out the window, maybe at the cars, maybe at nothing.

"You might as well take a seat and get comfortable." I backed into the rocker, but Ruth didn't budge. "Did you know Nana wasn't your real mother?"

"Who?"

"Nana. Did you know she was *not* your real mother?" I waited, but there was no response. "Do you remember the ranch? Where you grew up?" Still nothing. "Ever kill anyone?"

That got her. She fixed her eyes on me and stiffened her spine along with her face. She pressed her lips until they disappeared.

"I'm not the murderer." Silence lasted while she situated herself on the side of the bed. Her tiny pink slippers dangled like a child's and I wondered how innocent little Betty became such a soulless woman. The large framed print above her head distracted me. Something about it was off. It hung crooked, but that wasn't it. A watercolor beach scene in the moonlight. Small waves rolling in as what looked like children cut from old photographs, taped to the glass, were playing in the surf. I got up for a closer look as Ruth continued to ignore me.

"That's Joe," I mumbled. My brother when he was about two. "And me." I was just a toddler on a rocking horse that someone had cut out of a photo and artistically placed on the glass. There were a dozen old cutouts of Joe and me taped in place—back when we were little, before we knew of the hell to come. Guess that included my mother.

"Did you do this?" I asked, but she only lifted her chin and stared. "Heard you robbed a bank, Ruth."

She grinned.

"Please." She finally met my eyes. "They think Nana killed people. That she may be a serial killer. I'm begging you to talk to me. Tell me what you know." I sat next to her on the bed. She'd become small. "There are human remains on the ranch and I know Nana didn't do it."

"Don't be so sure."

"Come on."

"Ask her for her diaries. I found them buried in a metal box on top of Blue Mountain when I was twelve. Thought it was odd. A circle of fresh dirt. And a shovel leaning against a juniper tree. Like she wanted me to dig. Daring me. I thought I'd find a buried treasure. Not secrets that would ruin me. All she had to do was take the shovel with her when she left and my life could have been tolerable. Maybe even good. Leaving that shovel was no mistake. People like her don't make mistakes." Mother was regaining her memory. It was a calculated miracle.

"That must have been awful." And I meant it.

"I don't think about it." Mother shrugged and it reminded me so much of Nana.

"What happened to the diaries?" I asked.

"I have no idea. I read them all that day. The next day they were gone. Along with the shovel."

I stared out the window at a random blue Honda Accord parked in the lot. Rain speckled the rusted hood. "You knew Nana wasn't your real mother?"

"She'd written the entire sick story down to the last morbid detail. Evidence of her insanity. Wish I'd never found them. There are ugly truths and pretty lies. I'll take the pretty lies any day of the week."

Tears streamed along her wrinkles deep as the creeks that ran down Blue Mountain. We shared the burden of being children of rotten mothers. Poor little Betty—whom no one wanted besides Nana. And poor me, whom no one wanted but Nana.

I set my hand on hers, suddenly understanding the torment she must have endured. Ruth, the young girl, reading Nana's diaries. Reading the shocking words over and over: *Her real mother hanged herself. Roy was not her father; an Indian named Dink was her dad and he was murdered because he couldn't live without his daughter, Betty.*

My mother's pain and guilt for loving Nana—the only mother she ever knew—must have created a terrifying maze of emotion especially when it came to turning her in for murder. I couldn't imagine how something that horrid would affect a child and it blew a hole in every bit of hurt and resentment I'd carried all these years. Tears I didn't know I had for my mother came. I hugged her and she hugged me back and in less than an hour we purged our demons for what seemed like a lifetime.

I said, "I'm sorry."

"You have nothing to be sorry for." Mom kissed the side of my head.

"Do you want to go see her?" I asked.

"Who?"

"Nana."

"Who?" She winked, and I understood that the brilliant memory-loss game she was playing allowed her to stay here and away from Raymond.

"I have to go."

"Please come back." She squeezed my hand.

"I will," I said and walked to the door. "Nana told me to tell you something."

"What?"

"She said she loves you."

Mom smiled. It looked good on her. I couldn't remember if I'd seen her smile before and warmth filled my insides as I opened the door.

"I love you Jessica Juniper," Mom said and I finally understood much more than the reason for my middle name.

"I love you too, Mom."

I smiled all the way to the truck.

The wine had worn off completely, but I felt better than I had in months. Even though my life was currently a shit show, I felt I now had a shovel. I had hope. Hope and God and an understanding of my mom gave me strength and an appetite. My body screamed for sustenance. Meat. San Andreas had no fast-food joints and little chance for a better than decent meal. Gloria's Grill was up ahead, so I pulled in and pigged out on a double cheeseburger and a side of sweet potato fries. I hadn't eaten that much in months.

Along with the day, I was fading fast, but come hell or high water, Nana was going to give me the truth before visiting hours ended. All of it, right now, I decided as I burped up burger and chewed a handful of Tums. No more pretty lies. I had to have the ugly truth and I'd use the dogs as leverage. That'd get her. I wouldn't claim her precious dogs until she confessed and explained everything. They could stay caged at the animal shelter until hell froze over. No doubt that'd hit a nerve and sway her my way.

Nana was sleeping so hard she seemed to have one foot in another world. Drool leaked from the corner of her mouth. I grabbed a tissue from my pocket and gently wiped her chin. The scar that pulled at her upper lip had faded and blended so well over the years that I had hardly noticed it. I stared at that scar as a mix of emotions knocked around. Made me wobbly and weak. I backed into a chair and sat. Waited. And waited. Watched the slow rhythm of her heartbeat on the green monitor. Watched her sleep. She looked as peaceful as ever.

Maybe it was my full belly on top of being completely drained, but I wanted so badly to crawl into that bed next to my Nana. Put my head on her chest like I used to and sleep without a care in the world. What was the worst that could happen? Could I be arrested or kicked out for lying next to my dying grandmother? I doubted it and lay down quietly alongside her. The side that didn't have IV tubes flowing from her hand. She didn't move. The blipping sound of the heart monitor like pulsing wallpaper never changed its beat. I faced her. Her mouth hung as breath moved slowly in and out.

"Close your eyes." She said it but her mouth never moved and I closed my eyes for a just moment.

The soft ding of an alarm sat me up, wondering where I was—an alarm chiming like a frantic doorbell. Outside the window, only black. It was night. How long had I been asleep with Nana beside me in her bed? A nurse rushed in and I stood.

"Mrs. Williams, please step outside."

"What's going on?" I asked, but she didn't answer. She jerked the stethoscope from around her neck, stuck the headset into her ears, then pressed the bottom against Nana's chest. "She's just messing around. Nana. It's not funny." *Any minute now. Laugh. Please.*

Nana's jaw hung slack as the nurse removed the stethoscope from her ears and lowered it back around her neck. She produced a pen light from her shirt pocket and lifted Nana's eye lid. The light in Nana's eye went out and the nurse said she was sorry.

"No." I knew Nana was dying but the shock of it cut me in two.

"You'll have to wait outside the room, please," a doctor I hadn't seen before said as he rushed through the door to Nana. I took a long look at her lying there. A painful smile on her face. The tiny limp body made me dizzy, like moving in a dream, and I knew this time it was no joke. The room became a hazy, heavy blur as I turned and walked out. I moved down the hall like a tranquilized animal just before it goes down. With no idea where I was going, I went.

Nana had slipped away. Dead. Died right there next to me in her sleep. I stopped. *Exactly how she'd have wanted it. She wasn't alone and knew she was loved.*

Footsteps echoed as I pounded down the exit stairwell. A surging weakness made me stumble and fall. My shin cracked the edge of the metal step. Pain was a welcome distraction as I sat, hugging my leg to my chest with both hands. I made the most of my painful shin because I didn't want to cry anymore. Not ever. If I did, I knew I'd never stop so I laughed and tears broke to spite my best efforts—dripped down my face as I hurried outside for air.

Trying to walk off some of the hurt, I wandered the dark and empty hospital parking lot before sitting on a red curb and burying my head in my lap. Shivering and crying without my coat, I wrapped my arms under my thighs.

"Dear God, Grant Nana eternal rest. Let light perpetually shine upon her. With your mercy, may you forgive and allow her soul to finally rest in peace. She was loved. Amen."

After a long while of staring at nothing, I forced myself back inside. The nurse met me just outside of Nana's room. "I'm so sorry Mrs. Williams, I know how difficult this is." She rubbed my arm.

Hearing the words made it real and I nodded. Cold and numb inside and out.

"Last night, she insisted I tell you to 'Get the sack from the tree.' An oak, I think. Sometimes when people are dying, they—"

"Yes. The oak," I nodded and walked into Nana's room. Her bed was empty. I grabbed my coat and left. The oak was now my main priority and a welcome distraction.

PART II

CHAPTER
EIGHTEEN

It was nearly nine o'clock by the time I got home and threw the horses some hay. Down to four bales meant two more days of feed for them. Then what? I'd called and left messages with at least a dozen old friends I knew would love to own the well-bred mares. The price was right. Free! That was two weeks ago and not one of them had called back. It was impossible not to speculate as to the reasons why.

Sleep came in short increments as I compared the woman I'd become to the girl I used to be. That girl would never have stayed married and be so completely loyal and committed to a lying, cheating, horse murdering monster. Had I justified Nana the same way I had Mark? The soft rain quit and a long-lasting silence fell. Sometime silence is the worst sound.

With dawn came more rain. Hard and fast. Although sleep was mostly elusive, it was good to wake without a crippling hangover. It was barely light out, but no point lying in bed fretting and staring at the ceiling. *Coffee*. Maybe something other than Pepto Bismol for breakfast.

As the coffee spit and sputtered into the pot, I went through the stack of mail piled on the kitchen counter. Mail from Mark's clinic had been forwarded to our home address. Mostly junk. Equine supply catalogues, pharmaceutical newsletters, flyers for the latest in therapeutic horseshoes. The trashcan was filling fast.

An envelope marked *Important Recall* in red letters caught my attention. It was addressed to Mark personally, but mailed to the clinic. I didn't think much of it until I reread the letter. It meant to inform Mr. Williams DVM of the recent recall on the radius compression plate LOQTZQ 2.5. I assumed it was regarding the plate used to reconstruct Mark's arm back in 1999 and now was all that was left of him. But it didn't make sense. Why would the company mail it to his office? His office didn't exist back when Mark had surgery.

Little hairs on the back of my neck stood erect when I saw the order date: June 17, 2019. The same day I bailed Mark out of jail. It was like the moon had suddenly emerged from behind a cloud and illuminated my world. Gears in my mind grinded trying to work the pieces into place. It got easier and easier as the entire story fit together perfectly. I'd allowed Mark to gnaw me down to nearly nothing until the simple recall of a compression plate pricked a pinhole into the darkness.

The smell of coffee pulled me to the pot. I poured a strong mugful before the batch was even halfway done and drank. I didn't need Dickless Tracy at the FBI to understand why Mark had ordered an orthopedic plate exactly like the one screwed into his arm. That no-good cock-sucking mother-fucking bastard was still alive. The rotten piece of shit had planned his own murder. He'd planted evidence in the hog pen he knew would eventually be discovered. Did he know about the bodies? He had to—but how? It was like doing high school algebra and the harder I tried the more convoluted the entire problem became. But the simple part was clear. Mark was alive. Finding that fucker would prove Nana didn't kill him—and give me a valid reason to get up in the morning.

As the caffeine hit so did doubt. I wondered if I'd made a mistake, jumped to a conclusion without enough evidence, but everything about it felt right. Mark would do anything to keep from going to prison, and the faking-his-own-death scenario was ideal. Hell, I'd guarantee he loved planning every gory detail. To keep my anger from turning to rage, I refilled my mug.

"The best way to drive cattle fast is slowly." Nana's advice came to mind as if she were sitting next to me. *Now slow down and use your head.* If I allowed the rage entitled me, it would surely compromise my reasoning. I missed Nana. She would have known exactly what to do and I chocked down the lump in my throat with my coffee.

The sun came up somewhere behind dark clouds and kept the morning and the mountains in a dim gloom as I turned my truck around in the red mud. The logging road owned by Sierra Pacific Lumber and known to locals as Spur 15 ran east and west about a half-mile behind Nana's back pasture. Rear tires spun and slipped in thick muck. Then the entire truck slid sideways before I stomped the clutch and turned the knob—locking in the four-wheel drive. Crawling forward, I reached a section of granite and parked. For a while I just sat listening to the icy rain hit the roof and thought long and hard on what I was about to do. *Maybe I should just ask? Explain how I need to retrieve something, not sure what, from an old oak tree because Nana said so.* It sounded ridiculous. *Better to beg for forgiveness than ask for permission.* Nana's voice played in my head and I decided to get on with it.

Cold rain threatened snow and accentuated my bad mood as I pulled Mark's waterproof camo jacket out from behind the backseat. The big hood smelled of his spicy aftershave and shrouded my face as I picked my way around thick pines, cedars, and manzanita toward Nana's fence.

On the sidehill, slick pine needles against my leather-soled boots made hurrying a challenge I wasn't up for and I fell twice. The third time, I stayed down. On my hands and knees, I sank into mud red as a bleeding wound and wept. Again. "Stop it." I told myself through a tightened jaw. *Nana's watching and she'd never whine like a little bitch.*

Somewhere from the darkest muck of my mind, Mark slithered out. What he'd done to those poor horses and me kicked me into gear. I clawed myself forward through the sticky clay—vengeance overwhelmed grief. I accepted my fate from here on out and stood.

Wet mountain misery gave off a pungent scent as I stomped through it all the way to Nana's barbed wire fence. Slipping between the barbed wires was not as easy as it used to be. I hooked the back of Mark's coat and left a foot-long tear before escaping. Would I be arrested if they caught me here? What would I tell them? I should have planned better and concocted a story. I'd never get to that tree without being seen. And if, by chance, I got lucky and made it to the tree, would I even be able to still get my ass up it? Probably not. Thank the Lord Nana's dogs were gone. They would have barked and bayed and given me away.

Rain and wind mingled with snowflakes that stuck to my lashes as I got closer to the old tree. I scanned the area then listened and waited for I don't know what. A raven barked from somewhere above as I approached my old friend Miss Dendrola Tree. She seemed to have shrunk some over the years. The poor thing was more than half-dead and nowhere near as tall as I remembered, but every bit as massive in girth. It would have taken four of me with outstretched arms to hug her. Much of the trunk was cloaked in a brilliant green moss almost like lichen. Maybe I could climb her after all? I hoped the old rope ladder still hung from her backside. I took one last look around and saw no one. No movement.

I hunched over as I trotted around the trunk to the rope ladder, now frayed and wet and black with rot. With both hands I took hold and tugged. It held so I pulled myself up and set my boot into the first loop. The entire thing gave and I landed on my back gasping for air.

Air. All I wanted was my next breath and it wasn't coming anytime soon. If only Nana would have allowed me to nail up the wood ladder like I'd wanted to do years ago I'd be up the tree by now with little trouble. Nana would not allow nails in trees. So, there I was, flat on my back in the mud. Soft mud. Part of me wanted to close my eyes and stay there until the police put me in a warm cell.

Breathing eventually returned. I looked for another way up. None of it looked easy. The knobby rounds where I'd planted my feet and climbed effortlessly decades ago were now slick with wet moss and not suitable for my much bigger feet or my much bigger self. I needed to be where the tree forked and it was at least four feet above my head. *Shit.*

Thick bark like protective scales broke off in fat chunks every time I dug my fingers in for a solid grip. I just needed a boost. Or a ladder. Snow and the crime scene investigation start time were encroaching. I had to hurry. Soon eyes would be everywhere and I wouldn't stand a chance of retrieving whatever was in the tree.

A ladder would solve my problem. Like a wounded animal I moved toward the boundary of cedars for cover and snuck along the pasture toward the barn. I unsnapped the chain from around a small aluminum corner gate that was seldom used. It squeaked as I pushed it open. I froze, hoping there was no one around to hear it. Nana had asked Jim to remove this *"useless little shit gate"* more than a few times. I swung the gate slowly closed when the idea arrived. I inspected the height—it was about eye level and lightweight. It should work perfectly. Rusty wire held the gate to metal T-posts on either side.

The old wires busted as my cold hands worked to unwind them. The gate fell with an oversized clang, but the boisterous wind and rain covered for me. It was the first time I was grateful to be in a downpour. If someone was coming to inspect the noise there was no point in waiting around. I lifted and dragged the gate back along the cedars.

The gate was light, but dragging it through the mud was a workout. I was out of shape and breathless by the time I reached the oak. Wet and stiff with cold, I seemed to move in slow motion as I wedged the gate against the tree trunk, then stomped it into place to test its compliance. It felt sturdy enough, but I climbed each rail like it could give at any second. With both arms, I reached the fork and pulled myself up like I was attempting to summit Everest. It was ugly, but I did it. *Thank you, God.*

The hole had grown bigger due to rot. I reached in and felt around—nothing but pulpy debris. With my back against the dead limb, I looked into the hole and saw only black. I reached in again, deeper this time and felt something smooth, grabbed onto it and pulled hard. It came up toward the mouth of the hole, then stopped. Stuck. With both hands I held some sort of soft handle and worked the thing back and forth and side to side until it emerged. A black dry bag, the kind people used for rafting, about eight or ten inches in diameter and a little over a foot long. *How the hell had Nana stuffed the bag into that hole?*

A ladder. She could have hauled a ladder over in the tractor then easily climbed up. I wedged the bag between my legs and reached in again to make certain I'd left nothing behind. That's when a voice came.

"Probably some sicko trying to get pictures of the crime scene. You know, so he can make a buck." It sounded like a man's voice crackling over a walkie-talkie. I tossed the bag to the ground and rappelled down the gate like an expert. "I'm investigating the northeast section now." That was a woman loud and clear and way too close. I grabbed the bag and ran like hell for the thickest section of manzanita I could find. "I have movement!" she said—and I knew I was in trouble.

CHAPTER
NINETEEN

Adrenaline fueled my stride as I ran on shaky legs. Every breath stung my lungs until my chest ached from the cold. Plumes of white puffed from my mouth like a freight train while I fought my way through thick manzanita for cover. Icy branches cracking, poking, and stabbing my face. My cheeks burned as I slid the bag over one shoulder like a purse, put my forearms in front of my face, and crashed through the brush.

"I need backup!" Her voice was distant and panicked. Backup meant I'd be caught, and there was no telling what was in this bag. I dropped to my hands and knees and crawled downhill. It was slow but with less resistance from the red knifelike branches that refused to give way. My gloves soaked through. Remnants from the manzanita got in my mouth, shit in my eyes and ears, and something was in my bra scratching the hell out of my right boob. *Keep moving!*

It wasn't long before my manzanita cover thinned and became useless. I stood up and ran as hard as I could through tangles of knee-deep mountain misery. Running had never been my thing and I seldom had call for it so of course I sucked at it, and fell. On my belly, I crawled behind a wide cedar and listened in the wilted stillness. Nothing—except for my heavy breathing. Slowly, I tilted my head out from behind the tree. Just enough to let one eye see. Nothing.

I went on. Ran straight ahead at first, then zigzagged from tree to tree like I'd seen in a movie where someone wanted to avoid being shot. Being shot hadn't entered my mind until that very moment. They could shoot me. *If they holler at me to freeze—I'm not stopping. I could be shot. Shit. Go!* But how would I cross that damn barbed wire fence in a hurry?

"Hey!" Her voice sounded distant, but I wasn't slowing down. "Stop!" As I came to the fence, I tried not imagining what the bullet would feel like as it pierced my back. A lung? My heart? I flung the bag over and held my breath while trying to slip through the barbed strands like I had when I was twelve. With one leg through, I pressed the middle wire down hard with my hands and straddled for a moment before bringing my other leg and the rest of myself through. I did it. I was up, and on my way to grabbing the bag until Mark's coat stopped me.

Hooked like a fish, I threw my weight back and forward and tried to escape. Tried to rip free. I unzipped and pulled myself out of Mark's coat letting the fence have it. Between my foot tracks and the coat they'd eventually be able to prove it was me trespassing at the crime scene, but not today and probably not tomorrow. With the bag back over my shoulder I ran for the road. Ran for my truck. Ran for my life.

Pain stabbed at my side as the road came into view. Everything in me screamed *Stop. Walk. Catch your breath.* I kept moving, avoiding leaving tracks on the muddy road by staying up in the mountain misery until I reached my truck below.

The keys were inside the gas tank flap and I hurried with freezing wet fingers bumbling to grab them, open the door, toss the bag in, and start the truck. The diesel engine roared louder than ever as I rolled off the rock and onto the muddy red road.

Snow began to stick. Soon it would be impossible to confuse fresh tracks with old. The instant the tires gained traction I sped toward home taking only logging roads. No doubt in my mind the police would be swarming the main road in and out. All they'd have to do was take one look at me and they'd know I'd been the one prowling around their crime scene. My hair dripped and from the waist down I was soaked.

My jaw shook as I shivered knowing it'd be a long while before I'd stop. Cold seeped into my marrow.

I'd only been this awful cold once before. Mark and I were just married a month or so and he'd convinced me to ride up Devil's Nose to an old hunting cabin belonging to Jim's dead uncle. It was unclear who rightfully owned it now, but Jim claimed it didn't much matter since no one had used the place in years.

Buck fever had taken hold of Mark after he'd scouted what he called a monster the week before. Hunting was not my thing and I knew next to nothing about it, but I knew deer season had ended two weeks ago and if Mark shot a buck now, that'd be poaching. It was the first time I saw Mark as less than perfect.

We'd hobbled the horses in a small meadow surrounded by bushy pines that smelled like Christmas. Mark insisted we hike to the top of Squaw Ridge—something about the wind and positioning. It was brutally cold. The steep trail climbed out from the meadow with switchbacks that seldom flattened. Snowflakes salted Mark's black cowboy hat while I pulled on ski gloves.

Along the opposite side of the ridge, wind and snow whipped at my face as we sat against a downed log. Below, a narrow game trail tunneled through thick manzanita and spilled onto the creek at what looked like a four-foot cutbank. After two hours of glassing, my eyes burned. A throbbing ache pulled at my back and cold numbed my hands and feet. I couldn't wait for this day to end.

It was nearly dark when he filled my binoculars. Antlers too special to be mounted above some fireplace and sport a Santa hat. The thick neck and big body strong enough to keep that massive rack from being a burden. His furry ears twitched and Mark steadied his rifle—lowered his eye to his scope. With his finger on the trigger, he waited. Slowly, the buck stepped forward, as if on tippy-toes, and lowered his head. Through my binoculars I saw him nibble at the ground. Saw what looked like horse grain and lowered my binoculars. "Have you been feeding them?" I whispered. He ignored me and I lifted my binoculars back to my eyes. The majestic buck held that magical beauty that filled me with awe as the shot rang out and shook me to the core. Something unseen forced me back. My heart hurt.

The buck bolted and I hoped like hell Mark had missed. We stumbled and slipped as fast as we could—cutting across the switchbacks and down the ridge to where the buck had been. On his hands and knees, Mark inspected the ground and found drops of blood. The thought of that poor animal suffering made me mad and now I wanted to find him just as bad as Mark. We'd searched the dark with flashlights for nearly an hour before snow added to the fiasco.

"We're gonna find that fucker," Mark said in a tone that left little doubt.

"I'm freezing." I wrapped my arms around myself and shivered.

"Can you find the meadow and get the horses?" Mark asked.

"I think so," I lied. Guilt stung my conscience. "I have the trail map on my phone. I can just follow it back."

"Make it quick, okay?" He kissed me, but I felt nothing. My face was freezing.

For once, walking away from Mark felt good and I moved fast to keep the blood circulating. Snow came in fat flakes by the time I reached the meadow. It was impossible to see more than a few feet ahead. As I circled the meadow for the second time I finally caught sight of a steaming pile of manure and followed the horse's tracks. They were huddled in a stand of cedars.

It took two tries to mount my horse I was so cold and stiff. I'd only just started riding out when I saw a light in the trees. It was Mark. He limped up cradling his bad arm. "I fucking fell." He took hold of his horse's reins and slipped his boot into the stirrup. Empathy got the better of me and I quit being mad. "I landed on my bad arm." He pulled himself up into the saddle with a painful moan. "We'll come back in the morning. He'll be easy to find then." His horse's hooves dwindled into silence.

It was after midnight when we got to the cabin and I'd been cold for so long that I could not get off my horse. My brain said go—get off this damn horse and into the cabin, but my legs refused to move.

Before I knew it, Mark had my waist with his one good arm and jerked me down hard. I hit the snow with a dull thud as my horse jumped sideways. It was soft and wonderful to relax my body. Standing and walking would take too much effort. "Get up. Don't be a baby," Mark muttered and held out his hand. "I'm just as cold as you are."

No, you're not. You're much, much colder.

As the truck warmed, I held my numb fingers to the heater vent. It wasn't only the cold shaking my body. I was damn near convulsing from sheer panic and an overdose of adrenaline since escaping the long arm of the law. I'd never been in trouble. Not even a speeding ticket. A sick feeling gagged me. I rolled the window down fast, leaned out, and spit. In the side mirror, I caught a glimpse of myself. Manzanita leaves and debris stuck to my wind-burnt face. I pulled my ball cap off and picked twigs out of my ponytail as I raced through the storm.

Thoughts of Mark crept up as the forest flew by at forty-five miles an hour. Why hadn't I believed him when he showed his true colors plain as day on that hunting trip? It's a curse. He'd always held the power to render me helpless. We never found the buck Mark shot, but we did make love over and over again for two days and three nights in that cabin. That cabin held good times. Memories spilled like beads from a broken string. That cabin—*that cabin!* Holy shit, why hadn't I thought of it before? I needed to check the old hunt cabin. No way Mark would choose to rough it through the winter in that deteriorating old place with no running water or electricity, but I had to be sure.

Halfway home sleet forced the red Dodge off the muddy backroad twice. Windshield wipers fought to keep up as I turned south onto a graveled road I knew was partially paved. In a mile or so I'd make good time.

At the hay shed, I loaded the last bale of alfalfa, section by section, onto the tailgate. Hungry horses fought for position as I pulled the truck to a stop next to the pasture. After tossing heavy flakes into three big feeders the horses settled and each one went to eating. How would I feed the herd tonight if my credit card failed? Snow fell.

Warm water burned my icy skin as it showered down—thawing my body and mind. I'd promised to meet detective Rocha and Dickless Tracy at nine o'clock. It was a bit after eight and it would take at least forty-minutes to get there. Maybe I could call and reschedule—tell them I was sick? I rinsed and turned off the shower.

Rocha didn't answer. I left a message saying I'd be in just as soon as I felt better. A day, maybe two at the most. Seemed like all I'd been doing lately was asking God to forgive me. I didn't bother asking forgiveness this time. Figured with all the bad that'd been hurled at me these last few months, God really should cut me some slack. I was doing the best I could.

While coffee brewed, the black dry bag sat in a chair at the head of the kitchen table like a gift waiting to be opened. I undid the buckles, spread the mouth open, and reached inside. One by one, I pulled out stacks of quart-sized Ziplocs preserving what looked like journals from a lifetime, and set them on the table. At the bottom of the bag was a rusted Folgers coffee can with a white envelope taped to the lid. It looked like Nana's perfect cursive and was addressed to me. I couldn't resist. I popped the lid off the can and couldn't believe what I saw.

CHAPTER
TWENTY

C ash. Rolls and rolls of cash. I lifted one of the rubber-
banded rolls from the can. One-hundred-dollar bills
circled into five rolls almost as big around as my mug. It
looked like a lot. Where the hell would Nana get that kind of
money? Three slow and steady knocks hit my front door and
shook me away from my sudden wealth. I replaced the lid with
the envelope still taped to it and shoved it all into the refrigerator.
Two more knocks—harder this time.

In my sweats, I was the definition of rode hard and put up
wet as I peeked out the side window to see who it was. "Shit," I
whispered before opening the door.

"Hey." I coughed as realistic and as hard as I could into the
crook of my shoulder. My nerves tight as freshly strung barbed
wire. "Come in."

"No, it's okay." Rocha stepped back which meant he
probably believed I was contagious. "I wanted to offer my
condolences. In spite of my position, I am sorry for your loss."

"Thank you." I sniffled.

"Is there anything you'd like to share with me, Mrs. Williams?"

"No." I could feel my face getting hot as I considered sharing the recall notice with him.

Rocha ran his hand over his mouth. He looked as worn out as me when he lowered his arm and brow. "Someone was trespassing on our crime scene this morning."

"What?" I coughed. "Who? Why?"

Rocha lifted his brow and tilted his head with an I-know-it was-you look. "I was hoping you could tell me where you were this morning."

"Right here. Sicker than a dog."

"Why's your truck motor warm?" Rocha shoved his hands deep into the pockets of his gray Dickies.

"They repoed our tractor. I use my truck to feed the horses." I waited, but Rocha went quiet for once. My heart throbbed in my ears so I forced another coughing fit. "Please, come in—I'm trying to keep the house warm."

"You were at Blue Mountain. It's only a matter of time before we prove it. And it's only a matter of time until we unravel the crime scene. Evidence doesn't lie."

I filled the awkward silence by hacking.

"Hope you feel better soon better. I'll see you tomorrow." Rocha seemed sincere as he stepped off the porch then looked up at the falling snow as if it held the answers.

For a moment I wanted to stop him and hand over the recall letter. But it was best if they believed Mark was dead so that when I killed him, they'd never suspect a thing. He's was already dead, right?

I shut the door and locked it. Poured a cup of coffee and sipped—wondering how much trouble I was in. *Wouldn't life in a jail cell be easier? The money!*

I opened the fridge, retrieved the coffee can with the envelope, then hurried to my bedroom. The ancient wall heater revved and something inside whined as I shut the door. With the precious can and envelope on my bed, I cranked up the electric blanket and crawled in. Carefully, I peeled open the envelope. A heaviness in my chest as I unfolded two pieces of lined paper. The cursive was small and so perfect it looked like a font. The first line read, *If you're reading this I best be dead and gone...*

Here came more damn tears followed by endless amounts of snot. I wondered if they'd ever dry and wiped my face on the sheet and started again.

Dear Jess,

If you're reading this, I best be dead and gone or you're gonna wish I was. I can't imagine dying knowing you hate me. Never forget I love you more than anything in this world that's why I did it the way I did. To spare you the unnecessary burden of the awful truth. I saw what it did to your mother. You can find a good life and money ALWAYS helps. You're a good girl and you deserve better than what you got. Here it is—sit down...

The Mexicans Mark was in cahoots with on the horse killings didn't only kill horses. They killed people. Bad people who'd crossed them I suppose, and Mark swore that was the case the night I caught him and Jim dumping a body in my hog pen. Mark said he was being forced to dispose of the bodies but we both know he's a liar. He said they paid him five thousand dollars per head. He gave Jim five-hundred to help him. I shoved my shotgun into Mark's gut and asked him and Jim how many they'd dumped so far. Told them they best answer on the count of three and if the numbers don't match Mark's gonna have a bellyache for the rest of his short life. I counted and they answered. Five.

I thought long and hard and came to what I figured was the best deal for you. Mark paid me twenty thousand. I let Jim keep his money and over time I was paid another thirty thousand. That's yours. All of it. And please, scatter my ashes on Blue Mountain.

Love you,
Nana

Tears came so hard and fast that I buried my head in my pillow and bawled. Nana was not responsible for the human remains on her ranch. She took the blame. Went to jail and never exposed Mark because the long arm of the law would look to me as an accomplice. They'd charge me because who would believe I was dumb enough to not know what my husband was up to. They'd find out about the money and take it as evidence. Nana was great at seeing the bigger picture.

I fell back against my pillow and looked at the bigger picture. How could a loving God allow Mark to get away with this? If God wouldn't do right by Nana and me, I would.

No longer cold or tired or unclear about what to do, I reared out of bed and dressed in layers. Wool leggings, undershirt, and socks. Wrangler jeans followed by a heavy Pendleton. I found a woven winter hat and my dirty North Face jacket hanging on the back of the bedroom door along with Mark's waterproof

Australian duster that smelled like musty soap. I gave it a few good shakes in case spiders had homesteaded inside. After pulling on boots and gloves, I was nearly ready.

The hammerless .38 Smith & Wesson was hiding in the bottom of my underwear drawer. I tucked it into the inside pocket of my duster. In the closet mirror, I startled myself and stopped. For the first time in my life I looked and felt like someone I wouldn't want to fuck with.

The Feed Barn would deliver ten bales of alfalfa by two o'clock and I'd leave an envelope of cash tucked into the screen door as payment.

None of Nana's horses were very well broke. They were started as cutters, or reiners, or ranch horses, but had spent most of their lives as broodmares. Taking care of foals had been their only chore. I had to choose well. Getting bucked off and left in the snow was not part of the plan. Getting to Jim's uncle's cabin in one piece was.

Wendy, a soggy sorrel mare, seemed the best choice. She wasn't pregnant and was easy to catch. She stood quietly as I saddled her, then even opened her mouth as I slid the bridle on like she was looking forward to the ride. Snow was a foot deep and building fast as I led Wendy outside the barn and pulled my cap down over my ears. I checked the cinch one last time, took a deep breath, and stepped on.

Wendy pranced high and fast like she was leading a parade. Snow stuck in her tangled mane as she swung her head from side to side in rhythm with her gait. Fleeting breaths of steam billowed from her nostrils as she snorted up the mountain like The Little Engine That Could. I gave little slack in the reins the first half mile and kept my hand on the saddle horn just in case. Something I'd never have done only a few years ago. Back then if a horse wanted to fight or buck, I'd give it to him. Now, I couldn't chance getting bucked off, and wondered when it was I'd lost my nerve.

Snow stopped and made for a serene setting. After a mile, Wendy settled into a smooth stride, her footfalls post-holing the soft snow—hypnotic like the tick-tock of a metronome. I yawned. Sun broke through a set of dark clouds and turned snowflakes to diamonds. My face warmed and I was glad I could still appreciate the beauty in things until the possibility of finding Mark at the cabin toyed with me. I imagined him apologizing and crying for my forgiveness. On his hands and knees before me, I wondered what I'd say; hoped I'd never forgive him, but love seldom allows for logic or wise decisions.

I knew there was little to no chance Mark would be dumb enough to remain in the county or even in the country and thought seriously about turning around and going home. But making assumptions and excuses was something I had to quit doing. There was only one way to be sure and that was to see for myself. I guesstimated the ride up would take at least three hours. Maybe four in the snow on a fat broodmare.

Tiny bits of snow floated down between clouds when I thought I got a whiff of smoke. Wendy had made good time and the cabin wasn't far off—less than a quarter mile—when suddenly a fifty-foot cedar, packed with heavy snow gave and popped. Crashed across our path only a few yards ahead. Wendy dropped her entire front end as she snorted and jumped back. With a tight grip on the saddle horn, I rubbed her mane with the reins in my hand, trying to reassure her. "You're okay." I told her, "you're okay," hoping to convince us both.

We worked our way around the busted cedar and through a tangle of trees. I pushed aside a low-hanging branch and released an avalanche of snow. Wendy shook her head as I brushed snow off my face.

Approaching the cabin from the rear seemed the best option and I reined Wendy to the right, up through miserable manzanita for the second time in one damn day.

No roads led to the tiny cabin tucked deep in the woods, confined all around by a dense forest canopy that kept it in continual darkness. A steep hill grew behind it. The place didn't look near sturdy enough for full-time winter living as I approached. The roof saturated in snow. A tendril of smoke rose from the rusted stovepipe. My heart flipped. Wendy must have sensed my alarm because she nickered like it was suddenly dinner time. I pulled on the reins in an attempt to distract and quiet her, but if someone was in that cabin, there was no doubt they'd heard her. She nickered again.

CHAPTER
TWENTY-ONE

With Wendy's reins tied solidly to a high manzanita branch, I crept down the slope toward the cabin. My ears pricked for the slightest sound. A well-fed squirrel startled me as it raced up a dead pine and I slipped. Slid downhill on my ass until level ground stopped me. The back of the one-room cabin had no windows, just a warped plank wall that sat about two feet off the ground. I stepped behind a cedar and watched for what seemed like forever as snow gathered on my shoulders. Nothing. No tracks. No movement. Not a sound. I felt for the gun inside my slicker and held it tight to spur me on.

Up to my knees in snow, I ran in a way that can only be described as a lame penguin. I plowed more than ran, but made it to the corner of the cabin. There I rested until I caught my breath then pulled the gun from my slicker and gripped the handle the best I could with thick ski gloves. My finger barely wedged through the trigger guard. Like I'd seen on so many TV shows, I kept my back against the cabin wall until I reach the north side. Then I lowered myself under a dirty window with no idea of what to do next. Blast in—guns blazing and yell *Don't move motherfucker!* Or, just try peeking through the window and assess the situation?

Slowly, I turned and faced the wall. My heart stuttering as I slithered up enough to peek over the windowsill. Nothing but darkness inside. An old burlap sack curtain made it impossible to see anything, but still I strained my vision hoping to catch a glimpse of movement—when all at once Wendy nickered and something stabbed my back. "Don't fuckin' move."

"I won't." All the feeling left my body as I raised my arms and the gun. "I won't." Something tore the gun from my hand and pulled my glove off. I felt lightheaded. The world went completely off balance. I really wanted to sit down before I fell. My forehead pressed against the wall, I closed my eyes realizing in that long moment that more than anything I wanted to live. To go forward with my shitty life. And Nana—her story *had* to be told and I was the only one to tell it. "Please, don't kill me."

"Jess?" The voice was familiar. I knew him. Soon as I pushed the fright aside, my mind cleared. I lowered my hands and turned. His face was hidden behind a grizzled beard and long wild hair wet with snow. He looked like he'd become as much a part of these mountains as the trees. His dark eyes carried the burden of living in the wilderness.

"Jim."

He lowered his rifle. "What the hell, Jess?" I collapsed into his chest and hugged him like never before. He dropped the guns in the snow, then cradled and stroked my head like a father might do for a child. Although Jim was like family, I couldn't recall ever showing him one bit of affection and was sorry for that. We both could have used it.

"Nana died yesterday," I said.

"No." His body sagged as if someone had just let the air out of him and I swear I could feel his hardened heart breaking. "Figured she'd somehow outlive us all." His voice cracked. Avoiding eye contact, he backed away, then reached down and handed me my glove.

"She loved you," I said, and it broke him.

"She gave me a chance, trusted me, when no one else would." We stood there as if trapped in a sorrowful snow globe, and cried. Wendy's nickers dropped across the canyon.

The cabin was nothing more than a damp and dark twenty-by-twenty wooden box. No pictures on the walls or items that could be considered décor other than a cowboy bedroll pushed against the far wall. An unlit lantern sat on the floor nearby. The place smelled earthy like moldy bread but at least it was warm.

"Knew I shouldn't have started a fire, but a man can only take the cold for so long without a drink." Jim shut the door and leaned his rifle next to it. "Ain't had a drink all winter." He handed back my gun and I set it on a foldout card table next to the woodstove.

"Jim, that's the best news I've heard in six damn months. Good for you."

He grinned and nodded like he was both proud and embarrassed.

"You been up here the entire time?" I pulled my slicker off and draped it on the back of a rickety wood chair, hoping it would hold me as I sat.

"Camped out when it was warm. Once winter set in, figured there was no way in hell anyone's gettin' to me back in here." He grunted a laugh and raised his bushy brow at me while warming his hands above the woodstove. "You ride all the way up here to find me? Tell me about Effie?"

"No. I need to find Mark and thought this was as good a place to start as any."

Jim's face dropped. He chewed his lower lip.

"I know for a fact he's not dead, Jim. He faked his death just like he faked loving me."

"Don't waste your time on him."

"You have any idea what he put me through?!"

"Yes. Yes, I do. And I'm very sorry for it. But don't let it destroy you. Move on. You're a smart gal."

"I *have* moved on from what he did to me—but not what he did to Nana."

"What'd he do to her?"

"She got arrested! Went to jail! Everyone believes she murdered children and dumped them in the hog pen. I'm supposed to be okay with that while he's God knows where living it up?" I waited for Jim to agree but he didn't. "You should see what they've done to the ranch. They took her *dogs!*" I swallowed and breathed until I calmed down. "She should have died at home, Jim—in the place she loved. Don't you think Mark should pay for what he's done?"

"Yeah, but just let the cops handle it. Going after him is crazy."

"Would you say that if I were a man?" I asked.

Jim ran his grubby hand down his wiry beard. "Probably not."

"Why is it if a man hunts justice people think he's a hero, but when a woman does it, she's crazy?"

He shrugged and seemed to consider it. "Things are screwed up." He pressed his back into the wall and dropped his head. "Never thought they'd arrest her. Ain't no kids in those hog pens."

I let him wallow in his guilt a while to see if he'd confess.

"Jess, I swear to God if I'd a known, I'd a come forward. I knew what Mark was doin'." He looked at me a while, then down at his boots. "Even helped him a few times. I'd never a let her spend one minute in jail—"

"I know."

"She didn't—die alone...did she?"

"No. I was with her. We had a few really good days together and she shared a lot. Wants me to write a book about it."

"She tell you—" He stopped and shook his head. "You should. You should write a book. No one will ever believe it, but you should write it anyhow."

"Truth is stranger than fiction."

"That ain't no shit. True fiction." Jim laughed and I joined him. For a brief time, laughter outweighed pain. "I'll go to the cops. Tell 'em what we did. If the Mexicans don't get me first."

"No. This is on Mark. All of it. No one else needs to pay for his crimes." I looked Jim in the eye. I needed him to trust me. "One way or another, I'll find that bastard, so, I'm begging, if you know anything—this is your chance to do right, Jim."

He nodded with a thousand-yard stare. "Want some coffee?"

"Please. And I want you to tell me if you've got any idea where Mark's hiding."

He walked to the woodstove and grabbed a tin cup off a shelf. "Ain't got no sugar left." He poured thick black coffee from an old red pot that looked like it hadn't been washed since the cabin was built.

"I don't need sugar." My foot bounced while I rubbed warmth back into my knuckles. He was keeping a secret. "Why protect that prick?"

"It's not him I'm protecting. Careful, it's hot." He handed me the cup.

"Thanks." I sipped the burnt black liquid. It was old, strong, and bitter but warmed my insides just like the man who'd made it. The old chair creaked when I leaned back. "Come on, Jim."

He poured himself a cup. "Jess." He set the pot back on the woodstove. "Mark's kind of evil is best left alone. Trust me, you don't want no part of him or the folks he's in with. They're bad news." He rolled a torn office chair next to me, sat, and rested his elbows on his knees. Cradling the tin cup in his hands. "You need to understand somethin' about them Mexicans and their kind of bad. They don't beat you up and leave you crying for your mama. They chop your arms and legs off while you're still alive and can watch. I seen it, parts of people. They got no conscience." He turned pale. Swallowed hard and I could see he was scared. "Why you think I'm livin' like an animal?"

"Is it the cartel?"

"No, don't think so. Some fat bitch named Lupe is who Mark dealt with and a guy below her, Omar or Oscar, or somethin'. Lupe was runnin' the show and profiting off all the horses Mark put down."

"If you *had* to find Mark where would you start?"

Jim rubbed hard at the back of his neck and looked at his boots, then knocked them together until clumps of snow fell on the wood floor. "Had plenty a time to think on it. About a year ago, Mark give me a ride over to the Walmart. We got to bullshitting like always and somehow we ended up getting' serious—talkin' about regret and all. Can't even remember what the hell I said, but I'll never forget what Mark said." Jim leaned back in his chair and lifted his chin while he looked at me.

"First off, he made me swear to God not to laugh or ever repeat what he told me." Jim shook his head with a half-grin at the memory. "I shit you not, Jess. He looked me in the eye and said he'd die happy if he could kill a Sasquatch. 'Course,

I laughed. Laughed so hard I choked on my chew. What else could I do? Say, *Hell yeah* me too? I didn't buy it for a second. Thought he was just messin' around. Mark's not the type to believe in Sasquatch."

"Yes he is," I nodded. "Did he tell you why?"

"Nope. Just got pissed off 'cause I kept laughin'. Told me to go fuck myself, then got out of the truck and slammed the door. Few days later I apologized and he admitted that that was why he went to work for Lupe in the first place. Apparently huntin' Sasquatches ain't cheap." Jim didn't laugh but I couldn't help myself. "After that, I thought hell—he might be serious."

"He was. He told me about his obsession with Bigfoot two years after we were married. I thought it was completely ridiculous until he explained. Mark's dad swore he had a Bigfoot encounter when he was hunting grizzlies in British Columbia. The Great Bear Rainforest. Mark was nine and said when his dad came home, he wasn't the same. Some newspaper ran a story and things got ugly. His friends and family called him crazy or a liar. Accused him of making the story up just to get attention. Poor guy had to be hospitalized for a while over it. Mark said it was the only time he'd ever seen his dad cry. It destroyed the family." Wendy nickered while we sipped coffee.

"Mark got in a lot of fights defending his father's sanity and after about a year his dad disappeared. Mark's even been up to the Great Bear twice to hunt grizzlies, but in the back of my mind I knew he was looking for his dad—or maybe Bigfoot. Wanted to prove his dad wasn't crazy *or* lying. It was nuts, but you could see how something like that would affect a kid, then just eat on a person forever."

"Hell, it ate on me after he told me." Jim shook his head. "Imagine at nine, he didn't have much choice but to believe what his dad told him. No different than religion—or racism. A kid's mind don't reason truth, they just soak up all the bullshit adults tell them—'specially fathers. Tragic how shit like that gets handed down."

"Jeez, Jim. That's deep. I think I like you sober." I'd never thought of it that way. Never really thought of it much at all. Easier to just push it off to the side and not deal with the fact that my husband, an extremely well-educated man, would actually believe in Bigfoot. "I'm an idiot."

"No you're not. Love mucks up good thinkin'. Which might be why you figure you need to find him." Jim eyed me and raised his brow like he expected me to agree.

"Mark ever mention a guide? Some old guy up there who always hunted with him. Can't remember his name."

"Only person he ever mentioned was some gal..." Jim stopped. "Anyways..."

"Who?" I asked.

"It don't matter."

"Let me decide what matters. Who was she?" I raised my voice.

"He had some gal he was messin' with up there."

After all the hurt how could another blow possibly matter? But it did. Like razorblades slicing at my gut over and over again. I nodded.

Wendy nickered loud like she was on the brink of starvation.

"That sounds like Wendy."

"It is." I smiled. Impressed he could tell it was her by her nicker. "Know her name? The girl he was screwing."

"Naw. I wish you wouldn't let a grub like him burrow into you. But—guess I'd do the same." A smile moved Jim's hairy face and revealed a glint of his tobacco-stained teeth. "Being cooped up in this cabin takes my mind to wandering and I've thought about it *a lot*. Figure if Lupe ain't caught him, he's up north trackin' old Sasquatch."

"Sounds so ridiculous when you say it out loud." I rolled my eyes. No way I'm including this in the book, I thought. "Funny thing is, it makes more sense than anything else. And, Canada's extradition laws are tough."

"Yep. Look how long it took to get that Charles Ng fucker back here. And he killed a shitload a folks, *including* a baby." Jim got up and spit in an old plastic milk jug. "You got a passport?"

"Yeah. But, if Mark's up there, how'd he get across the border?"

"He knows people, Jess. Fake passports ain't nothin'. Hell, this fall, he could a gone from Washington or Montana a horseback, or even hiked." Jim sipped his coffee then stretched his back. "He could hunt and fish all the way up."

"I guess. Wasn't very good at it though," I said.

"Worst shot I ever seen."

"Least Bigfoot'll be safe a while longer."

Jim laughed. "Think he's real?" He scratched his chin.

"*No*. I think people want to believe. I mean, I'd love it if Bigfoot were real, but with all the cell phone cameras and—" The memory struck from out of nowhere like a rattlesnake when you least expect it. "Holy shit!" I jumped up and almost knocked the chair over.

"*What?*" Jim asked.

"Cameras. Game cameras!" I slapped the top of my head and my mouth fell open. "I got the Amazon bill a few weeks after Mark disappeared. Someone had ordered a dozen game cameras. Came to over nine hundred dollars. I assumed it was a mistake and disputed the charges." The clues were falling into place. I sat and gulped cold coffee.

Jim tilted his head back and sucked his teeth. "What a cocksucker."

"Motherfucker." I said it and didn't care that God heard. He'd let Mark get away with this shit. We sat in silence and soaked it in until Jim gave me an odd look and signaled for me to be quiet. He got up and peeked out the window.

"Looks like Wendy's ready to go." He turned back around and smiled. "Must have untied herself."

"I don't know how, but she knows you're in here."

"She was my buddy that one." Jim shook his head and looked back out the window. "I miss being at the ranch."

"You're too old to be living like this, Jim."

"Don't have to tell me." He swallowed his coffee, shook the grounds from the cup onto the floor.

"Ever been to British Columbia?" I asked.

He grinned. Set the tin cup back on the shelf above the stove.

"Can't just sit around waitin' for Mark to come walkin' through the door," I said.

"Nope. Don't think that'll happen."

"Come with me. We can figure this out together."

He seemed to be considering it. "Naw." He shook his head, but looked like he instantly regretted it. "I'm a liability, Jess. You best go or you'll be ridin' home in the dark and Wendy'll get cranky if she has to wait on supper." He walked to the door.

"Those Mexicans, that Lupe lady, probably doesn't even know you were involved. Come with me. Please, Jim."

"They know. And—" Jim shook his head. Seemed to be working out what to say. "Cemeteries are fulla people who knew too much, and making assumptions that're convenient will get me chopped into pieces. I'll take my licks right here in these mountains where I have a fighting chance."

"Winter in these mountains might kill you."

"I'll be fine."

"You always say that." I walked over and hugged him. "Love you." There was a good chance this would be the last time I'd ever see him.

"You take care a yourself." He hugged me hard for only a moment.

Avoiding my eyes, he opened the door. I pulled on my slicker, slipped the gun inside, and walked out.

"Love you too, Jess," he said as he started to shut the door, then opened it and leaned out. "And Jess, if you ever get a shot at Mark, you bury that son-of-a-bitch deep before his blood cools." He shut the door.

Riding down Devil's Nose, nostalgia occupied my time in the dwindling light. I thought about these mountains, their people, and the centuries of bones and secrets buried here. From the time when grizzlies and Mi-Wuks roamed this land. An icy wind bit at my face—stung my cheeks and reminded me that the native peoples had spent long winters on this section of the Sierra without the benefit of four-hundred-dollar coats. From earth and brush, they built pit houses fifteen feet underground. Rooftop ladders let them in and out and a firepit kept them warm. Better than the dilapidated single wide trailers they lived in now. *Better than being homeless.* I wondered how hard it would be to dig a pit house.

The temperature fell as fast as the light. The thought of not seeing Jim again sent a pang through me. I swiped at the snow stuck to my face. The darkening world blurred as my eyes filled with cold tears. *Enough.* I forced Mark into my mind and let anger boil my blood. *Could I ever really find him? What would I do if I did? Would vengeance ease the pain of grief?* I was counting on it.

CHAPTER
TWENTY-TWO

I t cost six hundred ninety-five dollars to have Nana cremated and would take at least a week before I'd get her back. I'd promised to scatter her ashes on Blue Mountain. A promise I intended to keep. Nana didn't live long enough to spit in her plastic test tube, but I did and had sent mine back the day after receiving it. I'd know my undeniable ancestry in a four to six weeks.

After a painless meeting with Rocha and Dickless Tracy that amounted to a whole lot of nothing, I was scheduled to appear in court next month over battery charges Gabby filed. Nights were spent sipping wine and Pepto Bismol while reading Nana's journals; her entire life was written down day by day with such rich detail and emotion that I had no doubt the story would write itself. Hidden in the very back of her most recent journal was Nana's will. She'd left Blue Mountain to me.

I contacted Bank of America to find out what was owed on the second mortgage Nana had taken out against the ranch and a girl with an angelic voice informed me that the second had been paid off four months ago. I could only guess how Nana had paid off the loan. Knowing that I could someday return to Blue Mountain and call it home again thanks to Nana brought an abundance of gratitude. The monster that had been squeezing and gnawing at my insides for so long had just died and rotted away. I could breathe again.

Beginning a vomit draft of Nana's story, researching the Great Bear Rainforest, and bear hunting in Bella Coola occupied the first part of February. It was no longer legal to hunt grizzlies in the rainforest. I scanned websites for bear hunts and eventually found a familiar name. Zack Lawrence popped up in an old article about hunting grizzlies in British Columbia, but I couldn't find a website or email address for him.

Maureen, my therapist seemed genuinely glad to hear from me when I called and scheduled an appointment. It felt good to send her the money I owed. Wells Fargo gave final notice of the foreclosure sale and refused my request to pay the back due amount. I had fourteen days until I was "required by law to vacate the property." The more I thought about it the less I cared. It was best to leave this place behind.

Most all of the furniture and appliances were sold cheap or donated. Wendy along with the rest of the horses went to Cowgirl Up, a therapeutic riding program. Day by day, I was chipping away at improving my situation and every now and then hope crept in, especially after an hour with Maureen. I bought a decent used overhead camper for six thousand dollars. At least I'd have a bed to sleep in until I could return to Blue Mountain.

The assistants and nurses at Paradise Ranch came to greet me with sincere smiles each time I visited. My mother couldn't hide the joy in her eyes when I'd arrive and she'd have to play the memory-loss game until staff left us alone in her room. Eventually, I'd asked Mom about the mill money she'd inherited. She explained that after marrying Raymond, they'd hired an attorney to retrieve the trust. Minus his fees and bearing interest, they'd received damn near a half million dollars. That's how they paid for the ranch, but ten years of Raymond's inept ranching skills eventually broke them.

On my last visit, Mom introduced me to her "friend" Charlie, an old black gentleman who doted on her like she was the Queen of England. He wrote and recited poetry for her. Taught her to play chess and never failed to walk arm in arm with her to the dining room for every meal. Before I left that day, I asked Mom if she'd eventually like to come live with me at Blue Mountain. She confessed that she was "entirely" in love with old Charlie and didn't want to spend a day without him. It lifted my heart to think that after a lifetime, she'd finally found true love. The old cliché *Better late than never* rang in my mind. *Lucky her.*

Valentine's Day, which also happened to be my sixteenth wedding anniversary, was closing in and there was only one way to get through it without drinking myself into a coma or pulling the radio into the bathtub with me. I had to hit the road. Tomorrow—February fourteenth. Roads were clear and there wasn't one good reason not to head north.

I printed out fifty 8x10 color copies of Mark's picture with the heading MISSING - REWARD. I'd buy a burner phone when I got to Canada and add a number to the posters later. Nana's cremains were under the driver's seat for moral support and the camper was packed.

Dread grabbed hold of me hard as I shut and locked the front door. It was no longer my home. The front door now belonged to the bank, as did the rest of the house. I unlocked and opened it. Let the critters and bears return to what had originally been their territory.

Staring at myself in the big picture window made me sick. Sick over what Mark and I had built together. How hard we had worked to make the place a home we could be proud of. I always imagined we'd have children and eventually rambunctious grandchildren who would love coming to grandma's house and would know they always had a place to go if life ever got too tough at home.

My cell rang. Caller ID read *Calaveras County Sheriff's Dept*. Law enforcement, I was pretty sure, could find me by tracking my phone just like they'd done when they discovered Mark's phone in Nana's hog pen. I did not want to be found. The ring seemed to get louder and I pitched the vibrating phone as hard as I could at the huge window. Glass exploded, then shattered and dropped like deadly jagged puzzle pieces. My spirits instantly lifted as I felt Nana looking down, laughing. *"Good girl! Good girl."*

The Calaveras County Animal Shelter didn't open until ten o'clock. I drove to the post office and mailed a check for two thousand dollars and a letter to Nana's attorney, Ed Manetti asking him to represent me, should need be. In the letter I explained Nana's and Mark's involvement in the largest mass murder in Calaveras County history. There was no good reason to share information about Jim or Nana's payoff money, so I didn't. Why test attorney-client privilege? Ed Manetti would share the information with law enforcement while keeping my best interests in mind.

Dogs barked and bayed and howled like miserable wolves caught and caged as I waited for someone to unlock the door at the shelter. The double-wide gray modular was originally where DUI drivers could take classes to lessen their sentence. I knew, because years ago I had dropped Jim off here twice. The door clicked and I stepped in. A woman with a severely sprayed blond bob and distracting D-cups stopped and faced me.

"How can I help you?" Her arched eyebrows gave a look of permanent surprise.

"I'm here to pick up Effie Hobbs' dogs. She died week before last and—"

"I need a certified copy of the death certificate."

"I haven't received it yet. County said they sent it a few days ago. But I'm sure you'd like to get her dogs out of here."

Her nametag read "Missee." She typed on her computer with long pink nails. "Says here that four of the dogs are pending adoption."

"What's that mean?"

"They are in the process of being adopted into *decent* homes."

I detected the hint of sarcastic judgement. "Good. Glad to hear it." Rather than argue the point, I knew the dogs were better off. "There were five dogs."

"Yes. The senior dog is scheduled to be put..." She leaned into her computer screen and squinted. "Jeepers, that was a close one."

"Can I have him? I'll pay whatever necessary fees."

"We offer a fifty percent discount if you're over fifty-five."

"Still got a few years to go." Eighteen to be exact. Did I really look that worn? Or was Missee just being snide? "How about a Valentine's Day discount? Dogs help ease the pain of loneliness, right?"

"They certainly do. And cats too. Don't know what I'd do without my kitties." Missee smiled. I could have figured this hag for a cat lady.

"At the moment, I only have seven. Lester died and I haven't replaced him."

"I'm so sorry."

Missee typed and squinted and continuously licked her lips. "The fees are one-hundred-ten. And there is a waiting period of one week."

"One week? For what?"

"To allow us time to verify the information you provide." She set a form and a pen on the counter.

"Okay. No problem." This *was* a problem and I was done playing games. "I have his pain meds for his arthritis and if he doesn't go for a walk at least twice a day he gets to where he can't hardly move."

"He has got himself a bad limp. It's his shoulders."

"I know, poor old guy. Can I please give him his pill and take him for a quick walk? Please?"

Missee looked around as if someone were watching. "No one else will be here for another hour." She stood and leaned over the counter. "I shouldn't but it feels like the right thing to do. Please have him back," she looked at her huge wristwatch, "by ten thirty. Okay?"

"You're the best Missee. Thank you *so* much." I smiled and followed her until she stopped me. "Wait here. I'll bring him out." She disappeared through a side door. The barking increased with an intensity that rattled the cheap paneled walls.

Old Duke limped through the door and his gray face sprang to life when he saw me. "Duke!" I knelt and rubbed his ears. Emotion sent tingles in my eyes and nose until his breath, like death, hit me and I leaned back. "Jeez that's rank, Duke."

Missee handed me the leash and Duke's nails clicked against the laminate floor as he pulled me out the door. "We won't be long." I smiled at Missee and she smiled back.

"Have fun."

"We will." The door closed slowly behind us.

Outside, Duke and I raised our heads to the sun. It was the first clear day in what seemed like a lifetime. The air was frigid but felt good mixed with freedom and invigorated both of us. I unsnapped Duke's leash. He ran and bucked as he followed me to the truck. Soon as I opened the passenger door, he looked up at me for a little help.

"Okay old man. Let's go." He wagged his tail and I swear to God he was smiling as he panted. I wrapped my arms around his chest and rear end, then sucked in a deep breath and used all the strength I had to lift him onto the front floorboard. Planning for five dogs in the truck, I had covered the backseat, floors, and front seat with old comforters and sheets. When I shut the door, Duke found the will to crawl up onto the seat. I ran around the truck and got in. With the sun in our face, we looked out the windshield at the road ahead and grinned.

PART III

CHAPTER
TWENTY-THREE

Once in a great while the world points you in the right direction, and when it does you'd best look. Images of the Great Bear Rainforest sprawled out across my mind for two days while driving north through California, Oregon, and Washington. I'd spent hours on the road daydreaming of hunting Mark through twenty-one million acres of rugged and tangled wilderness. The odds of finding him in a rainforest that stretched two hundred and fifty miles along British Columbia's coast were about as good as finding Bigfoot. I didn't care. Mark's Great Bear hunting trips always began from a town called Bella Coola. I'd start there.

From Vancouver British Colombia, Bella Coola is six hundred and twenty miles north. After waiting for over an hour at the U.S. Port of Entry, I pulled up to inspection station number nine and rolled my window down. The agent poked his red face out his window, took one look at me and my rig, then came around to my door. "Hello." I said with a smile.

He nodded. "Passport."

I handed him my passport and as he inspected it asked for my vehicle registration and proof of insurance.

After questioning me, checking Duke's rabies certificate, and searching the camper, the agent waved me through into Canada.

I hadn't an ounce of regret over my decision to come to Canada and decided to treat myself to a motel in Vancouver. Sleeping in the camper the last two nights with Duke had been cozy, but I needed a long hot shower.

Making reservations and even finding my way around Vancouver without a cell phone proved how dependent I'd become on the thing. Just off exit nineteen, I found a Travelodge. No pets were the policy and no way Duke was ever spending another night alone. The girl at the front desk suggested Motel 6 and drew me a map after questioning why I didn't have a map on my phone.

The cosmopolitan city was in constant cloud cover and impossible to appreciate. A cold day followed by a colder night made me grateful that the Motel 6 had a room on the bottom floor and with the exchange rate cost only forty-eight-fifty.

After we checked in, Duke and I walked a few blocks to find something for dinner. It felt great to walk and Duke seemed to enjoy the pats on the head, the ear rubs, and back scratches from strangers.

After a twenty-minute stroll, the streets became littered with trash, broken bottles, cigarette butts, and what looked like a used condom. The place turned into tent city. Homeless people camped along sidewalks for as far as I could see. Used and probably stolen goods sat out for sale on blue tarps. A greasy-haired woman who looked like she'd been dead longer than alive crawled out of her tent screaming, "I'll kill you, Kenny. You mother fucker. I slice you like a Thanksgiving ham." I could see there was no one, including Kenny, in her tent.

"Shut the fuck up crazy bitch!" A man's voice came from out of nowhere. If it weren't for Nana, I'd be homeless right now. These poor souls living on the cold street with no place to piss or shit or washup were no different than me. I clutched my crucifix, thanked Nana, and tied Duke to a pole outside of a Korean barbecue joint.

The smell reminded me of summer nights with Mark and our friends grilling meat over an open fire. Crickets, frogs, and laughter at home were now replaced by orders shouted across a flaming grill and a ringing phone no one answered. The cashier handed me four plastic sacks filled with a hundred dollars' worth of chicken and ribs.

I kept one bag for Duke and me and offered the rest to folks who seemed to barely exist. The "crazy bitch" who wanted to kill Kenny blessed me with tears in her eyes, then held out her arms for a hug. I wanted to turn and run. She smelled like urine as she closed in. The simple act of hugging this pitiful woman made me feel better about myself than I had in years.

Safe in our motel room, Duke ate his chicken breast without bothering to chew, then begged while I ate mine. A long, hot shower cleansed my soul. *When was the last time Crazy Bitch had showered? Who was Kenny? Why did I care?*

On the hard bed, Duke snuggled against me while I worked on Nana's story. Never had writing come so effortlessly. I had two chapters written by midnight and forced myself to stop. Having something to look forward to would be nice for a change.

Something crashed or banged or knocked on the door and woke me. I'd actually slept. What time was it? Where was I? It took a minute to remember. Vancouver. Motel 6. Did someone just knock on my door or was I dreaming? Duke didn't move and why should he—he was deaf. I slid out of the covers and stepped softly over the cold laminate. Next to the window I split the heavy curtains just enough to peek out. Smoke surged up from below my window as if someone were there smoking, but from my angle I couldn't see anyone.

The office phone rang and rang and rang. I hung up, then walked back to the window and peeked out again—relieved I'd put my money in the room safe. A shadow stood and moved down the walkway, only to return in less than a minute. Someone *was* out there sitting under my window. A flicker of light, then more smoke. What the hell was this guy doing? I worried about my truck being broken into until coming to the sad conclusion that there was nothing of value to be had. I went back to bed.

At daylight I took old Duke outside to pee and saw the smoking shadow from last night. The man was really a boy with his back against the wall under my window. Asleep or dead in the cold gray with only a hoodie to keep him warm. Duke was losing control and left a trail of piss as he limped across the parking lot to a grassy knoll and finished his business after five minutes of sniffing.

In the lobby I filled a tiny Styrofoam cup from a coffee urn and sipped. Duke watched through the glass wall as I stepped into the office and reported the kid outside my room to the clerk. She seemed interested and wrote my room number down. Said she'd get security right on it.

Duke and I rounded the corner to our room. The boy was up and leaning against the wall. I stopped. Duke wagged his tail and went to him without me. "*Duke.*" He couldn't hear me. The boy looked feral. His baggy jeans hung off him like a scarecrow as he knelt and rubbed Duke's back.

"Sorry." I grabbed his collar. "He's friendly. Obviously."

The boy looked up at me. It was cold, but beads of sweat and scabs blistered his face.

"You got a smoke?" His accent was odd. Slow like he was still learning English and his eyes were filled with a desperation that was easy to recognize.

"No. Sorry." I pulled the key card from my pocket and opened the door.

"How about...maybe a few dollars?" He hung on the word "dollars." Pronounced the s like a z. Maybe he was high. He stood and pulled up his jeans. There wasn't much height to him. "Some spare change?"

"Let me see what I have." I dug into my pants pocket. The tips of his fingers were calloused an ugly yellow and his nails caked with grime as I dumped change into hands cupped as though waiting to receive communion.

"Good luck and God bless." I led Duke into the room. The moment the door shut I latched the chain and bolted it.

I packed and called Duke off the bed. "Let's go." Not sure why I kept talking to a deaf dog, but he seemed to understand and stood waiting for help to get down. It was amazing he had no trouble jumping onto the bed. I lowered him to the floor and opened the door. There was no sign of tweaker boy or security.

A police car sped in and parked alongside the office as I loaded my bag and Duke into the back seat. A tall, big-boned gal with glasses that took up most of her face stepped out of the cruiser and walked over. She scanned the area then said, "Ma'am we had a report of a Caucasian male with a black hoodie breaking into cars in the vicinity. Have you seen anyone that fits that description?"

"Yes. He was just here—about twenty minutes ago."

Her partner, an older man with silver sideburns and a bulbous nose wasted no time getting from the cruiser to the office. "Thank you, ma'am. And please, if you see him again give us a call."

"Okay." I didn't feel like explaining how unlikely that would be since I was leaving and didn't have a cell phone.

Outside of Vancouver, the Trans-Canada Highway clung to sheer granite walls. Ragged cliffs and white mountain peaks loomed in the distance while the Fraser River raged below. The river was rimmed in an icy white that shimmered when we crossed over it at a place called Hope.

"Ha! Maybe we should just live here, huh buddy?" I rubbed Duke's ear but he didn't move.

From Hope the highway meandered with the river cutting its way through the canyon. Radio stations turned to static.

After two hours of the same Sheryl Crow CD, we reached Hells Gate. A big red building said so. "We've been here before, huh Duke?"

Highway 1 cranked hard to the east and Duke sat up as I merged north onto the Cariboo Highway. I moved the readers from my ball cap to my face to double-check the directions I'd written down last night. Highway 97, Cariboo Highway-North, was correct and it was only 9:30 a.m. "We're making good time."

A delicate snow fell on and off for the next few hours. Eventually, the town of Williams Lake sprawled out like a real city—situated between the Cariboo Highway and Highway 20 to Bella Coola. The lake hid somewhere under the ice and two feet of heavy snow. A large section of snow had been cleared down to the ice and kids played hockey. Smoke stacks blew heavily and crowded the sky as I turned into the Walmart parking lot.

I bought a prepaid flip phone, a bag of chips, dog food, three big bottles of Pepto, two boxes of red blend wine, and left Williams Lake behind.

"Only six more hours to Bella Coola." Duke and I crunched chips as we left the valley floor. Soon the truck's tires spun on the slick roads. I cranked the knob locking the wheels into four-wheel drive. Slowly, we climbed icy switchbacks toward the Chilcotin Plateau. Appreciating what must have been amazing views was out of the question with near whiteout conditions as we topped the plateau.

Descending "The Hill," a steep grade with zero guardrails, in the snow, was far worse than I'd read. The graveled road narrowed into a skinny single lane in spots and was dangerous in the best driving conditions but with the storm it had become downright treacherous. The truck slid sideways toward a sheer drop no one could survive. I controlled my panic and straightened out. Seconds later my hands began to sweat and fear flushed me. More than anything, I wanted to pull over.

White flakes shot hard at my windshield. I couldn't see more than a few feet ahead and dropped the truck into first. With a death grip on the wheel, I prayed we'd survive. Fuzzy red lights flashed ahead. I braked softly, pulled off the road, and tucked in behind a semi with its hazard lights flashing. "Thank you, God." Duke looked at me. "Let's get the hell out of here."

Opposite the road side and only a few feet away from the camper, a wall of black rock disappeared up into the snowy sky. I post-holed my way through the snow to the back of the camper as Duke plowed behind me. The doorknob was covered in black road slush. I wiped it away with my glove and noticed it wasn't locked. I'd locked it last night at the motel—I knew I did—since being in such a rough area. Butterflies swarmed my stomach as I hung my head assuming I'd been robbed and opened the door. Duke could hardly wait to get out of the cold and looked up for help. I lifted him in and climbed up behind.

Inside the camper, everything seemed to be in place. Dirty dishes still in the sink. Books strapped in place on a shelf. A plastic bag of dirty laundry under Duke's table bed and the pile of sleeping bags in my overhead bed. That punk probably tried to break in last night and something or someone interrupted him. The camper smelled funky like stale cigarettes and felt like an icebox. That smoking little shit broke in—there just wasn't anything worth stealing.

I started the propane heater and lit the stove for coffee. A blue flame coughed, then wheezed. Duke barked at my bed. "You're nuts. And you're not getting up in *my* bed. How 'bout a hot dog?" I opened the fridge and tossed him one of the hot dogs I used to hide his pain pills in. Duke caught the dog midair and swallowed it whole. "Jesus."

The camper warmed and Duke continued to stare up at my bed and bark. He'd started barking at walls, the couch, and sometimes the TV at Nana's house. Doggie dementia is real. It's called canine cognitive dysfunction and dogs over fourteen have a good chance of developing it. Duke was sixteen.

"Get in your own bed." His bed was where the small dinette had been lowered and cushions arranged into a mattress with a big comforter. "Hang on." I lifted him onto his bed and patted for him to lie down, but he continued to stand and bark at my bed. "Dude? What the hell?" I covered his head with the comforter.

I reached a coffee mug from the cabinet above and made a cowboy cappuccino by mixing coffee and hot cocoa.

While the drink cooled, I retrieved my laptop and the burner phone from the truck and returned shivering. Writing Nana's story was the best way to wait out the storm. Duke barked on and off with the comforter hanging off him like a cape. "Stop it!"

I sipped my coffee, then set my laptop on my pile of sleeping bags. Careful to not spill, I climbed up into on my bed. As my knees hit the mattress the pile of sleeping bags shifted then moved on their own. I jumped back, spilled, and wished I'd had my gun.

CHAPTER
TWENTY-FOUR

A sickening groan emerged as I ripped the sleeping bag back. "You!" He was so thin he'd hardly added to the mound of bedding. Black, stringy hair in his face as he curled into a ball and wrapped his arms around his middle.

"Help me." It was the boy, the smoking shadow from the motel parking lot. He must have broken into the camper and was probably hiding inside while the police were looking for him.

"What are you doing here?"

"Dying." He looked and sounded like death was a definite possibility. Shaking like he was cold, but sweating liked it was the middle of summer and he'd just stacked a ton of hay.

"You hurt or shot or stabbed or something?" I asked, but he just closed his eyes and rolled his head into the pillow. "I have a gun. I'll damn sure shoot you if you don't get out right now."

"Please. Ma'am..." He looked at me with red, sunken eyes. "Please, shoot me."

"*Shoot you?* You on drugs?"

"No! That's the problem." He started to cry like a little boy. "I need a shot."

"You got a phone?" I wanted to call an ambulance, but hadn't bothered to take my prepaid phone out of the packaging. Let alone figure out how to use the damn thing.

"Naw. Got jumped yesterday. Bitches hooked *all* my shit." He rolled over—the far side of his head shaved down to the scalp. "Got any pain pills?"

This kid's suffering was tangible and if he were an animal, I'd seriously consider putting him out of his misery. He brought his knees to his chest in the sleeping bag and groaned.

"I have Tramadol. You want that?" It was Duke's pain meds and I'd taken them once when I hurt my back.

"Anything. Please." He sat up. "I'm gonna barf."

"Shit." I grabbed the pot off the stove as fast as I could and held it under his chin just in time. His retching reached obnoxious volumes and was damn near contagious. I gagged and looked away, but the vinegar stench followed.

With saliva strung from his lips and his head hanging over the pot, "I'm sorry." He retched, but it sounded like nothing hit the pot. Once he settled back and closed his eyes, I set the pot in the sink and went to the door.

"I'm gonna get you some help. Be right back." I hopped out and sank into the cold. Snow up to my knees and still coming down hard. I worked my hood over my ball cap and zombie walked to the semi parked ahead of us. At first, I knocked on the driver's side door like there wasn't a kid dying in my camper. When no one responded, I banged with both fists. "Hey!"

Snow had stacked up on the step under the driver's window. I grabbed the handle next to the door and stepped up. A woman's face met me at the window. She was pretty in a pale and plain sort of way. "I need help!" I did not step down. "I need you to call for help."

She rolled the window halfway down. "What?" she asked softly like she'd just woke up. Her spiky blonde hair poking out in every direction.

"There's a kid in my camper needs help. Can you call an ambulance on your CB?"

"CB? Lady, I hate to tell you, but it ain't the seventies. I don't have a CB and I don't do convoys."

"Shit." Can you call on your cell? He needs help *now*." Snow caked my eyelashes and I blinked too much.

"There's no service until you get to Bella Coola." She pulled on a heavy, puffy coat. "How bad is he?"

"Seems pretty bad to me. He's throwing up and all sweaty and shivering. He looks awful."

She tugged a beanie down, then shushed me away from the door and opened it. "Sounds like food poisoning to me." She climbed out of the cab and dropped into the snow.

"I think maybe he's on drugs."

She stopped and shoved her hands deep into her coat pockets. "This your son?"

"No. I... I found him in my camper. Didn't know he was there."

She shook her head like she really didn't want to be bothered. Then went ahead of me into the camper.

It was warm. I flipped on the lights and lit up the harsh reality. The boy was on his back with his eyes closed and didn't move. "Hey." The truck driver tapped, then shook his arm. "What's your name?"

"Jed."

"Jed what?"

"Baxter," he mumbled.

"What are you jonesing from, Jedidiah Baxter?"

"Heroin."

"Shit... How old are you?"

"Fifteen. You got some somein' for me?"

"Yeah. Advice. Next time you want a hit remember what you feel like right now. Never forget the pain." She turned and opened the door. "He'll live. My boyfriend did." She climbed out.

Wait!" I yelled and stuck my head out the door. "I have pain pills. Tramadol. Should I give him some?"

The truck driver shrugged, then nodded. "Can't hurt."

I shut the door and found the bottle of Tramadol in the drawer. Opened it and shook out two pills.

"Think you can swallow these?" He didn't answer. Just moved his eyes my way and I showed him the pills in my palm. He opened his mouth like a baby bird and I dropped them in. He swallowed. "Want some tea?" His body shook like he was being electrocuted. "Shit, kid? You okay?" He didn't answer, just pulled the sleeping bag up under his chin. I pulled a paper towel from the roll and wiped his sweaty face.

"Talk to me. Please." Jed whispered.

"What do you want to talk about?"

"Anything. Just talk. I want to listen and not think."

When he said it, the situation turned weird, like an upside down deja vu. "I don't know what to say."

"Just talk. Don't stop."

Without a doubt, I'd heard his exact words and this scene had played before—a dream—somewhere, somehow. I thought of Nana. Of what she'd do if she were here. She'd talk all right— and it'd be more of an interrogation than a conversation. But when it came down to it, she'd do all she could to help him. "Okay. Your name's Jed. Mine's Jessica. I'm from California— heading for Bella Coola. The Great Bear Rainforest really. It looks incredible."

"Why?" Jed asked with his eyes closed.

"Why what?"

"No one goes in winter."

"Good. I'm not really a people person. How 'bout some Pepto Bismol? It helps my stomach. It's in that cubby on your right."

"No."

"Tea?"

"Kay."

Barf filled the pot so I took it outside and dumped it. Cleaned it out with a handful of snow, then brought it in and washed it out good before boiling water.

"Tea'll be ready in a minute." Sitting next to Duke, I couldn't think of anything else to say. Seemed like only a minute ago I was his age and the hick-kid drugs consisted of pot and spray paint in a paper bag. Pot paranoid me. I tried it once in junior high during lunch break. Sitting in algebra class it hit like lightning. My heart went nuts. Convinced everyone knew I was high and giving me the death stare, I ran out of class and called Nana. Told her I was sick. She found me lying in the wet grass alongside the school parking lot. I lied—said it was the meat piroshki I had for lunch. She didn't buy it for a second. "Lie to me again and I'll leave you here." And she meant it. I confessed I'd smoked pot. Nana looked at me and smiled. "Thought you were smarter than that." She held out her hand and helped me up. Never did I ever huff paint or try pot again. Vodka and beer became my drug of choice. And more recently wine. Red to be exact.

Duke laid his head on my lap. "When I was fifteen, I was going to high school rodeos, doing chores, and saving for a truck. Couldn't wait to drive to school. Riding the bus for an hour and a half each way every single damn day was a nightmare. The curvy backroads made me sick. I threw up on the bus at least a dozen times my freshman year. You go to school?"

Jed barely shook his head.

"I couldn't wait to drive—just take off. See what all was out there. Now I'm pushing forty and it's my first time out of the states. At fifteen, you could have given me a million guesses and I'd never have come up with the shit show I'm in now." What an ass I was for thinking my life was crap when this kid was in absolute hell. I'm sure he'd had it a lot tougher for a lot longer. I'd never had to spend a night outside freezing on a motel sidewalk. "Sorry. Didn't mean to try and out-suffer you."

Little water bubbles formed inside the pot and I turned the burner off. I drowned a tea bag in a mug with water from the pot. An earthy sweetness steamed my face.

"You want honey or sugar, or something?" He didn't answer. "Want me to keep talkin'?" He didn't answer. *Good.* He'd fallen asleep. Dread that he might be dead entered and I stepped up onto Duke's bed to see if Jed was breathing. I couldn't be sure and softly set my hand on his chest. It did not rise. Then it did and I breathed with him for a while. Here I was again, standing by for life or death.

It was good to have a conversation where what was being said didn't really matter and would not end in a prison sentence if I misspoke. It was nice even if I was the only one talking. I added two packets of honey to the tea and sipped. Duke snored and I wondered what the hell to do with this child. There was no way to get him back to Williams Lake down to Bella Coola. The roads were worse than before and it would be dark soon. Not worth the risk. Waiting out the storm was the only real option. I'd work on Nana's story and pray he'd make it through the night.

CHAPTER
TWENTY-FIVE

L ast night I dreamed of Mark. Of making love or rather
trying to—some random thing kept stopping us the way
it does in dreams when you really want to do something
important. Oddly, killing him was easy. In my dream I shot him
in the heart—but he didn't fall—just pressed his hands to his
heart and looked at me like he was thoroughly disgusted. Then
Mark became Roy. Lying there dead and bleeding on a front
porch I'd never seen before. In a time and place that made no
sense. Nana walked up and smiled. *"Fuck him."*

The semitruck's engine rumbled. I sat up, my heart racing,
and looked at the time: 5:00 am. I'd slept some and lay back
considering the vivid dream. Retribution was a responsibility
Nana and I could not ignore.

Duke snored next to me as I crawled out of his bed. An icy
air engulfed me soon as I opened the door and peeked out. Snow
had stopped and was now around two feet deep. We weren't
going anywhere until a snowplow cleared the road and I dug out
the truck.

The boy looked peaceful as he slept so I got back in bed with Duke. We snuggled while I reconsidered what I was doing there. I knew trying to find Mark was a serious kind of crazy and I considered turning around as soon as the road was cleared. I could take this boy to a hospital in Vancouver. But the urge to prove everyone had misjudged Nana, Mark—and me—was too strong. Mark should pay for what he'd done and I was the only one in the world who would see to it.

I needed a gun.

Just before sunrise the elegant grind of a metal snowplow against ice sent a rush of excitement. Massive tire chains rang like church bells on Sunday morning. The lady truckdriver revved her diesel engine a while, then pulled out. I tugged my boots on, then gloves, and my coat, and went outside.

The storage door on the side of the camper was frozen. I bent down and breathed heavy on the latch like an obscene caller until it opened. A bit lightheaded, I wiggled out the shovel and went to work.

Snow was to the bumper as I dug under the front tires and made a path to the road. Sweaty and out of breath, I began freeing the back tires.

Duke barked in the camper. I cleared a space just beneath the door and helped him down. He pissed and plowed his way through to the truck. Ready to hit the road as much as I was. But first—coffee.

Jed never woke when I set the pot of water to boil. I checked his breathing with my palm on his back then felt his clammy forehead. "The road's clear, but it'll be slow going down this mountain. I'll find you a doctor in Bella Coola."

He rolled onto his back and opened his dark eyes. "Day three's always the worst bitch." He moaned and rolled into a fetal position. "Can I get more pills?"

"The Tramadol? Sure." I pulled the bottle out of the drawer, put two in my pocket for Duke, and shook out two for the kid. "You need to drink a ton of water. Flush that crap out of your system." I had no knowledge of heroin withdrawals, but figured water couldn't hurt. He took the caplets and two bottles of water. I tossed the pill bottle back in the drawer and shut it. "Okay. I'll check on you in about an hour." Jed's jaw muscles flexed. He looked worse than he did yesterday. The shaking started again and he closed his eyes. "Try to sleep."

Descending the icy switchbacks was pure hell in the most spectacular snow-covered wilderness I'd ever seen. I shifted down into second gear. Miles and miles of winter wonderland stretched out below and made it damn near impossible to keep my eyes on the road and off the magnificence ahead. The single lane curved to the right and I hugged the mountain as a fat RV appeared around the bend.

"Shit!" I tried not to press the brakes too hard and held my breath. Uphill traffic had the right of way. At a snail's pace, the RV clipped my mirror. It cracked but didn't bust and I considered us both lucky.

The road spilled down the mountain and onto the valley floor. Snow disappeared completely in the low elevation and the sun woke in dramatic fashion. It was like we'd dropped through a seasonal time warp. No longer frigid, that spunk that comes with warmth brought Duke and I back to life. He stood with his front paws on the dash as I pulled over and parked next to a meadow as green as if it were spring. As I opened the passenger door, old Duke practically jumped in my arms.

A thick meadow, bordered by white peaks and sunshine, warmed my face. Sweet flora hit like an expensive candle as I inhaled. The essence soothed me until a hidden bird or critter chirped like the beep of a heart monitor, reminding me of Nana. Duke trotted lamely through the grass and lapped at a puddle, then looked at me with a drooling open-mouthed smile.

There was no traffic. Duke would be fine exploring while I went inside to check on Jed. The drawer had popped open during the drive and was blocking my way to the bed. I shut it with my knee. The bottle of Tramadol was on the floor with the lid gone. I picked it up. Empty.

It took a minute to register and when it did I jumped onto Duke's bed. Reached up and rolled Jed onto his back. "Hey." I shook him. No response. "Jed!" Nothing. I shook him hard as I could. "Jed!" His face vacant with a blue tinge. I set my fingers on his neck and checked his pulse. It was weak and slow. This little shit was going to die of an overdose in my camper because I left the Tramadol for him to do it. "Fuck!" *I'm such an idiot.*

I rushed to the truck and grabbed the cell off the dash. Checked for a signal. Two bars. I dialed 911. Not even sure if 911 was the emergency number in British Columbia.

"Hello. 911. Do you have an emergency?"

"Yes! There's a boy overdosing. He's dying. I'm parked just off the highway at the bottom of the hill into Bella Coola."

"Vehicle description?"

"Red Dodge truck with a silver and white overhead camper. How long?"

"I'm dispatching someone now."

"How long do you think?"

"I can't say ma'am. I'll stay on the line. Try to calm yourself. Do you know what he took?"

"Tramadol. It was for my dog."

"Can I have the patient's name?"

"Jed...something. I don't know. I... I can't remember. He snuck into my camper in Vancouver. I don't even know him," I said and waited for the operator's response. "Hello?" She didn't answer. "Hello?" I looked at the phone. The signal was gone. "Shit." I walked back and forth, lifting the phone to the sky as if God would send down a few bars. He or She didn't of course. Calm down, I told myself and tried calling two more times without success.

In the camper, I held Jed's hand. What could be so bad that this kid, who had his whole life in front of him, wanted to die? I checked his pulse at the wrist. Nothing. My heart dropped. I pressed two fingers against the carotid artery in his neck and prayed for a pulse. There wasn't one.

"Fuck!" I climbed into the bed and straddled him. Pinched his nose and opened his mouth. Pressed my mouth over his and forced breath into him. His chest rose. It'd been years since I'd taken the level-one avalanche course which included a half-day of CPR class. Mark and I had planned to get into backcountry skiing that year. It never happened of course.

How many breaths should I give him before heart pumps? I *couldn't* remember! Panic clouded my thinking. I gave him two breaths, then stacked my hands over the middle of his chest. Pushed hard and fast as I could. The song that the instructor had sung during the demonstration came back to me. It was the Bee Gees song, "Stayin' Alive." That was the beat, and I used all my weight with each compression.

"Ah, ah, ah, ah, stayin' alive—stayin' alive." I sang it over and over for one minute then back to mouth-breaths, all while wishing help would arrive. There was no way Jed would live if they didn't hurry.

Sirens arrived long before the ambulance did. "In here!" I yelled. "In here! Help!" Duke barked and the paramedics hesitated. "He won't bite. Get in here for Christ's sake! He's not breathing." I climbed off Jed as a man and woman crowded into the camper. "I'll get out. Let you guys do your job."

The woman opened a giant tool box as I squeezed past her. I walked with Duke, pacing the meadow, until the woman paramedic finally stepped out of the camper. I rushed over and followed her to the ambulance. "Is he going to be okay?"

"He's breathing. That's a good sign." She opened the back door. "But no guarantee you know. It's out of our hands." She pulled out a rolling stretcher and wheeled it to the camper.

"Where will you take him?"

"Bella Coola General."

"I didn't think the town had a hospital."

"It's small. Five rooms." She climbed into the camper and in no time, she and the man had Jed out using the bedsheet. They placed him on the stretcher and strapped him down. I followed them to the ambulance.

"He said his name was Jedidiah Baxter. I don't know him. He snuck into my camper when it was parked in Vancouver and I didn't find him until we were stuck in a blizzard halfway to Bella Coola."

As they opened the ambulance door, I confessed that I had given him the Tramadol, then explained about my poor CPR technique. And when they lifted and loaded him, I couldn't shut up. I rattled on about how the boy had spent the night under my window in Vancouver. They shut the door. I didn't bother to mention the cops were looking for him. Nana would have been proud. The boy had more than his fair share of shit right now.

The lady paramedic stopped and put her hand on my shoulder. "That boy would *not* be alive if it weren't for you." She seemed to be waiting for an answer.

"Thanks." I'd become so accustomed to blaming and being pissed off at myself that I honestly hadn't considered that what I'd done had saved Jed's life. The guilt that I'd made the Tramadol available pretty much occupied my mind. "Thank you." I swallowed tears welling behind my eyes. All that had happened hit me and it wasn't even lunchtime. "I'd sure like to check on him."

"Hospital's easy to find. Or you can call. Got to go." She jumped into the driver's seat and the ambulance left with its lights spinning. That's when the realization of what I'd done hit. Although I was the dipshit who made it possible for the kid to OD, I was also able to save his life. *I saved his life. Me. I've never done anything that important.* A feeling that could be called euphoric came over me and I'd never felt better. I wanted to pump my fist and whoop. Just how Nana felt when she had taken a life.

Bailey Ridge Campground was just shy of Bella Coola. Trees and mountains and greenery galore. Still wound tight from saving a life, I checked in at the office. A guy who reminded me of an older Asian Nicolas Cage, with better skin, was hunched over a book, reading with frowning concentration. He flipped the thick book over on the counter. *The Odyssey.* He oozed intelligence under a knit cap and didn't charge me the usual five-dollars-a-day dog fee. I paid for one week and bought eight bucks' worth of shower tokens. Since it was off-season, I had my choice of sites. I chose number twenty and backed in.

It was a secluded spot next to the bank of the Bella Coola River and surrounded by trees and rugged peaks and every now and then a soft ocean breeze that reminded me of clean laundry. Duke sniffed and wandered while I made camp and hooked up the electrical cord and water.

With all the trouble this morning I hadn't eaten and went from fine to famished in the space of a minute. I made a peanut butter and jelly sandwich then sat at the picnic table in my cozy little camp. A distant honking broke the quiet as geese passed overhead. Duke waddled up and sat staring at me as I ate. Those big brown eyes were irresistible and I handed over the crust.

The Bella Coola River was wide and purred. Deep turquoise water shimmered and sparkled like nothing I'd ever seen. It was intoxicating. Gratitude humbled, then overwhelmed me as Duke and I followed a path that led upriver. Movement caught my eye. I stopped. Looked around. Across the river I spotted a small black bear on the shore watching me.

"Wow." He or she stood. Sniffed the air a while, then gave me one last look before disappearing into the brush. I didn't move. Sat right there on the sand and stayed a long while. Taking it all in.

The world would be a better place if everyone had access to this much elaborate nature. Grace lives amongst the trees and river and mountains, I mused.

On the way back to camp I gathered an armload of kindling and dumped it next to the firepit. Someone had left a stack of firewood while I was gone. It had to be the guy in the office.

Before dinner, I cleaned the camper and pulled the sleeping bags off the bed, then took the one Jed had slept in outside to give it a good shake. I reached in and pulled the inside out. Something tumbled from the bag. It thumped heavy on the ground. I looked around. Nothing. I stepped down off the camper and looked under the truck. I found it. My gift from God.

CHAPTER
TWENTY-SIX

Wet wood hissed, cracked and popped when I tossed another log into the campfire. Blue and orange tongues licked the dark. There was something mesmerizing about the flickering flames. Mostly, I believed I loved fire for the warmth it offered, but to Nana it was much more. For her, it seemed, fire was a force that consumed. I couldn't stop staring. Sparks swirled above only to be lost in a canopy of treetops that shut out the stars.

I dragged my folding chair out of the smoke and sat with my hand in my coat pocket cradling the loaded gun I'd found. A mix of wine and Pepto coated my stomach as I wondered: what kind of trouble followed Jed? Why would a kid need a loaded gun nearby? I felt sorry for him and wished this world wasn't filled with so much suffering as I went to the picnic table and refilled my cup from a box of red blend.

As I drowned my sorrows with wine, the guy who'd checked me in walked by wearing a blue plaid wool coat I'd wear myself. "Hey, I like your coat."

"Thanks." He walked up. "Everything okay here?"

"Yeah, great. Thanks."

"Good. Good. I'm Kevin by the way."

"Hey. I'm Jessica. Nice to meet you."

"Nice to meet you. Need anything, let me know."

"Okay. This your place?"

"Yep." Kevin let out a breath. "Keeps me busy and out of trouble." He shrugged." So, gotcha some big plans tomorrow?"

"No. Just, playin' it by ear."

"If you need recommendations—maps and whatnot—swing by the office. We've got kayaks and bikes too. No charge."

"Thanks. Hey, would you like a glass? Or a cup I should say?" I held my plastic cup up. "It's not the best, but—"

"Sure. I'd never turn down a drink from a pretty lady."

I went inside the camper and grabbed a plastic cup off the counter. When I came out, he was sitting at the picnic table petting Duke. "This is one cool dog." Something about Kevin radiated goodness.

"Yeah. Old Duke. He's about sixteen now." I poured a tall cup of wine and handed it to him.

"Thanks."

"Of course." I sat across from him at the table.

"You got lucky with this weather. Most tourists don't chance coming up in February."

"I had to. I'm kinda looking for someone."

"Someone specific, or in general?" He smirked and drank.

I lifted my cup to him. "Specific—unfortunately." My daypack was on the table already stuffed with a roll of Mark's missing person flyers. I unzipped it and brought them out, then set one in front of him. He held it up toward what little light was coming from a lamp pole. "Who is he?"

"My husband."

"Whoa." Kevin looked at me and rubbed his graying head. "Do we know why he's missing?"

"Came up here to hunt. I haven't heard from him since."

"That's no good."

"No."

"I'll ask around. Put some flyers up for ya."

"Thanks."

Kevin didn't pry. We drank our wine and he did most of the talking. He explained that he was happily divorced and had two daughters. One lived with his ex in Vancouver and the oldest was spending her inheritance and his retirement at UCLA. He was amusing and I liked the way he carried the conversation for nearly two hours before we said goodnight.

It wasn't until I was nearly asleep in the camper that I realized I'd hardly thought of Mark all day and only briefly when I gave Kevin a flyer. I chewed on that fact a long while. That was progress. Definite progress.

I thought about the gun. How I'd come to acquire it could not be ignored. *No way it was just coincidence. No way. It was a sign. An honest to goodness opportunity to kill Mark.*

I let my imagination run wild and visualized finding the bastard kissing on some hot girl in a dense forest. I walked up and pressed my gun into his heart as the girl ran away. The shock that filled his face before I pulled the trigger made me smile. *Boom.* His cold heart obliterated. "Jesus." The desire to kill Mark was destroying what little faith I had left. The more I thought about it, the more I came to justify that what had happened to me and Nana was *not* fair, or just, and if God didn't want me to punish Mark, then He or She should end my desire to do so.

A late-night rain had come and gone, but left a dense fog that shrouded the surrounding mountains in white. Kevin walked up as I sat at the fire drinking coffee. "Good morning. Another day in paradise, eh." He stepped closer and through the wood smoke, I got a whiff of his tangy lemony cologne.

"I've never seen anything like it. These mountains are huge. They'd humiliate the Sierra."

"I spent a winter screwing around in Lake Tahoe when I was a lad."

"No kidding."

"Skiing was good. Not big like here, but fun." He sipped his coffee as Duke waddled over to him. "Hey old man." Kevin knelt and rubbed Duke's ears.

"Hey, you ever hear of a guide named Zack Lawrence?" I asked.

"Old Zack. Sure. Everyone knows him."

"He used to guide bear hunters or something, right?"

"Yep. Used to take the fancy-pants trophy hunters into the Great Bear so they could get a grizzly. I'm talking big-ass monster bears," Kevin grunted and stood. "Yeah, Zack." He shook his head and smiled. "He was kind of an outlaw for a while there. But he quit all that. Does viewing tours now. Takes groups out to where they can watch bears do their thing. You know, get their selfies with grizzlies eating salmon behind them."

"Is he doing that now? I mean this time of year?"

"Don't think so." Kevin crinkled his brow.

"Maybe I could call him?"

Kevin's laughter was as light as wind chimes. "Zack isn't good at what you call customer service. Lives completely off grid. No cell service or internet. His gal-pal slash secretary left, now he returns calls when he gets to town and has cell service. Might take a week or more. No telling. If you're in a hurry just go see him. Heck, that's an adventure in itself."

"Where's he live?"

"Over on Four Mile reserve. Not far. Don't unhook your rig and all—take one of my camp bikes. The blue one's practically brand new."

"Perfect. Thank you."

"Swing by the office when you're ready and I'll set you up with a map and a bike."

"You got a stapler I can borrow?"

"You betcha."

Fog gave way to sun as I rode toward Four Mile reserve up a long empty highway. Under swirling clouds, I shifted gears to ease the resistance and paced my peddling against an ocean breeze filtered through miles of evergreens. The scent was invigorating and the temperate climate ideal for riding. No cars had come or gone in nearly an hour.

I turned onto a side road and stopped. After double-checking my map, I grabbed a bottle of water from my daypack and drank. The reserve was a native Nuxalk community of homes on unfenced spacious lots separated by swaths of brush. Dogs rested on porches, in yards, and one, a husky type, slept in the middle of the road. For a moment I thought he was dead until he lifted his head just enough to see me. Children played tag and screamed and waved as I rode by. It did me good to imagine children with happy lives.

The Bella Coola valley was clear and I could see for miles. A sugar-coated glacier beckoned and grabbed hold of a passing cloud. The natural beauty stirred something in me. I felt strong and pedaled faster, until the pavement ended. According to Kevin's map, I should go east on the dirt road here. I rode two miles until I reached the only cabin as far as I could see. It had to be Zack's.

Dogs barked as I stepped off my bike and waited in what might be considered the driveway, but no one came out. Not even the dogs that barked and bayed from nearby.

"Hello?" I yelled and walked my bike toward the side of the cabin. A log barn came into view. "Hello!" Dogs were kenneled next to the barn. If someone were home surely they'd come to investigate by now.

Walking my bike back to the dirt road, I stopped at the mail box welded atop a wagon wheel and shoved a flyer inside. If Zack and Mark were old hunting buddies like Mark had said, Zack would at the very least get in touch. On my ride into Bella Coola, I stopped and decorated every telephone pole and bulletin board with my flyers.

A massive and elaborate totem pole with wings stood guard in front of the Spirit Bear Café. As I opened the screen door a little bell dinged above my head. The few customers turned and looked my way as I sat at a corner table for two. The server, a twenty-something with pimpled cheeks and a man bun, handed me a menu and said salmon burgers with homemade slaw were the day's special.

"I'll take that." I smiled and handed back the menu. "And a Pepsi. Please."

"You got it." He was light in his loafers as he sped back to the kitchen.

When the check came, I asked the server if I could leave a flyer. "Maybe you could put it in the window? My brother's missing." I stood and handed him a flyer. "We think he may be lost in the rainforest."

The guy shook his head and placed his hand over his heart. "Are the Mounties out looking for him? They live for this."

"Huh?" *The Mounties?* My heart skipped several beats. *Are you shitting me?* "The Mounties. Yes. I'm just...helping." The thought had never entered my mind. I was advertising myself into prison if they found Mark murdered. It wouldn't take Dickless Tracy to put it all together. I just happened to be in Bella Coola looking for Mark then he just happens to end up dead. What was I thinking? The sensation of falling made me grab for the table. I hadn't the slightest clue what I was doing.

"I'll give this to the manager. She'll put it up." He walked away.

"Actually, maybe I'll take that one back." I held out my hand. "I'm having new ones made. I'll drop it by tomorrow."

"Oh. Uh...Ohhh-kaay..." He handed over the flyer. I took it and paid him with a twenty from my pocket.

All the flyers needed to come down fast or I might have to explain to law enforcement why I was in Canada looking for my dead husband—or worse, why I killed him. It wouldn't take much effort on their part to look into Mark's case. I jumped on my bike. Pedaled fast the half block back to the telephone pole where only an hour ago I'd stapled a flyer. It was gone. I hurried to the next intersection where I'd hung flyers. Gone. I checked each and every pole and bulletin board at the grocery and post office. Nothing. Not one flyer left where I'd put it. Except possibly the one I'd left in Zack's mailbox, and I wasn't riding back there.

Who the hell took my flyers down, and why? Maybe you're not allowed to hang flyers around town. Maybe the locals think a missing person flyer is bad for business—tourists don't want to think something bad could happen in paradise. Wherever the flyers had gone, something about it felt very wrong.

CHAPTER
TWENTY-SEVEN

Maybe I should have gone to the Mounties and explained everything, but I had no solid proof Mark was in Canada or even alive. I rode hard back to camp to rethink this mess before I got myself into deeper shit.

I brought Duke and a bottle of Pepto out of the camper and walked upriver. With my shoes and socks off, I rolled up my jeans and let the cold current wash over me while I thought long and hard about how I'd rationalized my responsibility to teach Mark right from wrong. I'd conned myself into believing I owed it to Nana to clear her not-so-good name. Stopping Mark from hurting anyone else might give me a sense of worth I'd lacked for so long. But it was all bullshit. Anger and hurt were the only real motivation. I saw it all so clearly—without Maureen's psychobabble.

Sun slapped my skull. I'd always had the heart of a coward when it came to Mark. I wasn't cut out to be the great avenger; I'd find a better way to purge my demons. I sat in the warm sand

and pushed my wet feet down until they disappeared. The hush of the trees and river disoriented me. Duke sat down next to me and I lay back.

Tree tops swayed under a perfect sky. The majestic rainforest had a profound effect on me. All I had to do was let Mark go and release the debt I felt I owed Nana. Why should I care if people believe Nana was a killer? She was!

It had to stop here and now. Why not let this place lift my heart and bask in its undeniable glory? Hiking and fishing and working on Nana's story could replace my ridiculous pursuit of Mark.

Kevin was in the office when I returned the bike. I thanked him and gathered hiking maps for the Great Bear Rainforest from a stand.

"Gonna do some hiking, eh?" Kevin asked.

"Yeah. What do you recommend?"

"Not going alone," he said with a straight face and handed me a more detailed map from behind the counter. "You'll want this map. On the house."

I saw the $12.99 price sticker. "Thank you." I took the map. "I either hike alone or don't go."

"I know a *great* guide. He knows the area really well and is extremely knowledgeable. The only downside is the guy has a cornball sense of humor and sometimes, no always, talks too much, but I think you'll like him." The last thing I wanted to do was spend money on a guide. Kevin crossed his arms and puffed his chest, then finally grinned.

"We could watch the sunset from Purgatory Lookout."

I laughed. "How much does this guide charge?"

"Usually a lot. But it just so happens he has an empty seat in his Jeep that's already paid for." He made a dorky face. "You don't even have to hike—there's an old Forest Service road to the lookout."

"Okay, sold." This was a good opportunity to keep busy and practice forgetting Mark.

"Great. How's about I pick you and Duke up at four?"

"Works for me." He remembered Duke's name *and* invited him. *Very cool. Hope he's not a serial killer.*

I'd bring my gun just in case.

The Forest Service road to Purgatory Lookout offered spectacular alpine views. The Jeep rattled by several ponds glowing golden in the sunlight. Geese honked as we made our way between soggy meadows leaving tall grass swaying in our wake. Duke sat in the small backseat taking in the scenery as he drooled. We were all smiles. The road, if you could call it that, dried as we climbed. Slowly we scrambled and bounced past a talus boulder slope.

The sun was well on its way to setting when Kevin stopped the Jeep and we stepped out at the top of Purgatory Lookout. I hurried ahead toward the view of the Noeick River valley below feeling like I could fly across the valley—all I had to do was try. Purgatory Glacier was miles away but in my face. "Wow." My mouth dropped as the sun set the icy behemoth on fire. The glacier went from turquoise to violet right in front of my eyes, then the sky lit up with a variety of pinks and tangerines.

"Not bad, huh?" Kevin walked up with Duke.

"It's like... seeing God or something." I stood on top of the world. "Amazing."

Kevin handed me a brown opened bottle. "You brought beer?"

"Always. Cheers." We tapped our cold ones and drank.

"That's good. I don't really like beer, but that's nice," I said.

"I brew it myself."

"Of course you do." I smiled.

The lookout was a wide swath amongst the trees with a few slabs of granite perfectly placed for Kevin and I to sit, drink, and watch Mother Nature show off a climactic sunset. Sometimes silence is the best sound.

Lightning pulsed and lit the sky above distant mountains as the Jeep bounced down the trail. Foam erupted from my second bottle of beer and flowed onto my lap. I sucked and slurped the brew as Kevin smiled and handed me a rag from under his seat. A cool dusk blued the previously golden pond and in no time the temperature and dark fell. Kevin stopped the Jeep, reached under the little back seat, and pulled out an army-green wool blanket. He tossed it over Duke who was curled up and shivering back there. I thanked him. *That was nice, but then Nana was always kinder to animals than people. Would my thoughts and opinions be forever tainted by the people I loved?*

Kevin unloaded Duke and me at our campsite. We hugged goodbye. It was a good hug. Not one of those fake hugs where someone turns their head away and leans in just barely touching your back. This was two arms wrapped around me followed by actual squeezing. Warm and real. As he drove away, I wondered what Mark was doing.

Instead of sleep, the night produced two more chapters of Nana's story, but kept my mind occupied and off Mark. I dozed somewhere around daybreak. Since I was out of the finding-Mark mode, after pancakes, I took Duke for a long walk on the river trail.

It was late morning when we returned to camp. I sat at the picnic table thinking about Jed and called the hospital twice. The first time, the staff was too busy and asked me to call back in an hour. When I did, the receptionist said they could not share patient information over the phone. *Fine, I'll come for a visit.*

Kevin was on the phone when I walked into the office. I busied myself reading a variety of flyfishing brochures until he hung up. "Hey. What are you up to today?" Kevin asked.

"Just wondering if I could use the blue bike again?"

"Of course, you don't need to ask. Just grab it whenever you like." The phone rang. "Excuse me." He held up an index finger. "Bailey Ridge Campground could you please hold on for a sec?" Apparently, there was no hold button because Kevin covered the handset with his palm and whispered.

"You like to fish?"

"Yeah." I nodded.

"We're going out for halibut this weekend. You wanna come?" Kevin leaned towards me. "I'll bring beer."

"I'd love to."

Kevin gave me a thumbs up and put the phone to his ear. "Hey, thanks for waiting. How can I help ya?"

I borrowed the blue bike from behind the office and checked on Duke. I'd tied a rope to a tree and snapped him to it so he could enjoy being outdoors. I rode away while he slept in the midmorning sun.

The hospital was small. One story and built in an L-shape. "I'm looking for my son, Jedidiah Baxter," I said in pretend panic as I walked toward the front desk. The woman wore a white uniform right out of the 1950s. She never looked at her computer screen or asked any questions.

"Follow me," she said, and I did.

At the end of a light blue hallway, she stopped. "He's in here." She opened the door and held it for me.

"Thank you so much." I walked in.

"Your mother's here," she said from the doorway. Jed looked at me.

"Hi, hun." I hugged him. "How are you feeling?"

"With my hands." Jed's face stayed vacant.

The woman stepped out and shut the door.

"I'm glad you're okay." I stood and patted his arm.

"You saved my life." He didn't look at me.

"Yeah. I guess maybe I did."

"Why?"

"Why? Why the hell not?"

He closed his eyes and slightly shook his head—looked like he just might cry and I couldn't help but think of Nana—of Winnie, the little girl lying in a hospital beaten nearly to death while no one cared if she lived or died. A lump stuck in my throat. "Do you have any family?"

Again, he shook his head, then opened his eyes and looked at the ceiling. "Thanks, and all that shit, but you really don't need to waste your time here."

"I've got nowhere else to waste it."

He glanced at me and I was pretty sure the next words out of his mouth would be *fuck off*. After a moment a grin sweetened his face. "What's your name again?"

"Jessica Williams."

"Why'd you say you were my mom?"

"I called and couldn't get any information. Didn't want to chance riding all the way here, then them not letting me in. I just wanted to know if you—you know. Lived."

"You're weird, aren't you?"

"I suppose. But, not weird enough to bust into someone's camper and try overdosing on dog medication."

"Morality don't matter when you need a fix more than your next breath."

"I'm just grateful you're alive. And I'm sorry you're suffering." Feeling sorry for myself was impossible around this kid. His silence wasn't awkward. There was a mutual understanding in it.

"How long will you be in here?" I asked.

"Waiting for the psych evaluation. Last time it took a fucking week. And being underage I have to wait for someone, a legal guardian to decide if I should be released. Sign all the paperwork. But I don't have that so—hey! *You.* You could be my mom? Sign me out."

"I'm sure they'd want a proper ID. And since I'm not Canadian, I don't think that'll work. Why not stay? Better here than sleeping on the street, right?"

"True dat. The food's good. No maggots."

"I hope you're joking."

"I ain't. You don't live like this and not eat out of trash cans."

"Holy shit." I didn't want to believe him. I wanted to wave a magic wand and make it all better.

"It ain't that bad. Maggots are like rice. That's what I tell myself. Most stuff's only bad if you think about it. And obviously, sometimes I think about it. That's when trouble comes."

"You're wise beyond your years."

He looked at me like he appreciated the words. "I try."

"You keep trying. Don't ever quit."

"Okay." He got quiet and laid his head back onto his pillow.

"I should get going. You take care of yourself, Jed. I mean it."

"Think maybe you might come back?"

"I could. Sure. If you want me to?"

"If you want to. I ain't doin' nothing."

"Alright. I'll come by tomorrow. Bring you a salmon burger for lunch." I don't know why this made me happy, but it darn sure did.

That night, a full moon hung so low that I swore I could touch it as I stepped out of the ladies' room after a long hot shower. The jingle of spurs echoed out of the darkness. One footfall at a time. *Mark.* My heart hurled itself against my chest. The fight-or-flight response readied my fists. I spun and crouched like an Old West gunslinger as Kevin exited the men's room toting two plastic trash bags. A full key ring dangling and jingling from his belt as he neared.

"That's some moon, eh?"

A nervous laugh escaped as I caught my breath. "Wish I had a camera."

"I've got one. But it's a Polaroid and you can't get the film for the dang thing anymore. Guess it's time to update." He nodded, then looked at me kind of funny. "You like pot roast?"

Before I could answer he went on. Accentuating. Slow and deliberate with his words. "Pot roast, with thick brown gravy; tender red potatoes cut into bite-sized pieces, not those obnoxious huge chunks that you have to work around. Then the carrots. Baby carrots cooked to perfection. Not too soft though. But that's not all. Just to be sure and knock it out of the park— fresh warm sourdough with way too much butter. What do you think about that?"

"You had me at pot roast." I smiled.

"Good. I'll finish up with the trash and bring the cart around and pick you up. About twenty minutes, eh?"

"I'll be ready. Thank you."

Kevin's hair was damp, with an essence of what smelled like coconut. The deck behind his house stretched almost to the river. It was a perfect night to eat outside under that massive moon. We stuffed ourselves to the point of being uncomfortable.

"That was the best pot roast ever." I pulled a fresh napkin from the holder. Inspirational quotes on each of them.

"Glad you liked it. I ate way too much." Kevin refilled my wineglass.

I read my napkin. "The things you don't choose are what make you who you are."

"That's the truth."

"I'm saving this one." I folded it and stuck it in my shirt pocket.

"You know how long I've had these things?" He handed me a fresh napkin. "I bought these for my ex-wife. She thought they were corny and never used them." He scrubbed his head. "Sorry. Not supposed to mention exes, right?"

I laughed and Kevin pulled the entire stack of napkins from the holder.

"Here. Please—take them all." We laughed and it felt great.

"Dessert?"

"I'd love to, but I'm stuffed, really," I said, holding my stomach.

"Me too, actually." He held up his glass and we toasted: "To new friends."

"Yes. Thanks." I loved that he didn't know how pathetic and screwed up my life was. It was fun being someone else if only for an hour or so.

"Mind if I ask you something?"

"No. Not at all. Anything."

"Okay." Kevin leaned forward with his elbows on the table, then clasped his hands and looked down. "I uh... My sister-in-law, ex-sister-in-law, Kendra, is a Mountie here. I ran into her at the bakery today and asked about your missing hunter husband. She hadn't heard about it. Thing is—the rainforest is big, but the community here is small. She would know about any reports of missing people." He looked at me and squinted. I did not see that coming and dropped my gaze. Technically, it wasn't a question. Did I have to answer? My silence wasn't working. He waited me out.

"Huh. Weird." I shrugged and drank. "Maybe I should talk to her, see what's going on." I knew it was lame as hell but I had nothing better.

"It's none of my business. I'm not trying to stick my nose in where it doesn't belong."

"No. It's okay. I may need your nose."

He smiled and reached into his shirt pocket. "Here." He handed me a card. "This is Kendra's number. She said you're welcome to call her anytime and put her personal cell number on the back for ya. She's good people. You'll like her."

A bit of real sleep came after miles of peddling plus a bellyful of wine and pot roast. When the cell phone buzzed at six the next morning, I thought I'd only just fallen asleep and sat up fast. It took two more rings before I found the phone next to my pillow. "Hello?"

"I seen your flyer." The girl sounded young and slightly sarcastic. "And I for sure seen that dude."

"Oh." I fought to wake up. To think of what to say.

"Totally can't talk right now. I'm late as shit. Meet me at seven. I'll show you where he stays."

"Who is this?"

"Randy Johnson." She gave what sounded like a suppressed giggle. I didn't get it. "Someone at the bar had a flyer. It was super late last night and I got a wicked hangover. Gotta go. I work trail crew over at Lost Lake today, so if you could—like meet me there at seven—at the trailhead." She paused, then cleared her throat. "Go east on twenty, then left. North over the river. Right onto Saloompt Rd. Takes you right to the trailhead. Easy peasy. Lost Lakes. There's a sign. Don't be late."

"Can you text me the directions?"

She hung up. I couldn't remember what she'd just rattled off. "Shit." *Are you kidding me?* Lost Lake trailhead was all I had to go on. But did I even want to go? I'd given up hunting Mark and closed my eyes. It was too cold and early to get up and I pulled the sleeping bag up over my head.

Kevin's hiking map with all the lakes and trails in and around Bella Coola was on the counter. I could find the place if it were on the map. If I could find my reading glasses. More importantly, I had the gun, because something about this call seemed very, very odd.

I rolled out of bed and slipped on my Uggs, then went to the bathroom stiff and sore from all the bike riding. After dressing in record time, I noticed my sweater was inside out and left it that way. I unhooked the water hose and electrical cord from the camper and left them on the ground. The diesel truck warmed while I searched for my readers.

There was a scratched pair stashed in the glove box and even with the glasses on, I struggled to find the miniscule letters of Lost Lake trailhead. Frustration got the best of me. I growled until I finally found it and marked the way with a pen. Before pulling out, I thought about calling Kendra, Kevin's Mountie ex-sister-in-law, but it was so early, and what would I tell her? I pulled her card out of my back pocket and looked at my phone. Three bars were enough to make the call.

The rising sun broke over the blue mountain ridgeline shooting spectacular white laser beams out from above a snow-covered peak. The shadowed tree line turned as purple as a bruise while we sped east on Highway 20. Duke slept in the camper. It was almost light enough to see when I pulled down a narrow gravel road with a hand painted wood sign pointing the way to Lost Lake.

Left. After twenty minutes down the desolate forest road, I kicked off my high-beams and parked at the dead end. There were no cars in the circular lot. Nor were there any tire tracks in the mud. I unzipped my coat pocket with the gun in it and got out only six minutes late.

"Randy," I called without really yelling. Nothing.

I walked to the trailhead. It was dark and muddy and dropped at the start. I stepped down. Followed the overgrown path. My Uggs deep in the muck. You couldn't hike the trail without being bushwhacked. "Randy?" It was eerily silent. Thick walls of tangled brush like a soundproof chamber as I moved along slowly with only my heartbeat in my ears. The snap of a twig went off like a shot and I froze as if I'd hit a wall.

"Hey, Jess."

CHAPTER
TWENTY-EIGHT

There he stood towering above me on the trailhead like an apparition with a rifle slung over his shoulder. Smiling as if he were happy to see me. Something inside busted loose and banged my chest. Love reared its ugly head and crushed all the pain and grief and hate. He opened his arms and came to me, and I let him. Let him catch me from my never-ending fall even if just for a moment.

I didn't hug him back, just buried my face in him with my hands in my coat pockets. My right hand on the gun. I hadn't felt safe or whole since he left and when he wrapped his arms around me it was like nothing bad could ever get me. He cradled and held my head against his chest, our breath in perfect harmony. I cried. Love doesn't end just because you want it to. I wished it did.

"I missed you." His voice was as caressing as a tomcat's tongue.

I swallowed my pride like a disgusting wad of phlegm. Down and gone. "I missed you too." The familiar earthy smell, mixed with his peppermint soap, brought it all back in a flood of emotion. I sobbed. How could I love this horrible human? I was weak. Pathetic. And I accepted my fate.

"How did you find me?" he asked, rubbing my back.

"How'd you know I was looking?" I pulled away from him. Saw in his eyes there was no fear. There was never any fear. And why should there be? I was nothing to be afraid of even without his rifle.

"Zack had you on camera leaving a flyer in his mailbox. Came to my cabin yesterday and showed me the video on his phone. My buddy, Jolly, saw you plastering the town with my picture and he gathered them up. I have a lot of friends."

"Who was the girl called me this morning?"

"Randy Johnson?" He laughed. "Just a friend."

"Yeah, I bet."

"I'm just thankful you're here."

"No you're not! You'd kill me if you could."

"Now I'm a *murderer?*" He looked up and shook his head a while. When he finally looked at me, I could see the evil in his eyes. "I could have shot you soon as you stepped out of your truck. I could split your skull. I could kill you now and no one would ever know. But, why would I? I love you. You have no idea how many times I thought about calling or sending word." He held my face and looked into my eyes. With his thumbs he wiped my tears. "I love you. And I *am* sorry. With all my heart I'm so sorry." He pulled me into him as far as I could go and held on.

"You don't love me." I could pull the gun, shove it in his ribs, and shoot before he could react.

"Things got sideways, but that has nothing to do with love." He said it like he meant it.

"Nana died," I blurted and stepped back.

"Aw shit, babe. When? What happened?"

"They arrested her. Now everyone thinks she's a serial killer. All because of you. She didn't deserve that."

"No fucking way."

"I know everything. About the Mexicans, Lupe, dumping the bodies. Jesus, Mark."

"I did it to protect you."

"You shoved your dick into Gabby and however many others to *protect me?*" Something snapped and it was all I could do to not shoot him in the face. I roared. "You're a lying, horse-killing, piece of shit who dumps human beings like slop to hogs then lets an old lady take the blame. Who the fuck does that? Fake your own death, Mark? Really? For what? Money to hunt down a mythical creature? Do you realize how idiotic and *fucking insane* that is?"

He didn't answer. Just cried without tears.

"You know where you really fucked up?" I wiped my snotty nose on my sleeve. "You betrayed the one person who was always—*always* on your side. No matter what, I was loyal through all your wicked bullshit."

"I can explain everything, if you just let me." He took my hand and kissed it. "Please, babe. Come with me. Right now."

"Where?"

"I have a cabin on an island. The most beautiful place you've ever seen."

I laughed.

"You're still my wife you know."

"I know."

"Come on. Please come with me. You'll love it. We can fish and read and watch bears. I want you with me."

"You didn't want me when you had me!"

"I *know!* I get that now. That's what it took for me to wake the hell up and realize what I had. Give me a chance and I'll spend the rest of my life making it up to you. You won't regret it." He moved in. Closed his eyes and kissed my neck—the spot under my ear he knew gets me going. That warm fuzzy urge stirred and kicked like always. He sent a hot breath in my ear, then trailed kisses down my neck. I was on fire. He pressed himself against me. I weakened when I felt his hardness through my coat against my bellybutton. "We can start over, Jess." He slipped his hand between my legs and woke a carnal desire I'd thought had died. Our lips reunited like man and wife. My tongue slid onto his and fought for dominance until logic took over.

"Stop." I pushed him away, but he came right back.

"I want you so bad," he whispered and licked my ear. Shivers spiraled every which way. "I love you."

"You only love yourself."

His brow furrowed. He tilted his head, then smiled like he does when he's pissed but doesn't want you to know. "I want to make love to you. Like we used to. Come to the cabin. Just for one day. If you don't want to stay, then don't. You can leave whenever you want." He took my hand and pulled me down the trail. "I have a boat not five minutes from here."

I looked at my watch. 7:17. "Okay. But Duke's in the camper. I can't leave him."

"That pitiful old bastard is still alive?"

"Yep."

He stopped pulling me. "Jess, you should have put him down."

I turned and walked fast up the trail, hoping he'd follow me to the camper. No clue what I'd do once we got there.

Duke snored, but didn't move when I climbed into the camper and opened the narrow bathroom door. "I have to pee."

"Hurry up." Mark stepped inside.

The ugly black-cat clock the previous owner had screwed to the wall read 7:21. I shut the bathroom door. Inside, I pulled the gun from my coat pocket and lifted the leg of my jeans. The gun rode nice and snug inside the top of my Ugg boot. I flushed the toilet, washed my hands, and stepped out. 7:23. Time crawled on that awful cat clock, its eyes and tail swinging back and forth as if mocking me.

Mark seemed to take up all the space in the camper. I smiled, sucked an extra deep breath, and went to him. My hand went between his legs—kneading him. "I'm going to fuck you."

"Please do." His hot tongue like a snake tickling my ear. "Let's go to the cabin. Grab your things." The rifle slid forward under his arm. He shoved it back as I unbuckled his belt and filled his mouth with my tongue. I unbuttoned his pants, then tugged the zipper down.

"I can't wait anymore." I wanted him in the worst way. "Get naked. I'm going to fuck you like never before." The words came out of my mouth like they belonged to someone else—while my hands worked his pants down just enough to free his erection. He unzipped my coat and reached under my bra. Cupped, then twisted my nipples too hard. "I have to pee again." I adjusted my boobs back into my bra.

"You just peed."

"Think I'm getting a bladder infection." I stroked him with a slow, tight grip and he moaned. "Get your ass up in that bed— I'll be right back." I smiled.

Mark hesitated, blocking my way, staring down at me with a look I'd never seen before. I couldn't tell if he wanted me dead or in bed.

"You know how beautiful you are, babe? Inside and out. I love you and I'm going to spend the rest of my life proving it."

He kissed the top of my head, then slipped the rifle off and set it on the counter.

"I love you too." I glanced at the clock—7:25—then opened the bathroom door. Before shutting it, I caught sight of Mark pulling his boots off and I knew I had him. I took my time peeing then flushed the toilet a while. The water pump gurgling and sputtering as I thoroughly washed my hands.

"What are you doing?"

"I'm coming." I opened the medicine cabinet and brought down a bottle of Pepto and took a few swigs before putting it back. With my heart racing, I moved the gun from my boot to my back pocket. My sweater long enough to conceal the weapon.

Suddenly sweating like crazy, I stepped out of the bathroom. 7:28. Mark was in bed. His clothes piled on the floor. I opened the camper door and looked outside. "What the hell are you doing?" Mark asked.

"Thought I heard something." I left the door open and in one swift move reached the rifle off the counter and chucked it as hard as I could out the door. It landed with a splash in a puddle somewhere. In my back pocket, I felt the cold gun, and slid it out with my sweaty finger on the trigger.

"What the fuck are you doing?" Mark jumped down with a withering erection.

"Get back up there." I pointed the gun at his head. "I swear to God I'll kill you."

"Jess? Why?"

"*WHY? Are you kidding me?*" I screamed—wanting to kill him—and clicked the safety off. With my thumb I cocked the gun and steadied it at his head. "Get your ass up in that bed and don't move!"

"We both know you're not going to shoot me. I could take that gun—" He struck like a serpent when he reached for it. I closed my eyes and squeezed the trigger. Felt the jolt but mostly the terror. The blast was deafening and shook the camper. I opened my eyes. Smoke, then an acrid stench burnt my nose. My ears screamed. Mark slammed against the wall under the bed and we looked at each other in disbelief. *I just killed my husband.* Time slowed. I wanted to take it all back. Revenge felt awful like my soul being gnawed. Devoured. *Holy shit.* It was unreal. Like a dream. His face went pale, then morphed into the sinister monster he truly was when he saw blood blossoming on his shoulder.

He came at me. Grabbed the gun with his left hand, exposing his bad arm with the plate in it. The long scar like a target. With all my might, I smashed my fist down onto his forearm. Nailed the plate. Mark howled above the ringing and released his grip on the gun.

I jumped from the camper. Splashed down into the mud, then turned back toward Mark in the doorway. Like an expert I held the gun with two hands as I cocked and aimed. He stood bent, holding his bad arm with his right hand and his shoulder with his left. The rifle was to my left. I moved over and reached down keeping the gun on him. The rifle dripped with mud as I threw it aside. It slapped a big red cedar. Wetness soaked through my Uggs down to my socks as I repositioned, spread my legs, and straightened myself like a statue of a badass chick holding a gun on the devil himself. It seemed like an eternity. Standing in the mud, aiming, waiting, and watching Mark strain to figure a way out.

"Are you just going to stand there and watch me bleed?" Mark roared from the doorway.

"Toughen up!" Nana's words came with an overdose of adrenaline that sent effervescent tingles, not unlike an orgasm, throughout my entire body. The desire to share my overwhelming gratitude could not be contained. "Thank you, Mark!" I bounced up and down on the balls of my feet and shouted. "Thank you for forcing me to be a badass." My armpits sweated. "I could *not* have done it without you." *Nana would be proud.*

The sun rose—took shape in the sky and held the promise of another spectacular day. Mark slammed the camper door shut. My arms hurt and I lowered the gun. Shook my hands out to help the blood return, then breathed in the mountains long and slow. A bald eagle with wings spread wide glided by with a fish in her talons. I smiled at the vivid analogy.

It sounded like an engine purring closer and closer. Then an SUV pulled into the muddy lot. I almost cried, then began to laugh. Another SUV. Two Royal Canadian Mounted Police SUVs with lights flashing. I laughed. Three uniformed men and one woman emerged from the vehicles. They left their doors open and stood behind them like shields with guns on me. I raised my hands high over my head. "I'm Jessica Williams. The one who called Kendra Rogers this morning. Mark Williams is wanted in the US. He's inside the camper."

"Set your weapon down. And step forward. Hands up." I did as instructed.

"Is Mr. Williams armed?" a Mountie asked.

"He had a rifle. I threw it over there." I pointed to the big cedar and the Mountie headed that way.

A lady Mountie with big doe eyes under her hat came at me. "I'm Kendra." With knee-high black boots, she kicked my gun through the mud to a fellow Mountie, who grabbed it. Before I knew it, Kendra had taken my arm and rushed me to the SUV. "Wait in here." She opened the back door and locked me in.

"Come out Mr. Williams!" a voice demanded.

From the back of the SUV, I watched and laughed. Laughed even though it really wasn't funny. Helpless laughter burst from me like someone had tapped a gusher. I could not stop. Tears streamed down my face. There was a good chance this was hysteria.

Mark stepped into the doorway holding his bloody shoulder and cradling his arm. He had only his pants on and looked like he just might be sick or cry or both.

"I'm not Mark Williams. You've got the wrong guy!" Barefoot, he jumped down. When he slipped in the mud and fell on his ass I almost died.

"Put your hands up!"

"I can't! That rotten bitch shot me!"

"Okay. Let's get you to the hospital and sort this out."

Mark looked around, searching for me I suppose. I was laughing hysterically when he found me. He shook his head. I couldn't hear his growls but I could see them and could not resist waving a big middle finger his way.

"Told you I was going to fuck you." I cracked myself up. Nana had infected me and I loved her for it.

Kendra left Mark in the mud as she cuffed his hands in front of him. He squealed like a stuck pig. Two Mounties lifted him. Mark just glared at me as they led him to the back of an SUV and shoved him in, then left in a hurry.

Kendra opened my door. I stepped out weak with laughter that escaped every now and then.

"Good thing you called. I'm afraid to think what would have happened if you didn't."

I laughed. Swamped with adrenaline and genuinely fulfilled with the way things were playing out.

"We'll need to bring you in. I searched the database and found everything you told me to be true. But we have a problem."

"What?"

Kendra stepped close and lowered her voice, though her partner was off searching for the Mark's rifle. "Your gun. Where did you get it?"

"I found it. The kid who—"

"Stop! Listen very carefully. Our gun laws are extremely harsh. You got the gun from Mark—*right?*"

"Right." I chewed on what to say next. "He set it down?" It sounded like a question and I waited for her approval.

"Where?" Kendra asked.

"On the counter. In the camper. He had it in his jeans, I guess. The back pocket I think." I hesitated. "And when he took them off, he pulled the gun out. I saw him set it on the counter. Between the sink and the fridge." The lies flowed like good fiction. "Then he climbed up into the bed...I got scared and grabbed the gun. That's when he jumped down after me—tried to take it and I guess I pulled the trigger. I never wanted to kill him. Honest."

"Good. Remember every detail when they question you. Remember it the same exact way every time no matter how many times they ask."

"Am I in trouble?"

"Not if he was trying to kill you. It's clearly self-defense, but we have to prove it. Shouldn't be difficult with his background."

"What's gonna happen to him?"

"They'll take him to General—have him treated then transferred to Vancouver while he awaits extradition. That'll take months...maybe years."

That night I slept without the burden of murder upon my soul. I did not pray. Did not worry. Did not think of Mark. Just closed my eyes and fell asleep with Duke snoring next to me. Tomorrow would come and all I had to worry about was taking Jed his salmon burger.

EPILOGUE

I t was fitting that spring came early. It was always Nana's favorite time of year when creeks ran, pastures sprouted soft and green, apple blossoms filled the air, and life in general held promise. Although winter had come in like a lion, it hadn't lasted in the Sierra, or in Bella Coola where I'd spent the better part of a month with Kevin and Jed. We hiked and fished and had a blast hiding from the media.

They were relentless in their quest to get the inside story of what had happened with Mark. Letters from CNN, Fox News, and HLN arrived via special delivery to the campground. Offers from ten to twenty thousand dollars if I'd agree to an exclusive. Thanks to DNA test results, I decided to wait until I had dug up every bit of my new family tree and the book was complete.

The night before returning to the states, Kevin and I slept together under the stars on Purgatory Lookout. That one night in his bedroll could not have been better. His caring gentleness was novel and I learned I like to be spooned from behind all night. Kevin calls most every day now. Yesterday he bought a plane ticket to come for a visit next week, before the rush of summer campers. I figured it was best to wait and tell him in person that I was pregnant.

Regardless of his reaction, I was having this miracle baby. My drinking days were over. When I told Kevin I'd given up alcohol, he said he would too. I really, really liked this guy.

Grass grew over an inch tall where the sun had warmed it and smelled like heaven as Duke and I climbed Blue Mountain with Nana. Jim had offered to join us but I wanted to be alone, plus he was busy rebuilding the hog pens since all the crime scene evidence had been removed and sent to the California Department of Justice for DNA analysis. Jim wasn't cut out to be a backwoods recluse and was now at the ranch full time.

Detective Rocha guaranteed Jim's safety after a lengthy lecture on all the ways in which what I had done was foolish and worse, extremely dangerous. I agreed and promised to come to him first if ever I suspected my dead husband of being alive. Rocha laughed, shook my hand, and finally thanked me for allowing my attorney, Ed Manetti, to share most of Nana's letter with him.

Ed worked out a sweet deal with Rocha and redacted everything in the letter pertaining to the cash involved. Ed also refused to hand over the letter until Agent Lee and the FBI agreed in writing to keep Jim from testifying. To avoid being prosecuted for the crime of dumping bodies in Nana's hog pens, Jim shared all he knew about Mark's involvement with Lupe and identified her from an old booking photo.

Jim was charged with aiding and abetting and placed on probation for two years. It would be a long while, years probably, before the case would go to trial since Mark was fighting extradition from Canada.

Getting Jed over the border and into the US. was a piece of cake. He hid under the pile of sleeping bags in my camper, since he lacked a passport. He was adjusting just fine to hard work, three meals a day, and life on the ranch without drugs.

Mountain misery crept over the trail and tangled all along the western slope. I'd been climbing this mountain since I was seven. As I cradled the coffee can with Nana's ashes through the creosote-pungent brush, sticky leaves clung to my jeans like Velcro. Duke limped along behind and every so often I'd stop and wait for him to catch up. It was good—no great—to be home.

A warm wind blew like a wildness wanting out when I reached the top of Blue Mountain. Tall Jeffery pines standing like monuments. My name carved deep into the fleshy bark of the biggest tree twenty-five years ago. Nana was so angry when she saw what I'd done, she threatened to carve her name in me. She sat me down under that tree and explained how what I'd done could eventually kill it. The next day, she punished me with a gift, wrapped in silver with a lavender bow. I unwrapped it—*A Sand County Almanac* by Aldo Leopold.

Two Steller's jays squawked from their nest when I sat under their pine, grateful the big tree was still alive. Across the canyons, miles and miles of deep blue wilderness waited to welcome Nana. I set her ashes next to me and Duke sniffed the can.

"You loved her too, huh, Buddy." The sting of grief tore at my nose, then my eyes. I cried.

"I know you can hear me." I cleared my throat. "And, I know you hate poetry, but this is the last time you'll ever have to listen." I wiped my nose with my hand and stood. Lifting my chin, I took a deep breath and tried to stop crying.

"Do not stand at my grave and weep, I am not there, I do not sleep.

I am in a thousand winds that blow, I am the diamond glint on snow.

I am the sunlight on ripened grain. I am the gentle autumn rain.

When you awaken in the morning's hush, I am the swift uplifting rush

Of quiet birds in circled flight. I am the soft stars that shine at night.

Do not stand at my grave and cry, I am not there. I do not die."

Duke pushed his head against my leg and I rubbed his floppy ear. "I love you, Nana," I sobbed and left the coffee can on the ground as I peeled off the lid. I pulled out the Ziploc bag and stepped to the edge of the evergreen cathedral. Unzipped the plastic bag. Nana was not just ash and dust peppered with specks of gray bone; she was as much a part of me as my marrow and part of Blue Mountain forever.

ACKNOWLEDGMENTS

Mostly, I'd like to thank you dear reader. Without you, my work would remain silent. If you enjoyed *Blue Mountain*, please take a moment to share a review on Amazon or Goodreads or both. Your thoughts and opinions make all the difference to new authors like me.

Book 2 in the Calaveras Crime Trilogy is AVAILABLE NOW on Amazon.

I'd love to hear from you so please join the Reader's Club for fun and giveaways over at https://www.lisamichellestories.com.

I'm forever grateful to Pat Russell and the good people of Calaveras County for their endless encouragement when the going got tough.

To my read team, Randy Mundt, Frank Riley, Bruce Miller, Tim Hauserman, Susan Sanchez, Elia Bamberger, Dona Queirolo, Kathy Grimes, Sandy Kelly, Julia Marsili, Bridey Thelen Heidel, and all the folks at Tahoe Writers Works for suffering through messy drafts yet assuring me that this story had all the right ingredients.

Made in the USA
Monee, IL
20 November 2023

46821482R00173